R.H.TANG

THE HEAVEN'S BOXER

www.aethonbooks.com

THE HEAVEN'S BOXER

THE POWER OF NINE

THE FONT OF LIFE

[1]

"To me! To me!"

The crimson mechanical hawk soared effortlessly through a hail of unrelenting gunfire. The Overdrive World Champion—vermillionangel—was revered for his incredible control skills. Although the unit was an exhibition rental, he moved the avian Mech as if it were his own body, as if he'd been born with metal wings and Eternium talons rather than arms and legs. Even the few shots that hit him failed to inflict significant damage. He gently twisted back and forth, deflecting the gunfire off the laminated coating at the top of his wings and protecting the thin feather-knives.

Red lightning pouring from its talons and beak, the Paragon-class strafed the bunker three times before the defenders finally drove him away with a volley of missiles. The hawk fled back toward the skies, elegantly spiraling through the clouds as it drew the enemy fire away from its slowly advancing teammates.

Julian grinned with almost childlike excitement and leaned closer into his screen. The Vermillion Flier was awesome.

The current match was an exhibition promoting the game's most skilled Mech crafters. The stars of the top four World Championship teams were facing off against four Fortress Masters—veteran pilots the Overdrive administration had hired to create Fortresses, the equivalent of dungeons in traditional role-playing games. Unlike Overdrive's infinitely varied mission mode, the objective of a player vs. player Overdrive match was simple.

Eliminate all opponents.

Vermillionangel wasn't using his usual machine, the Vermillion Draco. However, the skilled crafter who'd created the exhibition Mech had evidently incorporated the inaugural World Champion's combat data. Repeated frontline assaults encapsulated vermillionangel's daring playstyle.

Julian pulled up the status screen at the bottom of the audience dashboard and analyzed the Flier's statistical information. The machine was perfectly suited to the World Champion's head-on fighting style and love of Wild-type Paragon units.

- General Data -
Pilot: vermillionangel
Machine: Vermillion Flier
Class: Paragon
Type: Wild
Designation: Ace Unit

- Statistics -
Melee: A-tier
Shooting: S-tier
Speed: S-tier
Maneuverability: S-tier
Defense: B-tier
Cohesion: S-tier

- Weapons -
Vermillion Beak (Full Custom)

Judgment Cannon (Full Custom) [x3]
Angel Wing Finale (Full Custom) [x4]
Vermillion Feather Dagger (Full Custom) [x20]
Vermillion Feather Epée (Full Custom) [x6]
Vermillion Talons (Full Custom) [x6]

- Abilities -
Liquid State Eternium
Vermillion Thunder
Vermillion Judgment

A diorama of the nearly impeccable Mech accompanied the full report. The Flier proudly cawed on the right-hand side of the screen. Because of vermillionangel's swift commands, the Vermillion Flier had spent most of the match as a nondescript orange-red blur. Now that it was standing still, Julian saw just how beautiful it was. Most pilots only built their machines to maximize combat skills, but the Flier was also a work of art.

Befitting its legendary pilot's name, the machine was all a single color—vermillion from head to toe. The avian wings looked biological rather than mechanical. Save for the keenly honed edges at the tip, the feather daggers and epées were identical to real feathers.

Vermillionangel's signature mono-eye sensors flared like golden bonfires across the Flier's body. There were five in total. One cyclopean eye blazed just above the beak at the center of the finely wrought head. The other four swiveled around the body on specially constructed tethers, providing perfect vision no matter the angle.

Julian felt a brief spark of jealousy.

He wished he could be skilled enough to pilot a Mech like the Flier. Julian was ranked just beneath the top five hundred on the server, but there was a massive gap between a simply reputable player and the World Champion.

If Julian tried piloting the Flier, his head would explode. He had no idea how vermillionangel could process five separate camera streams in the middle of an intense close-quarters battle.

Julian wondered how much the Flier would fetch if its crafter sold it. Overdrive's in-game economy was growing by the day. The other day, his favorite streamer—TiggerLuvr888—had sold one of his Mechs for just over a thousand dollars in a charity auction. There were even a few crafters who'd quit their day jobs to design Mechs full-time.

Sadly, Julian had no chance of joining them. He lacked the patience and delicacy to be a good crafter. The most powerful part he'd ever created was an 80% Custom, and that had been with his friends' help. Felix and Edwin had done almost all the work helping him make the Starlight R's latest sword.

After he finished marveling at the Champion's machine, Julian turned back to the main video. Rather than skipping to the live stream, he continued watching from where he'd paused the video.

Vermillionangel's gambit succeeded. With the enemies distracted, his team's sturdy Kingbreaker-class Grunts charged, spewing an unceasing barrage of explosive ammunition.

A swarm of flames engulfed the enemy bunker. Loud clanging echoed across the battlefield as the defenders inside furiously tried to escape, but the metal and stone roof crumbled before they could.

That was the cost of hiding behind cover for too long. There was no truly safe terrain in Overdrive. Anything, even an entire space colony, could be destroyed by the right weaponry.

The attackers cheered.

Then a guttural roar instantly silenced their celebrations.

When the smoke and rubble cleared, there was only a single machine remaining on the other side.

Even though everyone knew that Vile, the strongest of the Fortress Masters, would use a Hemoborn-class, Julian still gasped. Her machine was a mishmashed horror of rotting flesh and pristine metal.

For a moment, the world froze.

Then a poisoned heartbeat echoed through the air.

Julian winced. His fingers tightened against the screen, and his skin turned bright white. Julian had played Overdrive since the beta test, but Vile's designs still spooked him every time he saw them.

As he'd expected, Vile was the only player in the exhibition piloting a Mech she'd created herself. Her crafting skills were legendary. She was the number 1 crafter and the number 1 Fortress Master. A showdown between vermillionangel and Vile was a match between the greatest attacker and the ultimate defender.

Disgusting bits of rotting meat dripped to the floor as Vile's machine reloaded. Unlike any other class in the game, Hemoborn were cyborgs built from a mixture of biological and metal parts.

Julian hastily pulled up the status report on Vile's machine, wincing at the diorama on the right-hand side. Vile put just as much care into her Mech's aesthetics as the Vermillion Flier's crafter—it was just that Julian found the Fortress Master's tastes utterly repulsive.

Like her usual Frankenstein-inspired unit, her new Hemoborn class echoed a character from a traditional novel. Based on the split type, it must have been a Shifter, a versatile machine that could transition between variable forms.

- General Data -
Pilot: Vile

Machine: CWT-02 Hyde
Class: Cyborg
Type: Artillery/Attacker
Designation: Ace Unit

- Statistics -
Melee: S-tier
Shooting: S-tier
Speed: S-tier
Maneuverability: S-tier
Defense: S-tier
Cohesion: S-tier

- Weapons -
Smoothbore Flesh Cannon (Full Custom)
Hyde Gore Bazooka (Full Custom)
Machinegun Fingers (Full Custom) [x10]
Reinforced Steel-Infused Jaws (Full Custom)
Spine Whip (Full Custom)
Jekyll Blade (Full Custom) [x2]
Cackle Wings (Full Custom) [x4]

- Abilities -
CWT-78 Jekyll
Horror Level 10
Stench Level 10
Regeneration Level 10
Bloodlust Level 10

Julian reread the parts list twice just to make sure he understood what everything did. The Hyde was armed to the teeth. Although the Credits restriction on Ace units was far more lenient than the cap on Grunts—50,000 Credits vs. 10,000—it was still hard to believe that Vile could incorporate all those weapons onto a single unit.

It was only after taking a closer look at the diagram on the right-hand side that Julian understood.

The Full Custom weapons were smoothly integrated. When the Hyde transformed into its Jekyll mode, the Flesh Cannon and Gore Bazooka shifted into the Jekyll Blades. The Hyde's armor-plated ribcage detached and became the four Cackle Wings, providing the Jekyll with increased mobility.

The hideous CWT-02 Hyde was something only Vile could love, but the hulking monstrosity was undeniably a masterpiece of skill and creativity.

Players often speculated about a "perfect machine" where every statistic was in the S-tier. Mechs like the Vermillion Flier came close to that hallowed ideal, but they couldn't overcome the 50,000 Credit cap. Vile had accomplished the seemingly insurmountable task with her unique transforming design. The Hyde excelled in Shooting and Defense, and the Jekyll specialized in Melee, Speed, and Maneuverability.

Julian returned to the video.

The Hyde's muscular shoulders were as broad as the horizon. No wonder Vile hadn't attacked until the bunker collapsed. Julian doubted the giant machine could even move inside tight corridors.

Under normal circumstances, an enormous Mech like the Hyde would never bother ducking behind cover, but showmanship was a vital part of the exhibition matches. Both teams were trying their best to win, but they still had to adhere to The Mechanical King's requested conditions. Most lower-level games —even games around Julian's tier of play—devolved into one team camping behind cover. To make the exhibition more relatable, the CEO of the Overdrive Corporation insisted on emulating the experience of the average player.

A hideously swollen tongue flicked back and forth, licking

steel teeth that were jagged like a shark's. The creature's face was split in two—half flesh and half metal. A gaping gray eye—identical to a human's but fifty times larger—stared hungrily at the line of opponents. The Smoothbore Flesh Cannon and the Hyde Gore Bazooka were just as menacing and disgusting as their names suggested. The first was a hollowed-out leg grafted onto the left shoulder. The second was an enormous handheld cannon forged from bones and powered by a thumping heart. The colossal right hand, a fusion of flesh and metal swarmed by metal tubes, hefted the heavy weapon as if it weighed no more than a feather.

Just as the Vermillion Flier represented the World Champion's playstyle, the Hyde's supreme firepower embodied Vile's philosophy. The plainspoken woman believed in raw strength without any bells and whistles.

When Vile first burst into the Overdrive scene, her enormous Mechs had immediately seized the attention of the game administration. Their raw firepower and impenetrable armor led to an almost instantaneous game balance patch and a far stricter Ace Credit cap.

Back then, most pilots had pursued an even balance between strength and maneuverability. Vile had eschewed mobility entirely. Her Moby Dick didn't need to move when it had the firepower of a dozen Mechs. The giant machine was soon permanently banned from the Overdrive server. It was the sort of design that was so obviously game-breaking that everyone wondered why they hadn't thought of it first.

Even after the restriction, Vile steadfastly insisted that the majority of battles were won or lost before the guns started firing. Despite her unshakable piloting skills, she dedicated most of her streams to teaching crafting techniques. Her Fortress boasted a correspondingly formidable arsenal—every level had a personally crafted mini-boss. Despite untold hours of gameplay, Julian and his childhood friends Felix and Edwin had only cleared three out of the ten levels.

As soon as Julian hit play again, the Gore Bazooka spat a fiery globule of blood at one of vermillionangel's Grunt units. The revolting bullet was a third the size of an average Mech. The broken machine immediately crashed to the ground.

One moment, all the destroyed machine's health bars had been bright green. The next, the pilot was out of the match. It'd only taken a single shot to obliterate the cockpit in the torso, killing the pilot inside and eliminating them from the game.

Julian briefly pulled up the status screen, hoping to learn more about the Grunt's defenses. The kill was so effortless it looked like a glitch.

The diagram popped up on the right-hand side as the stats slowly loaded. The Guardian X's most unusual feature was that it lacked a distinct head unit. Instead, the entire Mech centered on its well-armored central spherical torso. A pair of glowing electronic eyes peered out from the top of the sphere.

- General Data -
Pilot: TiggerLuvr888
Machine: Guardian X
Class: Kingbreaker
Type: Artillery
Designation: Grunt Unit

- Statistics -
Melee: B-tier
Shooting: S-tier
Speed: C-tier
Maneuverability: C-tier
Defense: A-tier
Cohesion: S-tier

- Weapons -
300mm Heavy Bombardment Cannon (Full Custom)
6-tube Missile Launcher (Full Custom)
Reinforced Steel Sword
Reinforced Steel Shield

- Abilities -
N/A [Kingbreaker Class]

As expected for a Grunt unit, there were very few custom parts other than the weapons it needed to fill its role. TiggerLuvr888 had painted the Mech in his signature yellow and red, but otherwise, the Grunt cap of 10,000—as well as the limit of two Full Custom parts per Grunt unit—left relatively little space for personalization.

Julian sighed as he returned to the main video. TiggerLuvr888 was Julian's favorite streamer, and he'd gone down in a single exchange.

Like almost everyone else playing in the exhibition, Tigger's life had instantly transformed because of his skill at Overdrive. TiggerLuvr888 had been one of the very first esports players. He'd played competitive shooting games until his early 20s, but since then, he'd become a dad and computer engineer. Back then, gaming couldn't pay the bills. He'd more or less forgotten his youthful dream by the time Overdrive finally became popular. Tigger frequently mentioned on his stream that the only reason he'd first started playing Overdrive because his kids played. But despite his initially casual interest and rusty skills, his talent had quickly returned. During the last World Championships, the middle-aged man had finished in the Top 4.

And despite his skill and experience, he'd died in a single shot.

That was why Julian hated playing Grunts. Ace units had a

Credit cap five times higher than Grunts did. Grunts were just weak. Only a few Grunt enthusiasts argued otherwise, highlighting their unique properties like the ability to change their equipment before every match. In Julian's opinion, that was a paltry advantage.

In the in-game lore of Overdrive, Grunt units had to stay cheap for mass-production purposes. There were ways to get around the credit cap, but they involved sharp decreases to critical statistics, especially Cohesion. The often-overlooked statistic evaluated the crafting quality of your Mech. A horrible Cohesion meant your machine might spontaneously combust in the middle of a battle. Only one professional pilot was bold enough to continually gamble on low Cohesion—Sweetshot303, the legendary "Master of Minions."

The only advantage to specializing in Grunts was that competitive teams required three Grunts and only a single Ace. Getting good at Grunt play was an easier path to going pro, but there was no guarantee even then. Out of the players in the current Selection, Sweetshot was the only consistent Grunt user. Everyone else was a star Ace player who'd converted to a Grunt just for the match.

If anything, Sweetshot was the exception that proved the rule. He'd carried his feeble team to a second-place finish at the World Championships, but he could have won the whole thing if his squad had distributed their Credit resources more effectively. If someone led your team in kills every single game, you should just make them the Ace! Why would you have them use a weakling Grunt?

As if to prove Julian's point, Vile immediately destroyed the next Grunt unit with a rapid-fire barrage from her shoulder-mounted flesh cannon. As always, Vile fired in a way that minimized the need for accuracy. Instead of aiming directly for the enemy Mech, she took advantage of the terrain to bury her opponent beneath a mountain of rubble. The Guardian X had raised its shield, but there was nothing its pilot could do against an avalanche.

Julian winced and briefly turned away from the screen, cursing under his breath.

The flesh cannon's bullets looked like dismembered arms. Vile's machines were so frightening.

That left only vermillionangel and Sweetshot303 against Vile's towering Hemoborn.

A graphic popped up at the bottom of the screen, reminding Julian that his information on Sweetshot had been a little inaccurate. The Master of Minions hadn't just led his team in kills—he'd led the entire tournament. However, the Guardian X Sweetshot used for today's match lacked the extensive revisions he usually made to his frames. It was a standard model, not one of his hodgepodge "Patchwork" machines that sacrificed Maneuverability and Cohesion for raw speed and power. Because only Sweetshot303 could pilot his extensively hacked machines, using one in the exhibition would have been extremely unrelatable. The last time Julian had tried using one, he'd given up after crashing five times in two minutes.

Besides, the goal was to show off the latest top-of-the-line models. Sweetshot's forced customizations usually resulted in bizarre-looking heaps.

There was yet another thumping noise, and a revolting bullet of blood soared through the air.

Sweetshot and vermillionangel scattered to avoid the Hyde's repeated barrage.

The Hemoborn roared as its pilot's slight but taunting voice echoed across the battlefield.

"You boys plan on coming in?"

The Champion laughed but didn't deign to respond. Sweetshot's machine leaped into the air, landing on top of the Vermillion Flier. The pink and teal Guardian X's bazooka thumped and thumped, but Vile intercepted every bullet before it landed.

There was yet another barrage of crimson lightning. The flesh cannon on the Hyde's shoulder swiveled from side to side as it intercepted every shot.

Vermillionangel needed more power, and Julian realized what the Champion was about to do before he did it.

Bright red letters flashed across the screen.

OVERDRIVE ACTIVATED: LIQUID STATE ETERNIUM

Each of the four classes had an Overdrive boost accessible only to Aces. Liquid State Eternium was generally considered the most powerful. By liquefying the legendary metal they were built from, Paragons gained tremendous increases in strength, speed, and durability. More importantly, Liquid Paragons gained access to unique special attacks known as Finishers, which shattered the laws of reality to unleash devastating onslaughts.

The Vermillion Flier streaked toward its target, and once again, bright red letters flashed across the sky.

FINISHER: VERMILLION JUDGMENT

The red thunderstorm raged endlessly. Crimson lightning struck again and again. Vermillion Judgment, which the World Champion likened to divine retribution, was the Finisher vermillionangel used on all his Mechs.

The light was so intense that it covered the whole screen. Julian cursed and hastily turned down the brightness on his display. Sweetshot's bazooka fired endlessly into the rubble.

When the bombardment ended, the stage no longer resembled a military base. It looked like Earth after a meteorite collision.

The bunker's ruins had evaporated as if it had never been there to begin with. The ground had been torn asunder.

But despite the overwhelming display of strength, Vile's machine was still standing when the smoke cleared.

The Hyde was shattered and torn. The fleshy half of the face was shredded to bits. There was an enormous dent in the steel ribcage, and the metal arm was a molten slag. The flesh arm had been seared to the bone.

Green smoke curled around the Hemoborn as Vile activated her own Overdrive ability.

This time, the letters that splashed across the screen were mottled gray and sickly green, matching the Hyde's colors.

OVERDRIVE: UNDYING WILL

The Hemoborn's fleshy parts were an obvious weak point that invited direct attacks, but they also gave the Mechs access to extreme regenerative powers. The Hemoborn's Overdrive boost was unique in that it greatly boosted its machine's Cohesion stat, which normally couldn't be changed through any other means. By shooting the Cohesion up to ludicrous levels, the Hemoborn would continually reform after taking damage.

Of course, regeneration didn't explain how the Hyde had lasted through Vermillionangel's assault. It only explained how it could recover from it. The monstrosity had still tanked an S-tier Finisher to the face and survived.

The Hyde's defensive ability was the highest Julian had ever seen.

Vermillionangel gaped.

"Wait. How did you survive that?"

Vile laughed.

"You have no idea how strong this thing is."

[2]

The Vermillion Flier streaked toward the still-recovering Hyde. Hemoborn were highly vulnerable during their regeneration phase.

Under usual circumstances, a Hemoborn would retreat into cover to fully heal before reentering the fight. But vermillionangel had destroyed all the terrain, and Vile's Grunts had vanished after the destruction of the bunker. There was no cover to be found and no survivors to create it.

Although vermillionangel couldn't use his Finisher again, he'd win if he flew into close range. Sweetshot's bazooka thumped again, but the shot went wide. Someone unfamiliar with Overdrive would have accused the expert pilot of choking, but the reality was that the game itself had forced Sweetshot to miss.

As the red hawk drew closer and closer, it too fell under the dreadful influence of the Hyde's passive abilities. The immensely valuable innate passives were yet another benefit of incorporating the Hemoborn's highly vulnerable biological parts. Most Hemoborn only had a few basic boosts like Regeneration or Bloodlust, a unique performance-enhancing ability that sharply raised your

Mech's strength and mobility as soon as an enemy machine fell below 50% health on two or more parts.

The Horror and Stench enhancements were much rarer. According to the in-game lore of Overdrive, those abilities technically affected the enemy pilot. However, the game developers had wisely implemented a simple debuff to accuracy instead of simulating a horrible stink into their player's virtual cockpits.

With Horror Level 10, the Hyde dropped the movement speed of nearby opponents by 30%. Stench Level 10 meant that shots had an approximately 45% chance of going wide, and the debuff didn't factor in weapon size. Even if you were using an aim-friendly weapon like a bazooka, it would still force your attacks to miss. The mass-fire of Vermillion Judgment had rendered the buff useless, but now that the Finisher was over, the advantage had swung back to Vile.

Under normal circumstances, the Guardian X would dismount the Flier and shoot from out of debuff range, but the Grunt unit was a sitting duck without its teammate's mobility. Vile would gun Sweetshot down as soon as he stepped back onto the ground. The Grunt was just too weak. Sweetshot had no choice but to keep riding and hoping for the best.

As the Hyde continued reforming, it sent another spray of dismembered limbs at the Vermillion Flier from its steadily regenerating shoulder cannon. Vermillionangel's Mech was moving far slower than usual, but he wasn't the Champion for nothing. He specialized in daring assaults on entrenched positions. His slowed machine flipped upside down to avoid the first shot from the recreated gore bazooka. Sweetshot's Guardian X briefly set its own firearm aside to hang tight with both hands.

Red lightning wreaked havoc on the steel infused rib cage. The Hyde trembled, and the second shot from the Gore Bazooka barely missed. Sweetshot returned fire twice, but Stench forced both shots wide.

It was extremely unlucky.

Statistically speaking, the debuff shouldn't have occurred three times in a row. Landing even a single shot would have given Sweetshot's team an enormous advantage. Physical projectiles were far more effective against Hemoborn than energy-based weapons, which was likely why Sweetshot had armed his machine with a bazooka. The Master of Minions was an expert at using a Grunt's ability to change weapons before every fight.

During last year's World Championships, fans had taken to calling his Mechs Patchwork units not only because of their slapdash appearances but also because of his effortless ability to shift between roles. Sweetshot303 had played as a frontline Attacker, a backline Artillery unit, and a team-focused Support. He'd even incorporated transformation abilities into his machine to access the Wild-type for the final battle against vermillionangel.

Once again, Sweetshot had adjusted his machine to counter his opponents' Mech. But because of unlucky RNG, he'd missed all three of his shots.

When Vile raised her bazooka again, she launched the shot straight into the ground instead of aiming at her opponents. Rocks flew high into the air, obscuring the view of all three machines. Vermillionangel and Sweetshot were blinded.

But Hemoborn could smell.

The curtains of stone had little effect on Vile. The bazooka's revolting bullet smashed right into the backpedaling bird. One of the wings was torn right off, sending the Flier cartwheeling haphazardly through the air.

Somehow, the masterful Champion turned the situation to his advantage. Vile's shot had revealed her position. As his Flier fell through the air, vermillionangel fired his full quantity of feather epées.

Miraculously, over half of them struck vulnerable flesh. The monstrous Hyde was instantly marred with countless cuts. In particular, the Champion had landed two critical hits.

The first feather tore off the cannon at the base of the shoulder.

The second feather slammed into the vulnerable spot just beneath the knee. Vile cried out in surprise as the Hyde stumbled.

The Guardian X's bazooka thumped again, and this time, it struck true. Sweetshot had somehow accounted for the massive Mech falling over. He'd pre-aimed the lower angle, knowing that at least one of vermillionangel's shots would strike home at the vulnerable joint. The two pilot's synergy was incredible. It was hard to believe they hadn't played together before, that they were only a pair of famous names thrown together for the exhibition match.

The Hyde's freshly reconstructed face was instantly rent in half. Blood and shattered bone flew high into the air. Mealy brain sloughed to the floor. When he saw the brain, Julian paused the game and zoomed in.

The shot had nearly been game-winning. The Vermillion Judgment had melted the Hemoborn's face, but the enormous bazooka bullet had penetrated even deeper and almost killed the Hyde's pilot. Most machines had cockpits in the chest, but the cockpits of Hemoborn were located in the brain. The bullet had torn off a full third of mealy gray matter, leaving Vile exposed. Her hands were wrapped tightly around the controls, which she'd designed to look like nerve endings.

Julian replayed the clip.

Vile had shifted the Hyde's head at the very last second when she realized what was about to happen. Otherwise, she would have died. It was unbelievable. If Julian had been in her position, he would have lost before realizing what had happened. Julian was a skilled swordsman, but superstars were on a completely different level. He didn't know how he'd even begin getting that good.

The crippling damage remained when Julian started the clip back up again. The Hyde's Overdrive boost had ended. From here on out, the wily Fortress Master could no longer recover from the enemy duo's damaging attacks.

However, the gambit had taken its toll on Vile's opponents. They'd risked everything on attacking with no thought of what came after.

The flightless bird crashed to the floor, inadvertently crushing its remaining wing beneath its weight. The Eternium sparked and fizzled as it became solid again. Just like Vile, vermillionangel had spent the rest of his Overdrive boost.

The Guardian X was thrown off completely, skidding across the ruined terrain. Each jarring impact sent a spray of stone and metal high into the air. The health report flickered over its head as the spherical unit forced itself back to its feet.

Head: N/A
Torso: 31%
Left Arm: Destroyed
Right Arm: 15%
Left Leg: 22%
Right Leg: 40%

After falling from such great heights, the Mech was at the edge of unusability.

The ferocious Hyde lumbered towards its damaged foes, its speed sharply increasing with every step. The red aura around the Mech indicated that its Level 10 Bloodlust passive was fully activated.

Sweetshot raised his bazooka again. Without his left arm, the enormous cannon was poorly balanced. The veteran pilot compensated by falling to a crouch and balancing it on his knee.

The flightless Vermillion Flier sprinted forward like a dinosaur, spewing red lightning from its beak.

The scene was set for a final clash.

Then, with no warning whatsoever, a hideous mass of arms and legs burst from beneath the ground, wrenching Sweetshot to the floor.

It was a haphazard jumble of flesh and metal like nothing Julian had ever seen before. At first, he thought it was some sort of extraordinary ability, a Finisher for Hemoborn. Only Paragons had access to Finishers, but with Vile's crafting skills, anything seemed possible.

It was only when the status notifications appeared at the bottom of Julian's spectator screen that he realized the truth. They were Grunts. During the siege on the bunker, Vile must have ordered her teammates to bury underground and fake their deaths. They'd been waiting for the perfect moment to strike.

Julian wasn't sure if Vile had designed her Grunts herself, but the tattered machines were just as hideous as their commander unit.

The Mechs looked like zombies, and the substantial damage they'd taken only furthered their utterly terrifying visage. Unlike an Ace unit, a Hemoborn Grunt couldn't upgrade their Regeneration abilities using an Overdrive boost. The rotting flesh on their mostly metal bodies was slowly stitching itself back together, but the bones and sagging organs were still almost entirely exposed. Even most of their mechanical parts had been damaged. There was a piece of bunker buried deep in the head of the second machine.

Of the two Mechs grappling with Sweetshot, neither of them had a single part higher than 50% health. But there was little even the Master of Minions could do. The Zombie-like Grunts had a lesser version of the Hyde's Bloodlust passive. Their movements seemed almost Ace-like as they tore the battered Mech to pieces. Sweetshot furiously fought for position. He wrenched a revolver from his hip and lurched towards the first machine, slamming the gun straight into its head. Before Sweetshot could destroy the brain, a vicious kick from its teammate spent the spherical Guardian X tumbling towards the side of the stage.

Vermillionangel turned back to his dying teammate. The flightless bird streaked to its ally's aid. If he couldn't save Sweetshot, he'd almost certainly lose in a three against one battle. Even worse, he didn't know what had happened to the hypothetical third Zombie-like Grunt unit.

Had it been destroyed in the fall of the bunker? Was it lurking beneath the earth?

It was impossible to tell. Vile's strategy was like something right out of her beloved horror stories.

As soon as vermillionangel turned away, the Hyde transformed.

[3]

Even an idiot could tell that the Hyde had transforming capabilities. It was evident in the Mech's name. Julian hadn't spent a lot of time paying attention in high school English, but he wasn't an idiot. Almost everyone knew about Dr. Jekyll and his counterpart Mr. Hyde. Amusingly, Vile had reversed the two characters to befit her preference for bulkier units.

But Julian was still surprised when he saw what happened. Julian had fought against and alongside transforming Mechs—commonly called Shifters—before. He'd even used some. But he'd never seen a machine that shapeshifted like so quickly.

The change was instantaneous and as fluid as a splash of blood.

One moment, the hulking Hyde monstrosity loomed over its distracted foes. One second later, Jekyll leaped high into the air as the transformation ejected enormous chunks of flesh and metal. The machine wasn't precisely a Shifter, as the Mech couldn't switch back. The Hyde essentially served as a set of armor for the thin and highly mobile core Jekyll unit.

The bazooka became an enormous sword. The extensive ribcage damage meant the Jekyll only had two wings remaining instead of four, but the Mech still moved with unearthly speed, catching its panicked enemies completely unaware.

Vermillionangel was desperately trying to tear the Zombies off of Sweetshot, but he still had time to turn and fire. The Flier twisted and spat yet another gout of red lightning, perfectly timing the shot with the flesh and metal monstrosity's descent.

Considering the harried circumstances, it was a near-flawless shot.

But it wasn't enough.

Vile was a Fortress Master, an expert of defense and staying alive. The slender Mech somersaulted mid-air. A mix of dark blood and fuel burst through the air as the lightning evaporated the machine's off-hand instead of its exposed brain.

The Jekyll was grievously wounded, but the fight was over. Before Julian could even blink, the sword was stuck all the way through the crimson bird's chest. One second later, the Flier exploded.

There were two booming shots, and then the Guardian X stumbled to its feet. Sweetshot had somehow managed to kill both the enemy Grunts, but his Mech was so severely damaged that it couldn't even walk. It raised the revolver in its hand, aiming for yet another headshot. He didn't stand a chance.

The Jekyll reached deep into its back. Julian shivered as Vile yanked out her spine whip and slammed it through the enemy cockpit, instantly ending the match.

Julian was tempted to use a Hemoborn every time he saw Vile fight. Not every member of the class was gruesome. Others were Wild-types based on animals—amazing looking cyborgs like dinosaurs armed with a battalion of guns.

As the battle ended, a handsome pilot with a mane of long black hair and an enormous smile turned and waved at the screen. Even in defeat, Vermillionangel was every inch the charismatic Champion. He'd received an offer from Overdrive to become a

Fortress Master, but he'd turned it down due to his love of competing in tournaments. Prize pools didn't pay nearly as well as a sturdy Fortress Master's salary, but vermillionangel made most of his money from streaming. His stream had incredibly high viewership and was beloved by both competitive fans and casual players alike.

Every time he saw him, Julian became incredibly jealous. He had nothing against vermillionangel—he seemed like an awesome guy—but Julian constantly dreamed about being in the handsome man's position. Vermillionangel was the same age as Julian, yet he was a millionaire who got to play games for a living. He was the first Overdrive streamer who really took off. First came the fans. Next came the riches. Then came the media profiles. Vermillionangel's boundless enthusiasm and charisma made him the perfect representative for the Overdrive Corporation.

Vile stepped out of her machine and then dismissed it with a wave of her hand. Unlike vermillionangel, the bespectacled English teacher only gave a passing wave to the camera. Even after gaining worldwide fame, Vile was still very shy.

A stage rose in the middle of the crowd, and then the two masters of the game were elevated side by side. Unlike last year's hastily organized in-person World Championship, this exhibition was a virtual match. The Overdrive administration was coordinating everything behind the scenes to ensure a fluid event.

Ever the showman, vermillionangel bowed deeply for the audience.

"What an amazing event, and what an honor to fight for you guys using such exquisite machines."

He shook his head.

"The contest winners were far better crafters than I ever could be. Truth be told, their designs exceeded my ability. I couldn't bring out the full potential of the Vermillion Flier. Otherwise, we would have won."

To a degree, vermillionangel was just being polite. If he couldn't bring out the full potential of a Wild Paragon, nobody could. He was the absolute master of that category.

In Julian's opinion, the main reason he'd lost was simply that the Hyde/Jekyll machine was better.

"Next off, I wanted to thank the great pilots who fought alongside me. Sweetshot303, Peacock, and TiggerLuvr888. You played splendidly. Perhaps we would have had a better chance with one of you in the Ace slot. I should have been better prepared for Vile's scheme!"

Julian wasn't sure if they would have done better with someone else playing the Ace, but it was hard to disagree with his assessment that the Grunts weren't to blame. The battle had fallen into vermillionangel's hands, and although his chances of victory had been slim, he'd been the one to lose.

Grunts weren't expected to win the fight—they were just Grunts. Their role was to support the Ace or counter the other team's strategy on a shoestring budget. Julian had piloted Grunts a few times before—usually when he landed on a randomly matched group where he wasn't skilled enough to be the Ace. It was pretty unexciting, and it often resulted in his rank falling. It felt like Sweetshot303 was the only player who could significantly influence the game as a Grunt unit.

"And finally, my amazing opponent. It is always an honor to face you. I hope that next time, I'll be crafty enough to break your defenses. Despite your reputation for raw power, you proved that you've got some brilliant tricks up your sleeve. Tunneling Zombies!"

Vermillionangel shook his head, a giant smile on his face. The Champion was known for his sportsmanship. According to rumors, he was just as polite if you were lucky enough to end up in a competitive match or mission lobby with him.

The handsome man turned and bowed deeply to the woman who'd defeated him.

There was an awkward pause, and then Vile laughed nervously. The former teacher shyly stepped up to the stage.

"Yes. I wanted to thank everyone. Especially my teammates. I am so sorry about the bunker collapsing on you, Superbian. I should have had you guys get out earlier."

She sighed and shook her head. Even though she'd won, she was acting as if she'd lost.

A slight smile sprang to Julian's lips. He knew where Vile was coming from. The crafters and exhibition fighters put their full heart into their machines, and it would have been a disappointment to be eliminated before you even got a chance to appear in battle.

The former teacher meandered onto a few tangents before finally returning on topic. Unlike vermillionangel, Vile seemed like she was just a regular person. Her counterpart had been born to be a superstar. Vile was just insanely good at Overdrive, which made her the perfect Fortress Master, someone who designed Mechs and maps behind the scenes.

She turned back to the crowd again.

"Thank you for watching!"

Then she wavered for a moment before catching herself.

"Oh! Also, I wanted to announce that my shop is now open! I will be selling various Mechs and also opening up for a few commissions. All proceeds will be donated to charity. I also wanted to highlight the designer who created our Zombie Grunts! What amazing machines, I wish I came up with them myself! I'll also provide the link to her store, hang on here..."

Vile trailed off as she pulled up her status screen.

Julian waffled on whether or not to turn off the screen. Looking at her shop would only make him feel bad.

He needed to save money.

Julian still didn't have a job for after graduation, and the fear was starting to mount. He'd spent way too much time on Overdrive and too little time looking for internships. Now his complete lack of a resume was piling up, and it felt like everything was snowballing.

As of right now, there was no chance Julian could afford a Mech from either Vile or the creator of the Zombie Grunt. The Overdrive Corporation purchased frequently used Grunt unit designs and made them available in the general shop, but Julian was only interested in Ace frames. A Mech crafted by Vile probably cost around the $1,000 range. Tigger had sold one of his personal Mechs at that price. Although Vile's wares wouldn't be game-used memorabilia, she was an even better designer than the World Championship semi-finalist.

He should probably be looking for a job now instead of watching the exhibition. Maybe then he'd be able to buy something nice for himself.

But even though it'd feel terrible, Julian wanted to window shop for a while after seeing so many perfect Mechs.

After that, he'd get to work.

He'd already watched the exhibition anyways, and it wouldn't make too much of a difference to wait a few more minutes to get the link to the Zombie designer's new store.

But before Vile could say anything else, The Mechanical King barged onto the stage and shoved her aside. The bespectacled teacher nearly tripped as she scurried off the platform.

Julian facepalmed. Overdrive was the best game he'd ever played, but the CEO of the company was always acting like a huge idiot. He was always forcing his way into these events and making it all about himself. According to Julian's friend Felix, who was an aspiring professional player, almost everyone in the competitive scene thought The Mechanical King sucked. Not even the Fortress Masters liked him.

"Hello! Thanks for coming to my event!"

The Mechanical King flexed his enormous muscles. Overdrive's body scan meant that your avatars in Overdrive were identical to your real-world appearance, but that rule didn't apply to The Mechanical King. According to Felix, The Mechanical King wasn't nearly as muscular in real life as he was on the server.

"I am Drake 'The Mechanical King' Dunn, also known as THE DUNN! I'm the creator of Overdrive!"

Julian fast-forwarded the stream to catch up to the current time. He'd spent a lot of time pausing to look at status screens. He hoped that meant he'd be able to skip past the boring speech, but The Mechanical King was still talking when Julian's stream returned to the present.

Julian shook his head and gave up on getting the information about Vile's shop. He'd just check her stream later. The Mechanical King was comically long-winded.

During the last year's World Championship Final, vermillionangel had finally overcome Sweetshot's team after a grueling 7 hour set. Unlike every other match, the finals had been a best-of-five series. Each game had dragged on to over an hour of trench warfare after Sweetshot recognized that his team's weaker Ace couldn't compete with vermillionangel in high-speed shooting duels. The innovative Grunt pilot nearly won by dragging every match out and inflicting a massive mental toll on every player. By the time vermillionangel's team finally emerged victorious, all eight players looked like they wanted to instantly teleport back home.

Yet even after that set, The Mechanical King had kept them on stage for another two hours so he could give a five thousand word speech on perseverance.

Right now, it looked like he was going for a repeat.

Julian shook his head and closed out of the stream. He moved back to his computer and set his Overdrive control board aside.

The highest level pros used a full-body rig that could simulate their movements in the games. The control board was the cheaper alternative, a set of buttons and switches that he could put in front of his monitor in place of a keyboard.

A long list of job applications stared back at him. The first position was actually for esports development at the Overdrive Corporation. They were looking for someone who could help them set up events.

It'd be amazing to work there.

Hopefully, The Mechanical King wouldn't be the person interviewing him. There was a good chance that would happen—the Overdrive Corporation was still a small company despite its sudden outburst of incredible popularity—but Julian didn't want a lengthy interview. Julian didn't like interviews. He'd only done two before, and he'd flubbed both of them. It was hard talking about yourself.

There was a loud knock on his door.

"Yo. Yo. Julian. You in there?"

Julian hurried to the door.

Tyler had been his roommate since his freshman year. They'd been a random pairing, and while the two of them had seemed very different on the surface, they'd become incredibly fast friends.

When he opened the door, his best friend stared back down at him, fiddling with the knot of his tie. Unlike Julian, Tyler wasn't having any problems finding job interviews. He'd been working toward a career in finance since high school, and he'd spent every summer researching on campus or interning in New York. On top of that, he had additional connections through alumni on the school basketball team. People were practically begging to hire him.

"What's up?"

To his surprise, Tyler promptly pulled his phone out of his bag and showed him the video of The Mechanical King blathering.

"Yo, have you played this game before? I thought we could play this together. I know you like robot games."

Julian let out a bemused laugh.

"I do play this game. It's the game I've always been playing."

He'd explained Overdrive to Tyler before, but the words had always gone in one ear and out the other.

Tyler blinked and then laughed with him.

"Oh. Wow. My bad."

He smiled sheepishly.

"Hey, look, I knew it was a robot game."

His friend upped the volume, and The Mechanical King's whiny voice echoed through the room, praising himself for creating such a great community.

"Who is this guy?"

"He's the game owner."

Tyler laughed.

"Oh, I thought he was a player. Don't know why anyone would want to listen to some owner go on for half an hour. I think if that happened in the NBA, people would just walk out of the stadium."

"It might get even longer than that."

Julian peaked at the viewer count at the edge of the screen and smirked. The view total had dwindled from nearly a hundred thousand people at the end of the match to barely over ten thousand.

"So anyway, if you've been playing this game for so long, do you think you could teach me?"

Julian scratched his head in confusion. Julian had no idea where his best friend's enthusiasm was coming from.

Of course he wanted to play with Tyler!

After spending so much time passing the ball to him in the

post as they crushed teams in rec league basketball, it was about time for Julian to be the star.

Unfortunately, it hadn't worked out yet. The two of them had tried finding video games to play together before, but Tyler just wasn't much of a gamer.

"Of course! But what happened? I didn't even know you liked games."

[4]

Before Tyler could explain why he was suddenly interested in Overdrive, The Mechanical King clapped his hands over his head and said his first valuable sentences of the night. It was still somewhat jarring hearing the Overdrive CEO's familiar whiny voice from Tyler's phone.

"Alright. Now, time for the most important announcement of the day. I am announcing a new Selection process! In two months, we will open two new Fortresses! With a new Selection coming up, I urge you to chase a top five hundred spot on the ladder!"

Julian's eyes widened.

Selection was the most exciting time to be a highly ranked Overdrive player. It meant the game administration was searching for new Fortress Masters.

If you were one of the top five hundred overall ranked players on the server, you were invited to a series of special camps at the Overdrive world headquarters in Los Angeles. Out of that group, the game administration would select 2 Fortress Aces and 6 Fortress Grunts. Although the Grunts technically played a lesser role, the community colloquially referred to anyone employed by an official Fortress as a Fortress Master.

Fortress Masters were the equivalent of dungeon masters in traditional tabletop role-playing games. Overdrive had countless default missions run by AI, but the human experts' maps were far more difficult. Last year, fully clearing any Fortress and finishing the bonus stage of defeating the team that ran it granted your squad an automatic berth to the World Championships. There were millions of Overdrive players, but only seventy teams accomplished that task and qualified for the World Championships.

Julian had played the game since the beta during his junior year of high school, long before it became popular. But despite his experience, he'd only ever cleared two Fortresses, and he'd never come close to defeating a Fortress team. As Overdrive had grown in popularity, so had the wealth and prestige associated with becoming a Fortress Master. When considering the position's stability, it was even better than playing on a World Championship level team.

Tyler tapped the screen and paused it.

"What's the deal with this Fortress Master thing?"

Julian frowned.

"Wait, you want to be a Fortress Master? Is that why you asked me about Overdrive?"

Tyler shook his head. A bewildered smirk crossed his face.

"What? No. Why would I want to do that?"

"Well, you've never shown any interest in games before. I thought you might have seen how much the Fortress Masters make."

Tyler paused. Julian's best friend had never cared about games, but he did like making money.

"Wait. How much do they make?"

Julian shrugged.

"I mean, it depends on how good your Fortress is. But an officially sanctioned Fortress Ace makes about $110,000. If you're a Grunt, you make about $60,000."

Some organizations split the fees evenly between Aces and Grunts, but they were few and far between. Usually, the Master took a larger share of the earnings.

"Woah, really? That's a lot more than I thought."

"Well, it's a full-time thing. You need to monitor everyone challenging your Fortress. On top of that, the whole community is out there making guides on how to beat you. You need to continually mix things up."

"What about the big streamers? What do they do, anyways?"

The way Tyler said "streamers," it sounded like he was reading off a pile of notecards.

Julian laughed.

"What's gotten into you? Why are you suddenly paying attention to Overdrive stuff? Streamers are basically people who broadcast themselves playing. It's a full-time job for some people—if you make enough money doing it—but it's not exclusive. Like Fortress Masters can stream too, and so can pilots who contend for the World Championship. And then there are just people who just stream."

Julian stuck to watching Fortress Masters or World Championship teams. There weren't too many full-time streamers that caught his attention. Some of them were downright weird. DISTINCTIONMAN50000 was known for his selfish gameplay and bizarre attitude. Julian could never figure out why he was one of the most popular streamers on the server.

Of course, some players had a lot of viewers because they were beautiful women. If Julian were honest with himself, he definitely had a cyber-crush on one of them. Lilac was incredible at Overdrive—she was ranked in the top 100—but Julian usually watched her with the sound off. She was a hardcore rager.

"So how much do they make?"

"It depends, but if you have a ton of viewers, you can do really well for yourself. The game's been out for a while, but it only exploded in popularity recently. In the past, people could only stream part-time. Like my favorite streamer was a computer engineer until this year. But now I would say you can probably pull in six figures from streaming between donations, ads, and sponsorships. In even bigger games, there are people making millions a year."

"Wow! Why don't you do that?"

Julian laughed. As much as he wanted to make money playing Overdrive, the thought of becoming a pro streamer was even worse than becoming a pro crafter.

"I've tried streaming before, but I didn't get any traction. Streaming is hard. It's hard to talk while playing. I don't even know what I'd talk about. I tried once, but I just got discouraged and quit. I'm not a very exciting guy."

Tyler made an irritated face, which was so predictable that Julian had to laugh. Tyler was always getting on him for being easily discouraged. It was pretty unfortunate. Julian had enough self-awareness to know that he did a lot of quitting, but not the willpower to do anything about it. It was probably why he didn't have a job either.

But in this case, Julian was right. He couldn't be a streamer.

Tyler just didn't get it. He was only just now asking questions about Overdrive. He didn't get how the gaming scene worked.

Building up an organic audience was hard. There was a chance you could appear in a highlight clip and suddenly go viral overnight, but that was such a crapshoot. And even if you did get a lucky break, it was a lot of work to keep the bump. During his short-lived streaming career, Julian had once spiked to about three hundred viewers after he made it onto the second Fortress's high-light reel. But they'd all left soon after because he couldn't answer their questions about how he blocked projectiles with his sword. Julian hadn't responded to them fast enough, but it wasn't his fault. Deflecting attacks with the flat of your sword was incredibly mentally taxing.

It was ridiculous. Julian had no idea how people like vermillionangel could chat while making complicated plays.

Nowadays, the World Champion spent more time practicing privately than streaming, but he was bursting with energy whenever he started broadcasting. When Julian tried emulating the champion's energetic attitude, he'd immediately flopped. There was no way he could be more charismatic than a guy like vermillionangel. They were the same age, and the World Champion was already a millionaire celebrity.

Julian just didn't have anything to offer. The exhibition match proved it. Being a good player was one thing. Being a great one was quite another.

Tyler made a dismissive gesture.

"You already know what I'm going to say. Why don't you become a Fortress guy then? Shouldn't you be good enough to make this Selection process?"

Tyler smirked.

"You're certainly playing often enough!"

That had been the one point of contention between them during their first year when they'd shared the same room. Tyler woke up super early for morning basketball practice and went to bed correspondingly early. Julian always slept until noon and stayed up until two or three hammering away at his control board, creating such a racket that his roommate couldn't get back to sleep.

Julian shrugged.

"I'm alright."

He'd barely missed the Selection cut-off last time. They invited the top 500, and he'd finished around 520. It still bummed him out—he'd started the Selection process at 457 until a bad losing streak. But it didn't really make a difference. Even if he made the Selection, he wouldn't get picked to run a Fortress. Being in the top five hundred players was different from being one of the eight chosen pilots. Most Selection "contestants" just went to Los Angeles for a free vacation.

Julian was terrible at using Grunt units, and he wasn't good enough to be selected as a Fortress Ace. He would have happily switched Mechs to become a Fortress Grunt, but the chosen Grunt pilots were still usually picked from the top 100. Most of them were former Ace users who transitioned to Grunts in exchange for a high paying job. There were players capable of playing both roles, but Julian wasn't one of them. He wasn't going to spend all his time learning how to use Grunts if his goal was still so far away.

He thought back to the superstars' instant reactions during the show match. Julian couldn't manage that. He had great control skills, but he relied on instinct rather than quick wits.

But still, it would have been nice to go there and meet all the star players. TiggerLuvr888 had attended last Selection, although he'd taken himself out of contention to play at the World Championships. Julian would love to meet his favorite streamer, but the opportunity had slipped through his fingers last time, and he wasn't sure if he'd bother trying again.

There was an invitation for a one-on-one match waiting for him in his Overdrive inbox that Julian was trying not to think about.

If he won, he'd probably make the Selection. But if he lost again...

Dynamic was ranked in the mid-300s. Due to the ranked difference, Julian would immediately vault past the qualification line if he beat the skilled sniper. However, Dynamic had already beaten Julian twice in a row. If they played again, Julian would probably just continue falling down the ranks. That was how he'd lost his spot last time.

"Where would you put yourself compared to the people in the exhibition? I read that it was like an All-Star game."

Julian scoffed.

"Not even close. It'd be like if you had to play one on one against LeBron or something. I'm pretty good, but those guys are the best in the world."

Tyler's eyes widened.

"Wait, really? That good?"

Julian nodded.

"Yeah. Vermillionangel's team was the star players from the world championship. They basically got the best players on the top four finishing teams to play together. Vile's team—the one with all the scary Mechs—was made up of the four strongest Fortress Aces."

Tyler frowned.

"Wait a second. But didn't he just say you only needed to be in the top five hundred?"

"Yeah."

"What rank are you?"

"It varies because you can go up or down depending on how everyone around you is doing, but the last time I checked I was 531."

Tyler grinned from ear to ear.

"That's amazing! You can totally qualify! Making the Selection is more like making the NBA. It's not like being the best player in the NBA. Like yeah, there's a huge gap between LeBron and the worst player in the NBA, but that gap is infinitely smaller than the gap between me and the worst player in the NBA."

Tyler shook his head.

"I'm not one of the best five hundred basketball players in the world—not even close! Once you get into the top five hundred and apply to be in the Selection, you've got a shot. That's all you need, you know, a shot!"

He pointed at Julian's laptop and scoffed at the application on the screen.

"Come on, man—think about how much time you're already playing. It's practically a full-time job. Why would you apply to be a lackey when you get a shot to be a Fortress Master?"

Julian smiled.

Only Tyler would be so direct with him.

Well, that wasn't entirely true.

His parents were pretty direct with him too.

Once they heard about the last Selection process, they'd excitedly encouraged him to go for it. It'd been a strange experience having his parents encouraging him to play games—they'd spent most of his childhood telling him to game less and study more. Maybe they'd just realized that this was his best bet.

Julian wondered if they'd message him again about the new Selection. Overdrive was getting big enough that news about the game got reported on local TV stations.

He hoped his parents didn't know about it. They hid it well, but he could tell how disappointed they were when he'd failed to qualify last time around. Julian probably wouldn't make it this time either, unless he got lucky. The hail of gunfire that ended his second battle against Dynamic still gave him nightmares.

"I didn't even qualify last time."

"You could have."

Julian rolled his eyes.

Tyler always said stuff like this, no matter what the topic was.

He would just bull rush in, saying things like "anything is possible" or "you got this!"

"No, I couldn't have. I fell about 70 spots and didn't make it. I actually was in the mid-400s at the start."

Tyler shook his head.

"Stuff like that is just luck! Weren't there a few games you came close to winning that you didn't?"

"Yeah, I guess."

His matches against Dynamic had been pretty one-sided, but there'd been others. If he'd won those, he could have created a larger buffer.

"Well, you should definitely try again! There are millions of people playing, right? If you were only seventy spots off, that means you were super close! Like from a percentage point of view, you were like less than a hundredth of a percent away! And besides, you'll have me with you this time."

Tyler grinned and gestured Julian into his room.

To his surprise, his friend had purchased an expensive new Overdrive set-up. His board wasn't a full-body rig, but the latest control board still boasted far higher performance than the beat-up model Julian had used since high school.

Even more impressive was the new massive computer tower that took up half his desk. One of the biggest problems with higher performance Overdrive equipment was that they took up correspondingly more computing power. The best rigs instantly transmitted your commands to your Mech, making it seem like you were sitting right inside the cockpit.

Julian let out a surprised cough at all the expensive gear. Tyler rarely did anything halfway, and his wealthy family had the resources to support him.

His friend nodded seriously.

"Look. The season is over. My basketball career is over. I need something to do with all the time I spent training. I'm going to get good at this whether you take it seriously or not. But I'd want you to take it seriously."

He grinned confidently.

"In fact, I'll make this my second goal. I'm going to train with you until you become a Fortress Master."

Julian frowned.

"What's your first goal?"

Instead of answering directly, Tyler pulled out his tablet and scrolled backward. Instead of focusing on the duel against Vile and vermillionangel, Tyler zoomed in on the battle between Sweetshot303 and the two Zombie Grunts.

Despite the intense damage to his Mech, Sweetshot had landed two consecutive headshots.

"How strong are these Zombie Mechs? They looked super powerful."

Julian took the tablet and pulled up the status report.

- General Data -

Pilot: Harper7

Machine: CWT-141 Zombie Grunt

Class: Cyborg

Sub-class: Attacker

Designation: Grunt Unit

- Statistics -

Melee: A-tier

Shooting: B-tier

Speed: A-tier

Maneuverability: B-tier

Defense: A-tier

Cohesion: S-tier

- Weapons -

Zombie Steel-Infused Jaw (Full Custom)

Zombie Bone Dagger v2 [x2]

Zombie Blade Type-D (Full Custom) [x1]

Zombie Machinegun [x1]

Zombie Vulcan [x8]

- Abilities -

Relentless Level 8

Bloodlust Level 8

The Zombies lacked the Hyde's defensive abilities. Nevertheless, the combination of high level Relentless—which allowed continued attacks despite significant damage to your Mech—and Bloodlust passives meant the Hemoborn could fight like an actual member of the undead.

Although it was a mass-produced Grunt, all the parts were masterfully built. It was a miracle that Sweetshot303 had defeated both of them with such a badly damaged machine. He truly was the Master of Minions.

"Yeah. They're really strong. Under the right circumstances—like if I had low health points—they could even beat my personal machine, which is an Ace unit."

He quickly explained to Tyler the difference between Grunts and Aces.

His friend's eyes widened.

"So if someone can beat someone using an Ace with a Grunt, that means they're really good, right?"

"Yeah, usually. So this guy..."

Julian pointed at Sweetshot's battered Guardian X.

"He's known as the Master of Minions—basically an incredible Grunt pilot. He's been playing Grunts since he started, and he was the only non-Ace invited to the exhibition. He's actually way better than the Ace pilot on their team. It seems stupid to me. If someone is so good, why not just make them the Ace and build around him?"

Tyler ignored Julian's musings.

"So how long do you think it'll take for me to beat this guy? If I trained every day."

Julian let out a startled laugh.

"I mean..."

Where would Julian even begin? The difference between the Master of Minions and a total beginner—someone who didn't play video games at all—was an enormous chasm.

Tyler pressed forward.

"Look. I know he was second place in the World Championships last year. That was a real question. How long would it take?"

Tyler had clearly done a bit of research.

When Julian wavered again, Tyler explained exactly why he was so determined to get good at Overdrive.

"Sweetshot is Brandon. From back home."

Tyler's grin was almost childlike.

"This is a chance for us to have a rematch."

Julian blinked.

"Wait, really? That's Brandon?"

Now that Julian thought about it, Sweetshot really did look like the kid from Tyler's old photos. He was surprised he hadn't seen it earlier.

Julian knew all about Brandon. He'd been Tyler's teammate on their youth and high school travel basketball teams. According to Tyler, Brandon had been an incredibly special player. Their team was undefeatable with him on the court. He'd been good enough to go pro until repeated leg and knee injuries his junior year.

"Yeah. He sent me an article about the event when I texted him to catch up. Said he was doing a new thing now."

His friend's eyes glimmered with excitement.

"I need to fight him. You know I never beat him in practice. Not even one scrimmage. Maybe I'll have my chance here."

"Did you tell him you were interested in Overdrive?"

"Yeah. I asked him if he wanted to fight."

Tyler chuckled.

"He told me I better shut up and start practicing!"

His friend clicked the Overdrive icon and grabbed the virtual reality headset as the virtual world burst onto his monitor.

"Come on. Let's get going. I get my rematch against Brandon, and you go to the Selection. Let's make it happen!

[5]

Before returning to his room, Julian took one last look at all of Tyler's new equipment. Tyler's complete reversal on gaming would seem bizarre to an outsider, but Julian knew his best friend very well. Not getting to compete against and alongside his childhood rival had always been Tyler's greatest basketball regret, even more than not being good enough to make the NBA.

The equipment must have cost north of two thousand dollars, but it was nothing to Tyler and his family. After his finance signing bonus came in, Tyler would probably forget about the money entirely. In the old days, Tyler would have bought a new rig for Julian too. But by now, he knew that Julian would just refuse to accept it. Julian thought extravagant gifts were absurd, but to Tyler, it was like loaning a buddy a few dollars. His family was stinking rich.

Julian returned to his room and activated his headset and control board. A green light briefly flashed to scan his body. Moments later, he was back in the world he loved. As soon as he appeared in the lobby, he opened up his status screen and moved himself to the new player's landing zone.

Veteran Overdrive players could access the landing zone to

guide newbies through the new account process. The in-game Overdrive start-up guide was difficult to understand. Because Overdrive's popularity was blowing past their game management processes, the administration had outsourced a lot of work to its players. There were even veteran pilots who spent most of their time playing on maps meant for beginners to serve as guides and trainers. Julian knew a kid in high school who'd tried—and failed—to get community service hours by acting as an Overdrive guide.

"Wait. Tyler's not available?"

His friend sounded shocked. He hadn't picked his name yet, but Tyler already looked just like he usually did—a behemoth with neatly cut brown hair. There was no avatar creation process in Overdrive. The game just scanned you in. The only way to get around the body scan was by using a Guest account, which Julian had played on until his first year in college.

Julian laughed.

"No. Why would it be available? It's like an email. Your email isn't tyler@gmail."

"Oh. That's weird. But your name is Julian."

"Ah yeah, I've been playing since the beta test."

"Oh wow! You've been playing that long?"

"Yeah, I started in high school."

"Huh. When did Brandon start?"

Julian pulled out the account information, running a quick search for Sweetshot303 in the player-run Database. The Database was essentially a Wikipedia for notable pilots. Like most community-created content, it outperformed the game's innate account search features.

"About two years ago."

Dang.

Julian winced in anticipation of Tyler's obvious follow-up question.

"Why is he so much better than you?"

Julian had spent a lot of time playing Overdrive, but his improvement had been pitifully slow. It was only during his sophomore year of college that he'd broken into the top 1,000. There weren't really any guides or coaches. Even when Julian watched his favorite players stream, it took him a while to figure out what they were trying to do.

However, Tyler didn't ask why Brandon was so much better than Julian. Instead, he smiled as his new screen name, Tyler-Ford21, popped above his head.

"Great. I have less to catch up on. If he can get that good by training seriously, maybe we can too."

That was Tyler's overly positive logic to a hilt.

Julian was about to tell him that it wasn't that simple, but then he caught himself. For all he knew, it could be that simple. Brandon had succeeded through a combination of diligence and innate talent. Julian knew that Tyler was similarly determined, and he had no idea how good his friend could be. Since Tyler hadn't even played other video games before, he was a totally blank slate.

As soon as Tyler created an account, he immediately launched his status screen and dove into the guidebook. Information about the various available Mechs swirled in front of him.

Julian hadn't even understood what all the Classes did until his second year in the game. It took even longer for him to figure out the limitations of Overdrive's statistics system. The four Types were poor descriptions, and the rankings weren't particularly accurate. Even if two units boasted an S-tier classification for a stat like Speed, one could still be significantly faster than the other. There was a gradient within every tier. Until his fourth year playing, Julian had thought that an S was just an S.

Tyler wouldn't make those mistakes. Julian's best friend never did anything halfheartedly. Tyler still remembered his junior high school basketball playbook.

Tyler mused as he continued scrolling down the screen.

"I've played DND a couple of times before, so I have a basic grasp of this. So basically, your Class is like your race. And then your Type is like what people would normally call your job—like a mage or something like that, right?"

"Yeah."

"And then Ace is like if you're the star."

"Kind of. It's more about the Credit cap that I mentioned earlier. You don't necessarily need to be the Ace to be the star of your team. Just look at Brandon. Besides, that's only for competitive games or Fortress challenges. We'll be doing quests first. I'll try to pick ones where we can both use Ace units."

"It looks like there are some benefits to Grunts, though."

"I mean, there's a few."

"Didn't Brandon give some interviews about how they could be stronger under the right circumstances?"

"Yeah, but it's hard to say. So there are three big benefits— one for questing and two for competitive play."

Since Tyler wanted to train and defeat one of the best players on the server, Julian decided to emphasize competitive play even though most beginners spent their time questing and grinding for prizes.

"So there are two advantages in competitive play. The first is that you get to adjust your machine after seeing the enemy Ace unit and map. Grunts load into the match as frames, and then you get to equip the parts you want to use onto it. On the other hand, when you use an Ace, the Mech's equipment is already locked in. The other advantage is just that there are simply more spots for you on a team of you are a Grunt-user. Each team has one Ace and three Grunts. That's how Brandon ended up on a World Championship team in just his first year playing. He mastered Grunts."

Some players thought that was a cheap path to getting on a top team. After all, if you were playing a game with awesome Mechs, why would you deliberately choose to play a weaker machine? Julian sort of agreed. The one Ace three Grunt format was a stupid way to balance out competitive play. It was just to keep up with the in-game lore, but people didn't play Overdrive for the in-game lore. Julian couldn't even remember any of the stale characters or plotlines, which had all been ripped off of various mecha anime. It'd be way cooler if everyone could use an Ace machine.

"And then for quests, the big benefit for Grunt units is that they have a really low cost of repair. You can keep using them repeatedly. But if your Ace is damaged, you get put on cooldown unless you pay for repairs."

Tyler frowned.

"You need to pay to play this game?"

"Sort of. You can use either in-game currency or real money, which is called Credits."

Julian smiled.

"Most people think you're a sucker if you pay just to get rid of your cooldown—that's why they have it after all. But I'm not going to lie. I've done that a couple times before."

It was only a buck to perform a rapid repair your machine the first time in a week and then five bucks after that. On the other hand, it cost over 5,000 Credits per repair. If you used Credits to pay for a repair, you'd probably come out negative on missions. That was how the Overdrive Corporation tricked you into paying them, but it also worked.

"Hm. Looks like you can play more recklessly if your machine is cheaper to repair. That's probably why Brandon played Grunts actually. So he could practice more. I should probably start with them too."

Julian paused for a moment as he processed what Tyler was saying.

"Oh yeah. I guess that's true."

Julian hadn't thought about it that way before, but using Grunts did let you practice more. The Mechs were also more specialized because they only had 10,000 Credits to use on their parts.

Tyler was already thinking about everything.

Julian frowned as a troubling thought crossed his mind.

There were probably some hardcore map grinders who were good at using Grunts for the same reason as Brandon—to get back into the action faster. His childhood friend Felix had first started using the weaker Mechs to grind for loot.

An influx of grinders would make qualifying for the Selection difficult. Skilled Grunt pilots tended to be good at counter-strategies, meaning that they could win one-on-one battles despite their weaker units. They also excelled in the random team queues, which always got clogged with Ace users.

Julian groaned.

"You alright?"

"Yeah, was just thinking about the Selection. There's always some map grinders who make a run at the Selection. Grinders are pilots who focus on playing for player vs. environment—PVE—rather than competitive player vs. player—PVP battles. That means they usually aren't a part of the competitive ladder, but once they move into it, they climb super quickly."

Tyler scoffed.

"Come on, man! There were these 'grinders' last time too, and you still almost made it!"

Julian guessed that was true. He wasn't sure if it'd be worth the work to try again and lose, but hanging out with Tyler was always fun.

He'd ride it out and see how it went. He had been pretty close last time. Maybe it'd be easier if he studied more carefully.

Tyler was still reading through the guide.

"If you beat people, you just get parts? So you don't level up and get stronger. You just get parts."

"Yeah, more or less. I mean, you 'level up' by improving your piloting skills. There's no in-game mechanic. There are games out there where once you get stronger, you can access specific skills like 'Bombardment' to make it easier to shoot, but not in Overdrive."

Tyler nodded.

"Okay, got it."

He continued scrolling.

"Alright, what's this thing? A bet battle?"

"It's just what it sounds like—a battle where the winner gets the other guy's Mech."

"Woah, really? Won't people get mad if you take a nice Mech?"

"Yeah, they basically added it because people would make unofficial bets and then not pay up. If you notice, it isn't part of the three official competitive queues. It's just an option you can select for a custom created battle."

Julian laughed.

"Actually, there's been some pretty crazy grudges. There was even a real-life fight because of it. Someone flew across the country to try and get his Mech back. The game administration ended up permanently banning both players."

Julian had done a few bet battles before. It was actually how he'd won his current machine, which he'd renamed the Starlight R after extensive customizations.

Tyler just laughed and shook his head.

"So, how can I get a machine like the Zombie Grunts?"

Julian scoffed. First trying to beat the best Grunt-user on the server, next trying to get the best Grunt unit available. That was his friend to a hilt.

"I mean, you can buy one. Vile put a link to the designer's shop on her stream."

Tyler shook his head.

"Nah, I mean, I want to earn one. That's part of the game, right?"

Julian nodded.

"Yeah, it's like a big part of the game. People tend to disrespect you if you just bought your parts, especially if it's your main Mech. It's different for exhibitions or streams since you want to use fan-made machines, but you got to earn your Mech and then customize it. Otherwise, you know, people kind of think of you as a cheater. You know, they say you 'bought your way to the top' and everything."

"Yeah, that makes sense. Besides, if you didn't build a machine yourself, you probably won't know the best way to use it, right?"

Julian nodded. Tyler was quick to pick up on that all-important concept.

The importance of piloting skills put a cap on how beneficial spending money could be. Some players simply purchased the best Mechs by going to private markets or commissioning crafters. However, the highest-ranked Mechs were usually impossible for a regular person to handle. Even though Julian was in the top 500 pilots, he wouldn't be able to use a Mech like the Vermillion Flier. There were just too many features. He wouldn't know what to do with the incredible speed and mobility. Tracking five camera streams would be totally overwhelming.

"Yeah, exactly!"

"What does your machine look like?"

Julian pulled up his status screen and showed his friend his personal unit, a reasonably high-ranking Kingbreaker. Some pilots considered Kingbreakers boring. After all, they were based on realistic robots and lacked the distinctive characteristics of the other classes. Paragons had Finishers and Liquid State Eternium. Hemoborn had their biological parts. Spell Titans had access to a unique mana system that allowed them to cast spells like enormous mechanical wizards.

But Kingbreakers were the most reliable machines. Although their Overdrive bonus only provided a sharp increase in mobility, they had the highest base stats. Julian's favorite thing about them was their adaptive power outlets, which allowed them to use scavenged weapons from other Mechs. The other Classes could only use stolen weapons from either their own Class or various solid-type weapons. For non-Kingbreakers, the vast majority of beam or energy-based weapons were off-limits.

- General Data -
Pilot: Julian
Machine: Starlight R
Class: Kingbreaker
Sub-class: Attacker
Designation: Ace Unit

- Statistics -
Melee: A-tier
Shooting: C-tier
Speed: A-tier
Maneuverability: A-tier
Defense: B-tier
Cohesion: C-tier

- Weapons -
Close Combat Visor [x1]
Engine-Attached Beam Sword [x1]

Arm-Mounted Submachinegun [x2]
Reinforced Steel Shield [x1]
Enhanced Wings [x6]

- Abilities—

N/A [Kingbreaker type]

There weren't any S-tier statistics on Julian's machine, and his weapons were a good deal weaker than the ones seen in the exhibition. None of his parts were Full Customs, although the Engine-Attached Beam Sword was close.

The Starlight R still needed an actual long-range weapon, but the Cohesion was already at C-tier. It would be hard to attach more items without the whole thing falling apart. It was Julian's fault for being so bad at crafting.

Crafting was tough. There was also an RNG aspect, meaning that even experts like Vile frequently had to redo their recipes over and over again to get the optimal parts.

However, Tyler noticed none of the Starlight R's faults.

"Man! This is sick! I love the orange and gold! And the wings are awesome!"

Julian smiled back.

That was one of the coolest things about Overdrive. You built your Mech to suit your aesthetic and combat sensibilities. Even most of the lowest ranking pilots on the server loved their Mechs. After all, it was something they'd designed for themselves.

Even if Julian could control the Vermillion Flier, he wouldn't want to use it the exact same way vermillionangel did. He'd change and repaint it so it'd become his own.

Julian had colored his machine bright orange and gold. The visor, which protected his all-important eye sensors in close combat fights, was bright red. The six mechanical wings extended from the back in a loose circle-like formation. The flexible wing binders afforded him both speed and maneuverability. The parts were only about 60% of the way to becoming Full Customs, but Julian was proud of the work he'd put into them.

The beam sword was attached to his right forearm so it could swing into his hand whenever he needed it. The hilt was connected to the generator at his back through a mass of internal and external wires. Although there was a risk of damage from the exposed parts—targeting the fragile wires would likely cause Julian to lose his arm—the dangerous weapon gave him a strength that not even professional builds could match. Although most beam swords were narrow sabers, Julian's was a mighty broadsword, allowing him to overpower the opposition in almost any clash of blades. The crushing power allowed him to break through nearly any defense. Only his lack of back-up weapons kept his Mech from earning an S in Close Combat.

Tyler pulled up his probe again.

"Alright. My turn to get a Mech. Let's see what options I got."

He pulled up the beginner's shop, which presented a series of basic Ace units and Grunts. Intriguingly, although only the four most basic Aces from each class were available, you could purchase any Grunt from level one onward. Of course, a beginner wouldn't be able to afford any of the higher-tier Grunt units with Credits.

"Don't be afraid to just buy something and get started. You'll be able to change your mind after just a single mission."

Beginner parts were incredibly cheap. The game designers wanted you to try out every class. Julian had agonized over which to select—eventually choosing a Paragon—before realizing that after just a single mission, he had the money to buy all the other starter kits.

Tyler scrolled through the various descriptions. The four main classes flashed in front of them, complete with samples of what to expect.

Spell Titan: A Mech that relies on spells and the mana system to attack. Spell Titans include Mechs based on wizards, clerics, or paladins. These units rank the highest in terms of offense. They can most easily approach S-tier in their specializations, but struggle to achieve a balanced build with a sharp trade-off between Speed and Defense. Their Overdrive boost allows them a brief time period of casting unlimited spells and sharply raises their offensive stats.

"Yo, this one seems pretty cool!"

Julian grinned. The flashy Spell Titans were a good fit for Tyler's fiery personality.

"Take a look at the others first."

Paragon type: Mechs based on super robot anime. Built from the legendary metal Eternium, Paragons start with the lowest overall base stats but can dramatically boost their performance through the Overdrive mechanic. These Mechs have access to the Liquid State Eternium Overdrive boost, which sharply raises every single stat but for Cohesion. Their Finishers are the highest power attacks in the game, exceeding even the Spell Titans'. However, they are the hardest machines to repair, as they can only be rebuilt using Eternium.

Julian had used his Paragon class for a long time. He'd only stopped because of how hard it was to fix. Liquid State Eternium and Finishers provided the highest power ceiling.

"So what's the difference between Spell Titans and Paragons? It sounds like they are both glass cannons."

The descriptions did make it a little hard to distinguish.

"Bare Spell Titan frames are the glass cannons. You either build additional thrusters to try and dodge attacks or give them armor at the expense of sharply reducing speed. Paragons have better defenses, but without the Overdrive boost, they are weaker overall. When they say that Paragons have the lowest overall base stats, that means their usual performance in Close Combat, Shooting, Defense, Speed, and Maneuverability is the lowest average of the four categories. But that's just the average. Like Paragons have higher defense than Spell Titans and usually have higher offensive stats than the cyborg-like Hemoborn before their passives kick in."

"Oh, got it. And then their Overdrive boost makes Paragons have the highest average in everything, right?"

"Yeah. You don't see a lot of Paragon grunts for this reason. It's not really worth using them without Overdrive boosts or Finishers."

The next Mech were the Kingbreakers.

"This is the one you use, right?"

"Yeah."

"Why do you like them?"

"They are the most reliable. Kingbreakers are the easiest to repair and have the highest base stats overall. The other Mechs can surpass them in stats under the right circumstances—like Paragons with Liquid State Eternium or if a Hemoborn activates the right passive boosts. But in general, it's just hard to go wrong with them. Even the Overdrive is better than people think it is— by increasing your Mobility, you can usually tool an enemy around until they run out of their boost. Then you're back on the attack with your superior base stats."

Even after getting Julian's report, Tyler still pored over the information. Julian bit at his lip. He wished he'd known to study everything before he'd gotten started. He would have improved quicker.

Tyler quickly scrolled through the description.

Kingbreaker type: These machines are based on real robot anime. They are unable to use Special Abilities but have the highest innate stats out of all four classes. In addition, they can use salvaged weaponry from any other machine through their adaptive generators, although they can't use the associated special abilities. Their Overdrive boost sharply increases their Mobility.

Oftentimes, Grunts were Kingbreakers, but Julian had seen other successful Grunt types before. Spell Titan and Hemoborn Grunts were both competitively viable, depending on the strategy you were trying for.

Hemoborn: The Hemoborn are combinations of flesh and metal. The Hemoborn boast exceptional innate passive abilities that contribute to both offense and defense. After their boosts are activated, their firepower and strength of their metal components exceed even the Kingbreaker-class. However, their flesh parts are incredibly frail. Their Overdrive boost is unique in that it sharply boosts their Cohesion stat, leading to dramatic improvement in their regeneration.

On top of the Class, there was also the Type. Julian cut in.

"Let me explain the Types to you. The descriptions are horrible."

Tyler took a quick look through them anyways and then nodded. The four categories—Artillery, Attacker, Support, and Wild—pretty much didn't tell you anything useful. In fact, they were all actively misleading.

"Artillery machines sound like they added supportive fire from the rear, but all the designation means is that the Mech is used at long range. If you think of Artillery, what would you think of?"

"Hmm...Basically a well-armored machine that's like a huge cannon, right?"

"Yeah, that's what you would think, and there are a lot of Artillery Mechs like that. But here are two other examples that don't fit what Artillery means to regular people. Like a sniper would be considered Artillery too, just because it's long-range. Or maybe a highly mobile Ace unit that focuses on using weapons like rifles. So the description isn't that useful."

"So the Types are almost like your position. Like you can be a shooting guard in basketball, but there's a lot of different kinds of shooting guards."

"Yeah, exactly! That's a perfect comparison. The Attacker type has the same inaccuracies as the Artillery type. Like you would think an Attacker focuses on attacking, but a frontliner that focuses on blocking attacks and disrupting the other team is also classified as an Attacker. Or you can have a dedicated swordsman, like my Starlight R. The best way to think of it is as the opposite of Artillery. If it fights at close range, then it's an Attacker."

"Got it, got it. And a Support uses supportive items or Abilities, right?"

"Yes, but it's kind of a nebulous category. Like it's hard to say what makes the game classify a machine as a Support. Like this is just another example of how the categories don't matter too much. Like a tanky frontline disruptor can be classified as either an Attacker or a Support. The way the game decides to do it is pretty arbitrary. And then there's the Wild-type, which provides pretty much no information. It's just a Mech that doesn't look human. Wild-types can be frontline, backline, or supports, and they still get put in that category. In general, I would worry more about what your machine actually does than what the game claims it does. That's probably the best rule of thumb."

"So the red guy always uses Wild Types."

"Yeah, exactly. Like I would say he plays as a frontline Attacker usually, but again, the type doesn't matter. Like you don't even need all four types on a team. You can have a team with a Sniper and then three bodyguards that focus on flushing people out, with two that use bombardment and another that focuses on pistols in case people get too close. That would be classified as an all Artillery team, but it's still a balanced four-person group. Like you have elements of Support and Attacker in there as well."

"Got it, got it. So you really can put your own spin on it."

"Yeah, that's the best part of the game!"

Tyler grinned.

"Well, it looks like you're an Attacker. So I want to focus on supporting, right?"

Julian shook his head. That was what his old high school friend Felix had done, but he didn't want to restrict Tyler to any specific role. Julian and Felix had spent so much time playing as Attacker and Support, but if they did it over again, Julian wasn't even sure he would want to be an Attacker. Shooting seemed pretty cool, just hard to learn after six years of habit. It'd be best for Tyler to try every role.

"Don't worry about that right now. We're just at the beginning. I want you to try all styles just to see what you like."

"Wait a second."

Tyler suddenly stopped scrolling.

"These machines have horrible stats. Everything is C or D-rank."

"Yeah, of course. These are starting machines."

"What? That's ridiculous."

He pulled up the screen.

"Dude. Brandon's machines have so many S-rank stats!"

"Well, yeah, he's a pro who worked on his Mechs for a long time."

"Like you said earlier, I don't want to buy a Mech. But is there any way to earn a good one faster?"

Julian grinned.

"There actually is."

It was just Tyler's first night in the game, but he was already pushing Julian. His best friend had always been that way. Tyler had spent more time begging Julian to apply for jobs than Julian had spent applying.

"There's a mission we can do where you don't even need a machine."

He'd been putting it off for a long time, just because it seemed like a pain to go through a mission where you couldn't use your Mech, but there was no better time than the present. The map dropped exceptionally rare frames.

He pulled up the map information, and Tyler's eyes widened.

"Woah. We're going to steal those things? Won't people get mad?"

Julian laughed.

"It's just a mission. We're stealing them from NPCs—non-player characters. This is going to be hard. Look at that fail rate— you only have about a ten percent chance of making it through. You run in as a commando and steal these machines to escape. The problem is, the other side does have Mechs!"

Tyler just clapped his hands together.

"Hey. I don't even know how to pilot yet. Maybe one where we have to run around without a machine is the best."

Julian laughed again. That was probably true.

The prompt appeared, and Julian pressed yes after inviting Tyler to his party.

RANDOM PAIRING INITIATED

ENTERING MISSION LOBBY: THE RAID ON COLONY SEVEN

[6]

The friendly lobby vanished.

The two friends immediately found themselves in a dark shuttle. Three figures shifted on the bench opposite them, but it was hard to tell who they were. The shuttle's dim light made it hard to see, but Julian soon realized that the players in front of them were wearing jet black privacy armor. The man sitting in the middle was big and broad, with a protruding stomach. Two shorter people sat on either side of him, but Julian couldn't tell if they were boys or only short men.

Tyler let out a surprised breath as he looked down at his transformed clothing.

"Woah. Where did this body armor come from?"

"It's lent to you for the mission."

The Raid on Colony Seven didn't allow you to use any of your own gear.

Even the expensive privacy armor had been adjusted. Typically, privacy armor was one of the highest quality pilot suits, providing benefits to pilot movement and a layer of bulletproof armor. But now, the only remaining trait was how it blocked off their screen names.

Julian poked at the tight fabric on his arm and sighed. It was the weakest sort of material. This wouldn't stop a bullet, nor would it stop shrapnel from a nearby explosion.

The Raid on Colony Seven awarded a top-quality machine with all statistics listed at least B or higher. The high-quality parts gave significant leeway when it came to Cohesion, meaning that even someone like Julian could achieve an S-tier. Of course, such a promising mission had to have a downside. The map was devilishly hard to clear. It was hard to fight against a whole colony defense fleet without getting to use Mechs. That was just common sense.

The ten percent completion rate didn't quite do the difficulty justice. Most of that ten percent came from experienced grinders playing the mission over and over again. The win rate for the average player was even lower.

In addition to the three shrouded figures, there was someone else sitting in the far corner who Julian couldn't quite pick up.

His name and information floated above his head.

Liefield

Unranked

You only received a rank if you made the top 2,000 pilots. Overdrive had millions of players, so the vast majority of the player base showed as unranked. The game administration was currently expanding the ranking system to help more pilots show off their performance.

Julian thought that made sense. He'd gotten stuck at around the 2,010s four years ago. It'd felt so bad not getting to show off his almost just-as-good rank.

"Wait. You didn't know you got body armor? Is this your first time? Oh my god. Why did I have to get matched with you?"

Liefield's voice was very whiny and had a strange ring to it, like he was talking out of his throat. Julian sighed. It wasn't a good sign for their mission's success that their team had someone complaining before it even started.

Tyler just stared at the squat man. His friend had almost certainly played with troublesome teammates on his basketball teams, but ill-mannered Overdrive players were different. In traditional sports, you usually personally knew the guy who was causing trouble. Online, it was just a random stranger.

Julian peered at Liefield's helmet. The face behind the visor was clearly that of an adult. He should have known better.

"What are you talking about?"

The squat and bulky pilot faltered for a moment. Then he just put his head in his hands and stomped off. Instead of talking to Tyler directly, he loudly spoke to himself as he paced around the shuttle.

"Oh my god. This would never fly at work. Why is everyone so unprofessional? He didn't even know what the mission would be about. A total noob and then two kids. Why me? Why do I have to die because I got matched with bad teammates?"

Tyler still looked completely confused. Julian's friend could tell that he should be offended, but he just didn't understand Liefield's behavior. Unfortunately, people who acted like Liefield were somewhat common on Overdrive when you didn't have a full lobby. If Julian had to guess, he would have said that about 80% of players were just regular people looking to have a good time, but the toxic pilots with bad attitudes always stuck out. In missions like The Raid on Colony Seven, where the full lobby size was larger than the usual four players, you had an even higher chance of encountering them.

Liefield was a pretty common archetype—the chronically negative pilot who was terrified of direct confrontation but would spend the rest of the mission moaning and making passive-aggressive comments whenever something went wrong.

Julian stood to tell the annoying pilot to shut up, but then the fat man sitting between the two kids let out a jovial laugh. Even though the privacy armor completely covered his face, it was apparent that he was smiling.

"Don't mind him. He's just stressed out about the mission."

He turned to Liefield.

"Don't be such a spoilsport. Don't worry, Liefield. We're going to win this mission."

Julian blinked.

He thought he knew that voice.

The squat pilot didn't bother turning back to the masked man. Instead, he just kept on ranting to himself.

"Spoilsport? Spoilsport? He's the one spoiling my mission. Bringing along a bunch of kids."

His voice turned even whinier.

"Why me? Why do I have to die again? It's just so unfair! If I got a good Mech, I could carry all my stupid teams!"

Julian pulled up Liefield's status screen again. There was an offer to block or mute him, but unfortunately, it only prevented messages or friend requests. There was no way to shut off verbal communication.

Tyler shot Julian a bemused glance.

"Man, what is wrong with that guy?"

The three pilots sitting on the other side of him giggled. When the man in the middle told the two shorter pilots to calm down, Julian suddenly felt very nervous.

His vision was immersed in Overdrive's virtual reality, but Julian was keenly aware of his body sitting in the beaten-up chair in his bedroom. His hands were sweaty, and his heart was beating very quickly.

He tried bringing up the masked man's status information again, but of course, the privacy suit stopped him.

But Julian recognized that voice.

It had to be him.

He was an older dad who spent most of his time playing with his kids. Although only his face showed on most of his streams, he'd stood up on air a few times before, and this man had the same somewhat overweight body type. If Julian wasn't wrong, the man in the privacy gear was TiggerLuvr888, and the two shorter pilots next to him were his sons.

Julian tried his best not to gawk. They were wearing privacy armor because they didn't want to be bothered. As a player ranked in the top 500, Julian occasionally battled with or alongside professional players. He always felt bad when everyone started pestering them.

TiggerLuvr888 was Julian's favorite streamer, but that just meant he should be extra respectful. The two other kids also had their status screens protected. If only so he'd stopped staring, Julian pulled up Liefield's detailed information.

- General Data—
Pilot: Liefield
Rank: Unranked
Machine: Spectre
Class: Paragon
Sub-class: Artillery
Designation: Ace Unit

Since Liefield hadn't summoned his Mech, the full details weren't available. Spectre was a pretty common name for Mechs —unlike Pilot Names, you could name a Mech whatever you wanted. Julian was a little surprised to see that it was an Artillery-type, though. Most of the Mechs named Spectre were quick close-range Attackers.

The Spectre's despairing owner was still noisily stomping back and forth.

"Why me? Why do I have to get paired with kids and noobs?"

Julian had gotten angry at uncooperative or unskilled team-mates many times before, but he didn't see the point of throwing a fit before the game started. That just brought everyone down.

Of course, if Tigger hadn't been wearing his privacy armor, Liefield would be singing a very different tune.

Tyler sent him a private message.

"Yo, what's that guy's deal?"

"He's probably uncomfortable outside of a machine, so he's hoping someone can carry him to the prize. Unfortunately, our squad isn't looking that good for this mission. I'm not very athletic, but it looks like I might be the second most athletic after you. We got an old dad and two kids, and Liefield doesn't look that fast either. Like he probably just wanted someone to get him a free Mech. We're relying on you, star athlete."

It was sort of funny. Liefield was spending all his time whining about Tyler, but Tyler was probably going to be the most valuable member of their team.

One of Overdrive's dumbest features was how it estimated your avatar's physical capabilities based on the body scan. It was an utterly pointless and oftentimes inaccurate feature, but for some reason, The Mechanical King refused to remove it.

"LOL. Oh man, we're screwed. We can replay this if we mess up, right?"

Julian thought about telling Tyler his suspicions that the big man was TiggerLuvr888, but he decided not to. It'd be pretty unfortunate if he turned out to be another middle-aged guy with kids. Julian doubted it, though. Privacy armor was costly. Buying three full sets cost millions of Credits.

"Yeah—and you actually get a spare life on this one too, although you might still be in trouble just because of the mission timer. You need to escape before the full army comes back."

"Wait, so why is that guy throwing a fit? Can't he just play again?"

Julian laughed out loud. His friend had just started, but it seemed like he already had a better idea of what to do than Liefield.

"Yeah, some people are just crazy."

It could get frustrating to lose time on a failed mission, but dying wasn't the worst thing ever. The penalty wasn't very harsh compared to some other games. You lost either the lower of 4,000 Credits or half your Credits. There was no penalty timer.

The squat man moaned and moaned.

"No. No. I've tried so many times. People keep holding me back. Why me? I haven't gotten a hard mode machine yet. Why me?"

The shuttle landed. Although Liefield had been closest to the door, he immediately sprinted behind them. He actively pushed the kids out of his way to make sure he was in the back.

"No way am I leading. Nope. No way. You guys are in front. No way. I'm shotcalling from the back."

Considering his other behavior, that wasn't surprising at all. Julian was starting to get really annoyed, but the man Julian thought was Tigger just laughed.

"Alright, guys. Just follow my lead, and you should be alright."

Julian's suspicions rose even higher. Tigger always preached relentless positivity on his stream. The veteran pilot had lost a close match just last night after one of his teammates stopped cooperating. The stream chat had gone crazy condemning the player who'd spent the whole game hiding instead of helping, but Tigger just laughed.

"Not a problem. Just play it out and try to focus on having fun. Once the match is over, you can just not play with them again."

It seemed like he was taking the same attitude to Liefield.

He turned towards Tyler and reached out his hand.

"Hey, I can tell you're pretty new. Nothing wrong with being ambitious. It would be pretty cool to start with one of these Mechs instead of the rookie ones."

He offered Tyler a high-five.

"Let's get this loot together!"

Tyler grinned and returned it.

"Yeah!"

That was another cool thing about TiggerLuvr888.

Despite his incredible skill, he always reminded his viewers that he was just a lucky dad playing a game. He loved the Overdrive community and spent a lot of time helping out newer players. In addition to scrimmaging with various competitive teams, he also worked as a guide on new missions.

The door opened.

"Alright, guys. This mission isn't nearly as hard as people say it is. Just follow my lead, and we'll be fine. There's a secret path to avoid the enemy Mechs. We'll be in the hangar in no time."

Their party stepped forward.

A massive cyborg thundered on the far right-hand corner. It was a Hemoborn Grunt, specifically an enormous stegosaurus. Despite its frightening appearance, the Mech wasn't particularly menacing in a Mech battle. It lacked sufficient metal parts. The only enhancements were a helmet to protect the cockpit brain and a pair of wickedly curved swords that replaced the spikes at the end of the tail.

Julian had seen some incredibly powerful dinosaur-type Hemoborn before, but this one was just an average Grunt. The minor machine didn't even merit a full status report. Of course, fighting a dinosaur inside a Mech and fighting one with your bare hands were two very different things.

Tigger smiled.

"It'll be easier to fight that thing once we have Mechs of our own. We need to avoid it for now. I have a way."

Liefield jerked toward the big man like a drowning man grabbing a log.

"Wait. Wait. Wait. You've done this before?"

The big man laughed.

"Yeah, a bunch of times! Just follow my lead, and we should be alright. As I said, there's no need to be a spoilsport!"

He pointed to his two kids, whose screennames were still hidden.

"I'm Brian. This is Roman, and that's Robby. We've done this mission a couple of times before, but we're hoping to get some high-ranking Hemoborn this time."

The shorter boy chimed in excitedly. The smirk was evident in his voice.

"Vile is so cool! She's my favorite streamer! I want a Hemoborn, just like hers!"

That more or less confirmed his identity. Tigger had given himself a fake name, but his two boys were named Roman and Robby. He brought them up on his stream pretty often.

Julian smiled. He knew that most of the big names turned off their identification information when they wanted to avoid fanboys, but this was a night he'd remember. He'd print out the mission completed statement and stick it on his wall. TiggerLuvr888 seemed just as cool and patient in real life as he did on his stream.

Despite the hint, Liefield still didn't know who the masked man was. Perhaps he didn't follow the competitive scene. However, the squat pilot buzzed with excitement. The excitement of getting carried to a high-quality Mech had eliminated all of his worries.

"Yes! Yes! We've all done this before! This should be easy then!"

He waved his rifle around.

"Alright. I'll bring up the rear. You lead the way from the front!"

Ray let out a good-natured laugh and shook his head a little.

"Yeah, that's fine."

Despite Liefield's added confidence, he was still determined to hide in the back—he wanted to get carried to a powerful Mech without doing anything. It irked Julian, but TiggerLuvr888 always talked about how you didn't want to bother someone if they were set in their ways. The most important thing was to have fun for yourself.

With his favorite streamer watching him, Julian wanted to emulate his teachings. He sent Tyler a private message—alerting his friend of their available weapons—just to make sure Liefield wouldn't throw another fit.

"Hey man, you have a silenced pistol on your left-hand side, and each of us starts with two grenades in our pack. There's also a knife on the right."

"I thought you hadn't played this one before."

"I watched it on stream."

He'd actually watched it on Tigger's stream, but he didn't want to tell Tyler who he thought the masked man was. He didn't want to create a scene.

The group of them slowly crept forward with TiggerLuvr888 taking point. He had the gun carefully raised in his hand, and he peered around every corner before moving. They stepped through one corridor and then another. Instead of taking the main path, they slipped open a sewer grate and started creeping through in a single file line.

Nobody saw them. The massive Hemoborn Grunts lumbered outside.

TiggerLuvr888 was slow and unathletic, but he never let that become a problem. He'd already studied the map, and he knew where to go. He was the same when inside a Mech. There were plenty of pilots with better control skills or shooting accuracy. Tigger's thoughtful and team-centric playstyle meant he always took the safest path forward. That mindset had carried him to the World Championship semi-finals, where he'd lost to Brandon in an absolute nailbiter of a match.

Before long, they were close enough to the hangar that Julian could hear the NPC engineers working on the machines.

They'd just made it to the hangar doors when Julian suddenly heard a noise on the far corner.

Liefield let out a cry of fright, raised his gun, and fired. It echoed noisily against the wall. The silencer was useless if you fired your bullet right into a metal surface.

Tigger tsked.

"Oh, man. Next time, try to hold your fire unless you are sure you can kill them quietly. Especially if we don't see them yet. There's usually no need to fire blind."

Liefield let out an angry cry.

"What do you mean? I saw him! I did see him! I don't know how that missed! I was just doing my job! It's not my fault! I did my job! You guys should have finished him off!"

As if the bullet straight into the wall hadn't been enough, Liefield's screaming guaranteed that there cover was blown.

The NPC guards let out a cry of surprise.

"There's something there! There's something there!"

Liefield let out a cry of fright, shoving Tyler forward.

"Get in the way! Help me! Help me!"

Unfortunately, his terrified cries only further drew the enemies to their positions.

Tigger and his two sons drew their guns and started firing. Tyler pulled his pistol out, but his shots went wide. Julian sighed. He should have warned Tyler about that. Shooting a gun on Overdrive was nothing like shooting a gun in real life.

Liefield sprinted off to the corner, his hands held over his head. Julian drew his own firearm and turned to the other side to cover their backs in case any guards approached from behind.

His heart surged with pride as TiggerLuvr888 gave a nod of approval.

The expertise of the superstar pilot and his two sons soon made short work of the NPCs.

The taller one giggled.

"Man. What is wrong with that Liar guy?"

His dad sternly shook his head.

"Look, a lot of people play for different reasons. You got to be patient with everyone, you know? Maybe he's just having a bad day."

With the guards eliminated, the hangar was now undefended. Loud stomping echoed outside, but once they claimed the high-quality machines, they'd easily deal with the guard Mechs.

The mission was as good as won.

Tigger swaggered up to the door and opened it. Gold light glinted back out at them.

Julian gasped.

"Wow."

TiggerLuvr888 peaked inside.

"Ah, that one does look nice. It's not a Hemoborn, though."

He turned to Julian.

"You want that one? I saw you covering our backs there."

Julian wanted to agree before the words had even gotten out of his mouth. He had never seen such a beautiful Mech before.

But he didn't get to say anything. Gunshots rang out, and their whole team found themselves back at the spawn. It took Julian a moment to realize what must have happened.

Liefield cackled, his voice amplified a thousandfold by the speakers of the golden Paragon.

"Sorry, guys. That one's mine. I take a business mindset to the game. There's no room for feelings. At the end of the day, you gotta do what's best for you."

The shorter kid cursed, and Tigger glared at him until he said sorry.

"Come on, guys, let's do the mission again. We'll do it with just us. We should be able to figure it out with just five players."

There was no chance they'd make it back to the hangar in time. By shooting them in the backs, Liefield had doomed them to a mission failure. It was unbelievable. Julian was so angry he felt numb.

But there was nothing any of them could do.

They were just about to quit the map when Liefield let out an excited giggle.

"What is this? I've never seen this before?"

Bright golden letters flashed across Julian's visor. He let out a gasp of surprise.

REALITY SHAPER—HEAVEN'S BOXER ACTIVATED

REALITY SHAPING: CHALLENGE SYSTEM

The world changed.

[7]

Julian's machine flickered into existence. The Starlight R's orange and gold paint looked dull next to the golden machine's incandescent light, but his loyal partner was still a welcome sight despite his confusion.

He had no idea what was happening.

What was the Challenge System?

Liefield hastily shook his head.

"Nope! Nope! Not you. Not you. Too strong, not gonna do it."

The machine vanished, replaced by an orange and gold Grunt unit. The statistics flickered onto his screen as Julian stared, completely bewildered. The frame was one he'd bought almost two years ago for the few random queue matches where he didn't get to be an Ace.

He seldom used it.

Julian gaped.

How had Liefield done that? He'd demoted Julian to Grunt status at the push of a button. Julian called up his Status screen and tried to change his assigned machine, but nothing happened.

Liefield let out a sudden cry of fright.

"Wait. You? You? Why are you in my game? Are you trying

to bully beginners? Is that it? Why the hell would you be in this lobby? You're a pro!"

There was a loud clang as the three masks disappeared, and the screennames appeared above their heads. It was just as Julian expected. The man was TiggerLuvr888, and the two boys were his sons.

The veteran pilot took a look at the golden Mech and frowned. Julian thought he saw a flicker of sudden recognition in his suddenly stern eyes.

"What are you doing? How did you remove the helmets?"

Liefield laughed.

"What does it look like I'm doing? I'm challenging you to a battle! Not you, though, not you. You're too tough for now. But the kids and the noob. And the guy who doesn't have an actual Grunt. I can take them. That's how strong I am now. I knew I could do it if I had a strong machine! I knew it!"

He giggled.

"This Mech is amazing! I can challenge whoever I want! And I can pick their machine. They don't stand a chance!"

Julian still didn't understand what was happening, but it seemed like Tigger was catching on.

"Come on. You already got the Mech. And that guy's so new he doesn't even have a beginner unit. What's the point?"

Liefield scoffed.

"The point? What do you mean the point? I want to get parts and Credits, of course. Look, man. It's a tough world out there. It's like I always say. In the harsh world of business, you need to do what's best for you. You can't be worried about people's feelings."

TiggerLuvr888's kids didn't get what was happening either.

"Dad, what's going on?"

"What can we do?"

Like Julian, both of them had Grunt units. Their frames had

synched up to match his. All three of them were currently assigned the Defender Mk. II. To Julian's relief, the kids' machines were well-maintained.

Julian didn't know the Challenge System's limits, but it seemed like it couldn't just make someone's Mech worse. You could only pick a machine inside their inventory.

Tigger sighed.

"Alright. This is a Mech that I'd heard about a while ago, but I wasn't aware it was in the game. I thought it'd gotten canceled. The Reality Shaper series can alter fundamental game mechanics. Take the Heaven's Boxer. It's based on a Chinese martial artist, and it can challenge anyone to a fight."

"What?"

"That's ridiculous!"

The Ace designation flew above Tyler's head.

"It can even pick the arrangement of the other players."

Julian couldn't believe it.

"Yo, come on, man. My friend just started. He doesn't even have a machine."

Liefield sounded incredibly pleased with himself.

"That's the point! I'm making this a bet battle. I'll kill him for the Credits, and then take all three of your Mechs."

Julian hesitated.

Should he transfer a Mech over to Tyler? He didn't want to risk the Starlight R, but he had a few other powerful Ace units. Was it worth the risk? Wouldn't they just lose to Liefield anyways?

The golden Mech looked incredibly powerful. It wasn't carrying any weapons, but the radiant aura around it suggested that it could destroy any machine in a single hit.

If it were based on a martial artist, it was almost certainly a hand-to-hand combat type. Those machines were usually considered noob traps. After all, hand-to-hand combat rarely worked against someone with a weapon. But if the Heaven's Boxer were fast enough...

The machine was a total black box.

Julian couldn't even open up the status screen yet. Seeing the details of an enemy Ace was tied to whether or not you'd unlocked the base unit in the shop. Julian had unlocked all the base units by now, but this wasn't a machine you could buy in the shop.

Julian was just about to hand Tyler one of his Mechs anyways when TiggerLuvr gently waved him aside.

"Hey, TylerFord21. You should take one of my Mechs. This might not be the best way for you to be introduced to the game, but it looks like we don't have a choice."

"Oh, uh, sure."

Tyler had no idea who TiggerLuvr was. He'd diligently studied Brandon's tactics, but he hadn't paid attention to the other Grunt users in the exhibition match.

"Thank you!"

There was a brief pause as Tigger transferred his chosen machine. Julian wondered what Tigger would hand over to Tyler. Surely Tigger knew the risks just as much as Julian did. It was a strange situation. The expert pilot had to balance the advantage of giving Tyler the strongest Mech possible with the risk of losing it forever.

There was an enormous roar.

The two sons cheered, Julian gasped, and Liefield flinched before letting out a jealous cry of rage.

"What! I tried to buy that! You said it wasn't for sale! Now you're just giving it to him? Do you have any business sense?"

The Liger Soul—Cerberus Roar was the machine TiggerLuvr888 had used at the World Championship. The Mech was classified as a Wild type, but other than the three roaring heads that had replaced the chest and hands, the Paragon model had an almost entirely human-like figure.

It was the rare high-quality machine that'd been built to be as easy to use as possible. The yellow and red unit was focused on overwhelming firepower.

The main head boasted a proud V-shaped crest that slid down to protect the eye-sensors during close combat brawls. The cats' heads on the arms had overwhelming strength and firepower at all combat ranges. During the round of sixteen, the Eternium jaws had torn Lilac's transforming bomber plane clean in half. Tigger had battled to the top four before losing to Brandon in a vicious duel.

The Roar's Finisher had been the strongest in the whole tournament. The Cerberus Soulfire exhausted all the machine's resources—even vaporizing the very Eternium it was built from—to launch a devastating three-pronged attack from all the cats' heads.

Liefield laughed shakily.

"Well, it doesn't matter. I'm not going to lose to some noob. Soon I'll have all four machines."

Tigger's kids wavered, but their dad was quick to calm them down.

"Don't worry about the Roar. I like the look of this Tyler guy. I think he's going to win. We're going to get this gold Mech back too. He stole it from Julian."

Liefield's laugh was strained and high-pitched. Despite his feigned confidence, the sight of the Roar had badly frightened him.

"I'm not going to lose to two dumb kids and a noob. I don't know who this fourth guy is either, but that Grunt looks like it's about to fall apart. Some top 500 player he is. I'm good enough to be in the top 500 now that I finally have a decent Mech."

Julian grimaced. He really should have been paying more

attention to his Grunts. If he ever ended up in a lobby with a superstar like TiggerLuvr888, there was no way he could ask his hero to play as a Grunt.

This was an unusual situation, but his lack of preparation meant Julian had to fight this jerk without a properly maintained machine.

He could lose one of TiggerLuvr's legendary machines.

If they did, it would be Julian's fault. He took a quick look at their party. His Mech was by far the weakest.

- General Data -
Pilot: Julian
Machine: Defender Mk. II—Julian Custom
Class: Kingbreaker
Sub-class: Attacker
Designation: Grunt Unit

- Statistics -
Melee: B-tier
Shooting: C-tier
Speed: C-tier
Maneuverability: C-tier
Defense: D-tier
Cohesion: A-tier

- Weapons -
Close Combat Visor [x1]
Long Dagger [x2]
Revolver [x2]
Steel-Reinforced Blade [x1]

- Abilities -
N/A [Real-Class]

Julian winced at the D-tier in defense. He at least should have bought a shield or tossed some Credits into reinforcing the armor. The rest of the stats weren't much better. The only reason he had an A-tier in Cohesion was because he hadn't done much customization. He'd just tossed on his preferred close combat visor sensor and then added a few melee weapons.

Both the kids' Mechs put his to shame. All three of them were using the Defender Mk. II frame, but the stats were painfully different. Although both the sons had hoped to use their Ace units, their Grunts were diligently maintained.

The older brother had adjusted his machine to fit a more long-range fighting style. Julian nervously wondered if there were other strategies that Tigger's sons preferred. Tigger's kids must have had access to better Grunt frames and parts. Julian probably had forced them into picking a weaker frame just to match with him. In a competitive battle, the three Grunt pilots all had to use the same frame.

- General Data -
Pilot: Kingofkills
Machine: Defender Mk. II—Kingofkills Custom
Class: Kingbreaker
Type: Artillery
Designation: Grunt Unit

- Statistics -
Melee: B-tier
Shooting: A-tier
Speed: B-tier
Maneuverability: B-tier
Defense: A-tier
Cohesion: S-tier

- Weapons -
Explosive Machinegun (Full Custom) [x1]
Vulcan Cannon [x4]
Heavy Mortar [x1]
Grenade Launcher [x1]
Combat Knife [x2]

- Abilities -
N/A [Kingbreaker Class]

The second son was tuning his machine into a Support type to complement Julian and the Cerberus Roar. Thin wire arms emerged from the virtual hangar to equip his well-maintained base unit. Tigger's son's deft movements put Julian to shame. He'd been playing since the beta. Why was he forcing these young pilots to adjust to him?

- General Data -
Pilot: DivinelordFTW
Machine: Defender Mk. II- DivinelordFTW Custom
Class: Kingbreaker
Type: Support
Designation: Grunt Unit

- Statistics -
Melee: B-tier
Shooting: B-tier
Speed: B-tier
Maneuverability: B-tier
Defense: A-tier
Cohesion: S-tier

- Weapons -

Vulcan Cannon [x2]
Beam Spray Revolver [x2]
Particle Veil [x1]
Landmine [x10]
Smoke Grenade [x2]

- Abilities -
N/A [Kingbreaker Class]

Tyler fumbled around with the machine's controls and groaned.

"Oh, man. I don't even know how all these attacks work."

The Cerberus Roar awkwardly waved its arms around as Tyler tried to figure out what was going on. Liefield laughed cruelly.

"It's looking like a free win!"

But to Julian's surprise, TiggerLuvr888 was smiling.

"Yeah, that's it! Just figure out how everything works. You've got time before the battle starts. This is a tough fight for anyone, not just a beginner. Make sure you're ready!"

The Challenge System had essentially created the same circumstances as if you'd started a bet battle on the status screen. Both teams had adequate time to prepare and test their armaments.

Tyler raised a cannon and fired.

The beast at the chest roared, and a massive ray of golden light shot out.

"Woah!"

Tigger laughed.

"Yeah. There's a lot of firepower in that thing. It's just a simple offensive unit—no need for any excessive details. Got that trick from Vile."

Now that he mentioned it, Julian realized why Tigger had built such an easy-to-use machine for the World Championship.

His bracket had included facing off against Lilac in the top 16, Opt1c0n in the top 8, and then Sweetshot303 in the semi-finals. If he'd beaten Brandon, then he would have had to fight vermillionangel.

All of those players had better control skills than Tigger. The veteran pilot's best bet had been to spray as many attacks as possible, and it'd nearly worked.

Julian shook his head. That was another area of the game he'd completely overlooked. As fun as it was to create a Mech that amplified your strengths, it could be even better to build one that hid your weaknesses. TiggerLuvr888 was a true master of the game.

The head in the center roared again as Tyler drew an enormous sword from its mouth. His left hand held a composite rifle, a special weapon that could shift fluidly between a rapid-fire mode and a powerful sniping mode. The bayonet at the end ensured that it could be comfortably used at all ranges.

"Man! This thing is sick!"

Tyler waved the sword around excitedly.

The flaming blade made the air shiver.

Julian's eyes went wide as he pulled up the Roar's description. The Mech lacked speed and mobility, but it was the king of defense and stopping power.

- General Data -
Pilot: TylerFord21
Machine: Liger Soul—Cerberus Roar
Class: Paragon
Sub-class: Wild
Designation: Ace Unit

- Statistics -
Melee: S-tier

Shooting: S-tier
Speed: C-tier
Maneuverability: B-tier
Defense: S-tier
Cohesion: S-tier

- Weapons -
Pride's Sword (Full Custom) [x1]
Pride's Composite Rifle (Full Custom) [x1]
Cerberus Roar Cannon (Full Custom) [x1]
Tiger Roar Cannon (Full Custom) [x1]
Lion Roar Cannon (Full Custom) [x1]

- Abilities -
Liquid State Eternium
Pride's Roar
Cerberus Soul Roar

Despite the circumstances, Julian still couldn't help but fanboy at the amazing Mech. The Cerberus Roar had achieved a Top 4 placing at the World Championships. It was a legendary machine!

He couldn't wait to explain to Tyler what a special experience it was to pilot it.

Then he grimaced.

If they lost to Liefield, they'd lose the machine, and this would become nothing more than an exceptionally sour memory.

Liefield laughed and laughed, a nasty echoing sound that ricocheted off the empty walls of the colony.

"Oh my god. This is too good. I was going to pay you for that Mech, and then you're just going to give it to me for free!"

His golden Paragon flexed its arms.

"They can even fit on this machine too!"

Tigger ignored him.

"Alright, everyone ready?"

"Yeah."

"Well, it looks like his machine has no long-range weapons. Just take him out in a single barrage!"

The match started. Unlike a typical bet battle, where they'd launch onto a random stage, they'd simply returned to Colony Seven. There was only one change. Although the enemy Grunt units still loomed menacingly all around the map, the NPCs inside had vanished completely. The machines stood still as statues, leaving the players free to battle unhindered.

Their team raised their weapons. Julian sighed as he lifted his revolvers. The poorly maintained guns looked paltry compared to everything else's carefully maintained arsenal.

They fired as one.

The blasts streaked toward the Heaven's Boxer, leaving the golden machine with no room to dodge.

It vanished and reappeared right in front of the Artillery Unit.

Roman—also known as Kingofkills—let out a startled cry.

"What?"

"How?"

It had flown through the blasts, soaring through them without any harm at all.

Liefield cackled.

The golden fists lurched forward, one after the other. Even though Liefield hadn't activated his Overdrive boost, the speed was utterly blinding. Julian could barely see the arms pumping forward.

There was a cacophony of cracks and then the blue Defender Mk. II shattered to pieces.

Bright red letters flashed across their screen.

PLAYER TWO ELIMINATED.

[8]

TiggerLuvr's kids knew how to play.

Julian could only gape at the almighty onslaught, but Roman —the boy whose Grunt had been destroyed—immediately shifted to analyzing what went wrong. After losing a team battle, you reappeared in the "loser's lobby," which allowed you to spectate the game through your teammates' eye cameras.

"Don't rely on blocking. Its arms are too fast. It can easily get around your defense. We need to disengage and keep it at a distance."

If he were in Roman's position, Julian would have spent a couple of minutes complaining about his cheap defeat. If it were someone like Liefield, they might have just signed off immediately to start writing a furious email to the administration demanding the firing of whoever designed the Heaven's Boxer.

It always felt terrible losing to a new and likely overpowered Mech.

But Roman and Robby had grown up playing with their dad. They were shocked, but they remained analytical in the middle of the battle. They were playing to win. They wanted to become full-time pros.

Robby clenched his teeth, firing off a barrage of beams at the Heaven's Boxer. The blasts pinged off the gold armor, sending a mix of sparks and broken armor shards into the air. The Mech didn't carry a shield. It blocked with both its arms crossed in front of each other. Usually, directly shooting a Mech with a C-tier in Defense would result in its destruction, but Liefield had chosen his target well. He'd destroyed their only artillery Grunt. Julian and Robby didn't have the firepower, and Tyler just wasn't fast enough.

Before they could even blink, the Boxer vanished again, reappearing in front of Robby's Mech.

"What is that speed!"

Julian had never seen a Mech move so quickly before. It was moving faster than an S-tier unit empowered by a Mobility-enhancing Overdrive. It was moving faster than Vile's Jekyll after it received the Bloodlust Level 10 Passive.

The Heaven's Boxer looked like it had teleported.

Perhaps it had teleported.

Earlier, it'd flown straight through their gunfire without receiving any damage.

Robby cried out in fright, doing the only thing he could think of. His Defender Mk. II kicked back off the ground and fell straight down. The Heaven's Boxer's arms pumped back and forth through empty air. Liefield might have had a powerful Mech, but he wasn't a good pilot. He couldn't think on his feet. Before the Boxer stopped pointlessly swinging its fists, Robby fired his Particle Veil.

The Veil was a unique and highly expensive support item that disrupted all radar. The hasty addition of a smoke grenade straight on the floor completely obscured Liefield's vision, blinding him and allowing Robby to escape.

Julian raised his revolvers and fired at the smoke. The plink of

Eternium told him that his shots had landed, but the guns were simply too weak to inflict any lasting damage.

Tyler released a barrage of red and yellow lightning into the cloud. There was an explosion of stone, but this time, Julian didn't hear the corresponding ring of Eternium.

"Shoot, my bad guys!"

Tyler was learning fast. He'd quickly discovered that the telltale musical sound of struck Eternium would let you know if you'd hit a Paragon.

If only he'd fired faster.

With Roman already defeated, Tyler was their best chance to damage the machine from range.

Roman and Robby were quick to encourage him.

"It's fine! You need to focus on moving!"

"Don't worry! You're totally new! Just get out of there!"

Despite their age, the two of them were the veteran pilots here.

Even with how long Julian had played, he was just along for the ride. He should have been the one telling Tyler to flee. Instead, he'd just stood there watching.

It sucked. Julian had the control skills, but it was so hard to think quickly on his feet.

The Heaven's Boxer whirled awkwardly back and forth as their three surviving team members scurried away. For a brief moment, the smoke shifted and revealed the golden Mech's location. Strangely enough, Liefield was fleeing instead of charging straight at them. It seemed like the opposite play pattern of a typical melee machine.

Julian excitedly raised his pistol and fired, but once again, the bullets shattered uselessly against the pristine Eternium armor. Julian shook his head and cursed himself.

What was he thinking? Last time, he'd fired from a much

closer range and failed to do anything. Why would shooting from farther away be any different?

His Grunt was far too weak.

Robby had seen Liefield too, but he'd held his fire. The Beam Spray Pistols lacked the range to inflict substantial damage. His Mech specialized in restricting an opponent's movements so its teammates could finish them off.

Julian grimaced.

Robby should have brought a Mech with more individual strength. Supporting was well and good if you had a good team, but holding people down for Julian's weak Grunt and the still-learning Tyler was useless. Moments like this were why Julian disliked the support role. You could do everything right and still lose.

The son flickered at the bottom of his communications link.

"Don't fire next time."

Julian sighed.

"Yeah, that was my bad. I shouldn't even bother."

"No, that's not what I meant. Just tell Tyler to fire. If you shoot and fail to do damage, he'll know that we know where he is. That guy's not that good. He was just blundering around. If we get a good shot at him with dad's Roar, it'll be easier for us to get up close. Then we'll be able to do damage."

"Right."

Tell Tyler to fire.

He should have thought about that.

Julian was unfamiliar with long-range combat. He spent most of his games charging in with his sword, leaving the gunplay and support activity to his teammates. He was even worse at leading his team. That'd always been his friend Felix's job. During Julian's random queue matches, he usually just listened to whoever sounded the most confident.

"Let's focus on giving your friend a chance to take him out."

"Right, right."

Moments after thinking to himself that Tyler was their best chance to win, Julian had taken the opportunity away from him out of his excitement at spotting the Boxer.

Julian took a deep breath.

His heart was beating rapidly in his chest. He didn't want to lose the Roar, and he didn't want a jerk like Liefield to win.

But he had to think on his feet.

If a kid could do it, why couldn't he?

The smoke cleared, and the Heaven's Boxer stood on the far side of the map, right beside the door to the hangar.

Even though he'd just told himself not to, Julian instinctively reached for his revolvers before he caught himself. He had to set up Tyler to take the game-winning shot.

The only problem was that Julian wasn't sure if Tyler should try and fire now. After all, the enemy Mech had that strange warping ability. Wouldn't it be better for Tyler to wait until it jumped?

Apparently, Robby and Roman both felt the same way. Their communications wire was silent.

Julian waited, his every muscle tense. He replaced one of his pistols and drew the steel-reinforced sword instead. His sword was pretty high-quality, and he knew he could outduel Liefield despite the difference in Mechs. Liefield was unranked. If he charged, it'd be up to Julian to fight him off.

Julian's muscles tensed against the controls so tightly that he felt like his arms had locked in place, but the enemy Mech didn't move an inch.

It just hovered in front of the door with its arms crossed. Now that the Mech wasn't moving, Julian could truly appreciate its beauty.

The Mech was golden from head to toe. It was lean, yet strangely metallically muscular, with minimal armor save for a helmet and shoulder guards. There was gem in its forehead and another in its chest. They glowed with divine radiance, outdone only by the Boxer's eyes. The eyes were filled with beauty and menace. Julian had never seen anything shine so brightly before, either on the Overdrive server or in real life.

Would it attack?

Or would it stay?

Julian's mind whirled back and forth at the strange guessing game. It was like trying to guess what someone would pick next in rock paper scissors.

At the end, Robby made the call for him.

"Don't shoot. The status is available now. Let's just pull up his information and figure out what's happening. Don't attack until he comes near us. And we should group up. He can't punch all of his at the same time. He's only got two arms. When he charges, we'll counterattack."

"Oh. Right."

The option to pull up the data on his status screen had popped up above the Mech's head. That meant that they'd seen enough of the enemy machine to qualify for a data scan. Julian had been too anxious to realize it, but the fight had dragged on for quite some time.

He caught himself before he instinctively clicked it.

He had to be careful. If they all looked at the Mech, it would give Liefield an opening to attack.

"I'm going to pull up the status on the side. I'll keep an eye out, but let me know if it charges."

"Okay. I'll take a look after. We'll take turns."

Tyler stayed silent. His friend was too focused on trying to process everything. Even though the Roar had a simplistic design, Overdrive was still a complicated game. Tyler could use basic attacks, but little else. There was a reason why beginners usually trained with guides for at least a week before they got comfortable playing.

The three Mechs joined together, and Robby deployed a few of his landmines, putting them just a few body lengths away from them.

"I think that Mech can warp. Dad said it bends the rules of the game. But if it doesn't, the mines will get him. I can't put them right in front of us because we'll take more damage from it than he will."

"Yeah."

It was good thinking.

"Alright. I'm going to take a look now. Let's see what this thing can do."

After Robby nodded, Julian pulled up the status screen.

- General Data -

Pilot: Liefield

Machine: Reality Shaper—Heaven's Boxer

Class: Paragon

Type: Attacker

Designation: Ace Unit

- Statistics -

Melee: S-tier

Shooting: D-tier

Speed: S-tier

Maneuverability: S-tier

Defense: C-tier

Cohesion: A-tier

- Weapons -

None

- Abilities -
Liquid State Eternium
Reality Step
Challenge System
Mandate System

The statistics were even stronger than he thought they'd be.

It was virtually impossible to receive an S-tier on a random drop, yet the Heaven's Boxer had three S-tier categories. Bizarrely, the machine carried no weapons.

The most interesting aspect was the abilities.

Like all Paragons, the Heaven's Boxer had access to Liquid State Eternium. They'd already seen the Challenge System. Julian guessed the Reality Step must have been what the Paragon used to instantly destroy Roman's Mech, but he didn't know what the Mandate System did.

He'd never seen that skill before.

The letters flashed across his screen.

REALITY SHAPING: MANDATE SYSTEM

A golden arm tore the hangar door completely open. The Heaven's Boxer glowed brighter than a thousand suns. With a loud snap of its fingers, the Mechs inside rose.

All around the map, the dinosaurs got back to their feet and roared.

"What the?"

"Oh, no!"

"What's happening!"

Tyler was the most surprised.

"Wait. You can do that?"

"No. You're not supposed to be able to do that."

The army of Mechs charged towards them.

$$[\; 9 \;]$$

The army stomped toward them, coming from all corners of the map. The abandoned Grunt units stood again and the earth trembled beneath every footstep.

Julian let out a long sigh. It wasn't hard to guess what the Mandate System did. Calling the machine a Reality Shaper was right. No wonder Liefield had been so confident he could win the match. It'd seemed like a one against four, but the villainous pilot had an army lurking in the wings.

The dinosaur-type Hemoborn Grunts weren't particularly powerful, but they sure looked threatening when formed into a massive army. There were four of the stegosaurus-types Julian had seen earlier.

Because they were only AI Grunt units—weaker than even the Grunts used in standard competitive play—the status screen only displayed rudimentary information.

Name: Lightly-Armored Stego Grunt
Pilot: Mandate System AI
Class: Hemoborn
Type: Attacker

In addition to the stegosauruses, two other brontosaurus-types served as long-range artillery. They were lucky those machines were the same low-level Grunt quality as their stegosaurus counterparts. Brontosaurus Hemoborn had been considered underpowered jokes before the frame became a critical part of Sweetshot's repertoire during the World Championships. Now, most competitive Overdrive players acknowledged it as a top-tier Grunt choice. Their incredibly long necks gave them a shooting angle that no other machine could match.

Name: Lightly-Armored Bronto Grunt
Pilot: Mandate System AI
Class: Hemoborn
Type: Artillery

Worst of all were the five other high-ranking Mechs in the hangar. The Raid on Colony Seven contained six machines—one for each of the maximum number of players you were allowed to bring onto the map. There should have been one for each of them, but now Liefield controlled them all.

There were three Hemoborn types—two focused on close-range combat with the third dedicated to long-range artillery. Julian clenched his teeth tightly, and not just because of their high statistics. He always found the humanoid Hemoborn unsettling. Unlike the dinosaur-type Grunts, these units were based on giants.

One of the melee Hemoborn leaped into the air and landed cleanly on top of the fourth machine, a Kingbreaker class built to look like a fighter jet. The realistic Mech reminded Julian of Lilac's preferred strategies. Unlike almost every other player on the Overdrive server, she chose machines that resembled real-life weapons. Most of the time he tuned in, he'd see her using jets or tanks. Her signature unit, the one she'd used at the World Championship, was a Shifter bomber plane.

The last machine was a Spell Titan with ice-related abilities. Cool blue crystals glowed at the cyromancer Mech's fingertips as a blizzard began swirling behind it.

Julian cursed as he hastily scrolled through the status screens.

There were no S-tier rankings, but all of the machines were well-balanced. The Hemoborn had Bloodlust and Stench passives at Level 5, and the Spell Titan's abilities indicated it could freeze single units in place or summon a massive blizzard. It could even encase itself in ice for defensive purposes.

The fighter plane Kingbreaker was the least unusual Mech, but the quality of the parts was the highest.

The massive force reminded Julian unsettlingly of Dynamic's preferred strategy. The superstar gunner's Mech was called the Self-Supporting Sniper. The Mech combined a heavily armed artillery drone with a highly mobile sniping unit. The well-designed machine had totally overwhelmed Julian in both their previous matches.

It was almost like battling an entire army.

This time, they were battling an entire army.

Tyler cursed.

"What are we going to do?"

Julian's hands quaked at the controls. His mind scrambled for some kind of strategy, but he had no idea what to do.

The pair of brontosauruses roared, and a hail of bullets streaked toward them. The units both wore a gun battery over their heads like helmets.

The artillery-focused Hemoborn raised an enormous bazooka and fired. Like Vile's unit, the humanoid spat out a bullet of flesh and blood.

The cyromancer raised its hands high in the air. The storm blew faster and faster. Unlike the other machines' direct attacks, the blizzard would take a long time to arrive. But once it did, they were almost certainly dead.

Liefield laughed and laughed.

"I can tell most of you guys are new, so let me give you a tip. If I were you, I wouldn't mess with a high-ranking player like me. It's better just to play easy missions to learn the basics first."

Tyler ignored Liefield's mockery. Julian's best friend was wholly focused on the game.

"Come on, Julian! What should I do?"

Julian was far too terrified to get annoyed at Liefield's condescending statements. They were going to lose and give up the legendary Cerberus Roar. TiggerLuvr had shown them exceptional faith in lending Tyler the World Championship level Mech, but they had failed him.

Too late, he realized that there was an obvious counter. He should just ask Tyler to fire his cannons to counter the blasts. It was such an obvious gambit. Ace machines used it to defeat Grunts all the time.

But it was too late now. There were just too many shots. And besides, even if Julian had thought quickly enough to ask Tyler to cancel the blasts, they'd still lose to the all-out charge. And if they somehow survived, then Heaven's Boxer would finish them off.

The match was over.

All the shots missed them.

"What?"

In the corner of his screen, Robby looked at him like he was an idiot.

"They can't aim because of the Particle Field."

Oh.

Right.

Robby had thrown the support item down to escape from the Heaven's Boxer, but the powerful field remained in effect for five minutes. That was why Robby's Mech had to be so lightly armored in the first place. The Particle Field cost 7,000 Credits, almost the entire cap for Grunts.

In his panic, Julian had totally forgotten. He gritted his teeth. He should be playing so much better than this. It was the same effect he'd noticed during the exhibition. The top players remained calm even in the middle of a battle. That was the difference between Julian and the elites guaranteed to qualify for the Selection.

Robby sent the pair of them new information, indicating where he'd set his mines. His Mech carried two more in reserve.

"The melees won't be able to make it once they charge. Let's focus on getting rid of the brontosaurus-types for now. They are easy to knock out, but their shooting angle makes them the biggest threat."

Robby's instructions were clear and crisp, and his logic was sound. By setting up a perimeter of mines, Robby had ensured that they were safe until the Particle Field ran out.

Despite the low cost of his machine, he was playing far better than Julian or Tyler. They had a chance to win because of Robby's strategy. Instead of fighting all the enemies at once, he'd created a situation where their team could pick them off one at a time. It was fantastic support play.

Tyler's red and yellow super robot roared.

Both brontosauruses immediately fell.

"Aw yeah!"

His friend pumped his fist.

"Good job, good job."

Tyler immediately switched his focus to the stegosauruses, blowing one of them up with a fiery blast from his chest cannon.

"Yes!"

Robby shook his head, hastily stopping Tyler from firing at the next charging dinosaur.

"No! No! Save your fire. It's a waste. They'll die to the mines, and they're spread out so you can't shoot them all. You need to focus on the ice guy. Get rid of him before he uses the blizzard. Then get the gun giant."

Once again, Robby had suggested the correct order of operations. The Spell Titans were known for their light armor. Tyler probably could take it out, and the Hemoborn wouldn't be able to inflict enough damage by itself once the Particle Field ran out.

"Julian. You don't have the range yet, so focus on defending us from the plane."

Right.

The plane and the Hemoborn mounted on top had already reached Julian's position. In his focus on the long-ranged enemies, Julian hadn't even noticed it. He was such an idiot. Under normal circumstances, he might have fought better, but the thought of losing Tigger's Mech to Liefield had wiped his brain completely blank. It'd been the same last Selection when he noticed his rank slipping out of the top five hundred.

But now that the plane was here, Julian's worries didn't matter.

He drew his sword and then charged into battle. This was his element. He hastily stepped forward and swung, barreling into the jet with his massive blade. Although his Grunt unit was in poor condition, he was still fighting an AI. They were high-level units, but Julian couldn't count how many mission mini-bosses he'd beaten before. He couldn't count how many players he'd destroyed in furious close combat duels.

He knew he could do it.

The giant stumbled because of Julian's hasty charge forward. Julian fired his pistol right into the vulnerable flesh of the ankle. There was a loud crack, and then the unit stumbled off the plane. He smiled.

When he was in the middle of a close-quarters brawl, a strange thing happened to Julian's mind.

What had once been foggy and frightened became icily clear.

He could see the enemy machines' every move, sometimes before it even happened. It wasn't at all the strategic thinking Tigger's kids used. It was a heightened sense that told him what he needed to do to win. It was hard figuring out what his team as a whole should do, but Julian knew how to take care of himself.

Glowing red energy built at the plane's wings as it prepared to fire a pair of beams. Julian grabbed the top of the jet and forcibly pushed down to vault himself upward. The giant raised its club, but Julian dodged and viciously swung his sword. With its ankle injured, the melee-focused Hemoborn couldn't move fast enough to avoid the devastating blow to its neck. When facing multiple high-level units, the best bet was to simply land critical hit after critical hit. In a way, they were lucky the enemy forces contained so many Hemoborn. Their fleshy parts were far easier to strike than the other classes' vulnerable joints.

Blood gushed across his screen as the giant died.

Now it was time to nail the jet. Julian was already mounted on top. All he had to do was stab downward. The cannons weren't even facing toward him. Lilac's machines featured gimmicks to remove enemies that attacked from above, but this unit was just a base model.

The beam cannons underneath the wings fired, but it didn't do the machine any good. It had no way of hitting Julian.

Julian stabbed downward and grinned as the plane slammed into the ground.

He pumped his fist.

"Yes!"

Not everyone could win a 2v1 like that. Although he struggled with strategic thinking, Julian was ranked in the top five hundred for a reason—his sterling control skills. Few could defeat him in a clash of blades. At his specialty, he could compete with significantly higher-ranked opponents. He might even be able to defeat a superstar like TiggerLuvr888 in a sword duel.

"Dude."

Robby sounded angry.

"Could you hear what I was saying?"

Julian looked up and groaned.

One moment, he was happy and triumphant.

The next, the sinking realization of how hard he'd misplayed hit him like a hammer.

Robby's support unit had lost an arm, and smoke was billowing out of both legs. There was a massive dent in the side of the head as well. Julian figured he must have tanked a solid projectile.

The head was at about 20% health, and both legs had been reduced the mid-thirties.

By leaping on top of that plane, he'd left Robby's support unit totally exposed. He scrolled back a bit in the transcript of his log and saw the message he'd missed.

Robby had asked him to take the plane down first because it was capable of long-ranged attacks.

He groaned.

He hadn't even heard him. He'd been too excited to try and prove himself.

Beside him, the Cerberus Roar continued shooting and shooting. It was only then that Julian realized the Cyromancer had already been reduced to rubble.

Even Tyler was playing better than him. Julian wished he could have used his Starlight R. Then he would have shown Tigger his skills. Instead, he was stuck on his ill-maintained Grunt unit. Usually, he'd be excited for Tyler, but it was impossible not to feel jealous. He really wanted to put up a big game in front of his favorite streamer.

His friend cried out excitedly.

"Yes! Yes! I've got this now!"

The three feline heads roared again, eviscerating nearly all their opponents.

The only enemy left was the Hemoborn artillery unit. Tyler turned to gun it down, but stopped when Roman called out to him.

The older son had a more comprehensive vision of what was currently happening in the fight. Because he was sitting out, he could think of more advanced strategies.

"Leave it up for now. Julian and Robby should get behind Tyler. The Roar can tank blasts from a single A-tier Artillery unit without much of a problem, but the continued blasts will stop Liefield from just warping in. He only has a C in defense."

"Right, right."

"Good idea!"

It was another keen insight that Julian had overlooked.

In certain mission battles, it was worth keeping an opponent alive because to restrict the final boss's movements. This was technically a player vs. player battle, but the same principle applied. Liefield wasn't using a well-built team. He'd hoped to overcome them with raw numbers, meaning their side had a chance to exploit his allies' lack of synergy with the melee-range Heaven's Boxer.

Although Liefield probably should have attacked in the middle of the chaos, he remained timid despite the outrageously powerful machine. Julian had marked him as a coward when they played the mission together, but Tigger's kids had taken it a step further—they'd actively planned their attack around Liefield's cowardice.

"You go first!"

That'd been Liefield's mindset during the mission, and he'd kept that mindset after activating the Mandate System.

The remaining close-range units charged and promptly detonated the mines. The low-level stegosauruses died, but the Giant barely survived. A beam spray rifle to the face immediately took care of it. Robby's badly damaged machine couldn't move, but it could still fight.

The artillery unit continued firing, and Tyler continued blocking the shots. They'd completely lost sight of where Liefield was, but Robby fired out his remaining two mines behind him.

"Keeping them closer this time. If he lands on it, I'll probably die from the blast, but that's fine. Take advantage of his confusion and damage to defeat him."

The older son grinned.

"Good thinking."

Thinking.

That was what this really was about.

This wasn't about Aces vs. Grunts. Even if Julian had the Starlight R, he might have performed poorly against that massive army or the Heaven's Boxer.

The two sons never stopped thinking, and Tyler had remained calm enough to understand their discussion. It was about thinking vs. not thinking. Julian had won an impressive one on two victory, but he could have accomplished more with less skill if he'd been more careful and prepared his Mech better.

And although Tigger never explicitly mentioned it on his stream, he was continually going over the importance of strategic thinking. His most impressive wins came not from his skills, but from picking his matchups and executing them to perfection. If Julian remembered correctly, he'd also served as an in-game leader during his former life as a shooting game expert.

Strategizing enabled their team to defeat that enormous Mech army. The speed of Julian's blade had little to do with it. On top of that, Julian had severely underestimated the strength of Robby's supportive machine, which had given them the ability to translate their strategies into action.

The artillery unit continued bombarding the three of them, but to no avail.

Liefield hovered behind it with his arms crossed. His voice was a little shaky after the failure of his assault, but he remained confident that he'd win. After all, he had the Heaven's Boxer and the Reality Step.

"Well, that was unfortunate, but I'd happily trade all those machines for the Roar anyways. Still a good trade for me, still a good trade. It was worth doing that to wear you guys down."

The artillery unit's cannons thumped and thumped.

"What should we do?"

The kids sounded very unsure.

It was time for Julian to come up with a good plan, but he didn't know what to do. When it came to the play Tigger had praised him for earlier—turning the corner to watch their backs—he'd only done it because of his experience at Overdrive. It was only natural to watch your team's backs on an infiltration mission.

But this situation was unique. There was no way instinct could get him out of this.

How could you hit a machine that knew how to teleport?

Think.

Think.

Think.

But ordering himself to think was like bouncing his brain off of a brick wall.

Maybe someone else had been in this situation before. Perhaps it was something he'd seen on Tigger's stream?

Julian shook his head.

No, Tigger wouldn't be the answer. If Julian's hero had done something tricky to get out of this kind of situation before, his sons would have seen it. It had to be someone else.

Maybe Brandon?

He wasn't sure.

Unfortunately, he'd never watched Brandon's streams before, only his competitive matches. If a solution had presented itself in one of those high profile games, Tigger's kids would know about it.

Ah.

The realization hit him like a lightning bolt.

Lilac had won an artillery exchange before with using her bomber. It'd been an exceptionally clever gambit to turn around a horrible situation. After all, bombers usually won long-range duels by flying over enemy units. That time, the opposing team had been careful to fill the air with anti-aircraft fire to force her to stay on the ground.

"Tyler."

"Yeah?"

"Charge up a big shot at the artillery unit and make it seem like you're going to shoot it. Then, jerk at the last second and blast the Boxer. You might not get your full beam on it, but it'll slow it down."

The kids excitedly agreed with him.

"Nice! Nice!"

"Yeah—he's just standing there and posing! He's going to fall for it!"

Tyler took a deep breath. It was a slightly more complicated maneuver than just blasting people head on, but his friend should still manage. The two Mechs were standing next to each other. Julian wasn't asking Tyler to thread a particularly delicate needle.

The Cerberus Roar fired, jerking its cannons at the last second.

Liefield cursed.

His machine vanished, but not quickly enough. Tyler's sudden move had caught the arrogant pilot completely off-guard. No wonder Liefield wasn't ranked—he was somehow both cowardly and overconfident, not attacking when he should and sitting around when he should have bolted for cover.

The Heaven's Boxer's right arm was completely obliterated.

Liefield screeched angrily.

"My drop! My drop! My ultra-rare drop! You'll pay for this!"

Julian felt a thrill of pride at the success of his plan.

Without one of its arms, the Boxer would be much easier to deal with.

"Yo Julian, what should we do now?"

The Boxer had vanished entirely.

Julian's heart pounded in his chest. He was on a roll right now. He had to come up with the next plan too.

It was so unusual.

The Reality Step was clearly used to close the gap on enemy units, but Liefield was using it to hide instead.

Then he took a deep breath.

There was no need to panic. They were in an entrenched position with mines watching their back and the Roar watching their front. The Heaven's Boxer had no long-ranged weapons. It had to come to them.

If not, they'd find it.

"Tyler. Get rid of the artillery unit now."

It'd be best just to eliminate a confounding factor.

The artillery Mech was better armored than the others, but there was little a freshly dropped and completely uncustomized Mech could do against one built for the World Championships.

It eventually fell after a brief exchange of gunfire.

"Alright. Now just start blasting the terrain."

No matter where the Boxer was hiding, they'd find it.

The Roar fired and fired. Eventually, Liefield called out to them, asking for mercy.

"Hey, that was my bad. I was just so excited to test out the new Mech that I challenged you guys to a battle! I've had some time to think, and I've mellowed out a lot now. What do you say we agree to a tie?"

The kids just laughed at him.

"No way! No way!"

"You're the one who challenged us!"

Liefield's protests grew more and more panicked as Tyler continued eliminating the surrounding terrain.

"Come on! There's no need for any hard feelings! It's just a game! We can both learn from this and move on!"

"Okay, just give us the Mech back then."

"What? No! It's mine! Why are you kids just keeping a grudge over this? I already apologized! Once you're older, you'll see how immature you're being."

Tyler just laughed.

"What is wrong with this dude?"

"There's a lot of guys like him. Well, not a lot. They just stick out when you run into them."

Eventually, they'd decimated the entire stage. Julian felt incredibly jealous of the Roar's awesome powers. It destroyed the whole colony without running out of energy—and it still hadn't used its Overdrive boost yet. That was the strength of a World Championship caliber Mech.

He sneaked a look at the exposed Boxer. Tigger had said that he'd give the machine to Julian. Would he be able to build a Mech as powerful as the Roar if he had a base unit like that?

Liefield continued his whining.

"Come on. Look I already said I was sorry, I'm not sure how much more you want."

Tyler fired at him.

The Mech vanished, and it reappeared behind them.

They'd given Liefield no choice but to fight, but they'd already planned out what would happen.

The land mine promptly detonated, blowing Robby's severely damaged Defender Mk. II to pieces.

PLAYER 3 ELIMINATED

Liefield cried out in fear. The Boxer went reeling, but the burning machine could still stand.

Save for its missing arm, its parts had taken about 40% in damage, but there was still one last ability for Liefield to activate.

OVERDRIVE: LIQUID STATE ETERNIUM

The golden Eternium bubbled. Even without the Reality Step, Liefield moved faster than Julian could match. His broadsword swung into thin air as the Boxer's remaining hand slammed into the Cerberus Roar, obliterating the head. The heads roared and fired, but the force of the blow had knocked the other machine off-kilter.

All the head cannons managed were glancing blows.

Tyler hacked with the bayonet, but Liefield grabbed the arm and tore it clean off.

"Use it! Use the Overdrive boost!"

The two kids joined in the chorus.

"Overdrive! Overdrive!"

Unfortunately, Overdrive was a difficult-to-find setting on the default piloting screen. It was another example of how the game's design philosophies hadn't caught up to its popularity yet.

It didn't make sense to hide your defining game mechanic away, but in The Mechanical King's opinion, the Overdrive boost was something that had to be earned. He thought that spending hours poring through their control settings would make players appreciate Overdrive. In reality, almost every player used a guide to find it before binding the Overdrive boost to an easy-to-access key.

Unfortunately, Julian and Tyler had hopped right into a mission where you weren't supposed to need a Mech. Despite his preparation, Tyler couldn't have known that they were about to fight.

Liefield laughed.

"Oh my god! You're such a noob! You don't even have Overdrive unlocked yet!"

The Boxer slammed its fist into the Roar's shoulder. The metal held, but Julian could tell by the creak that it wouldn't last for long. He didn't have time to pull up the status screen, but Julian eyeballed it at having taken about 50% damage.

"After I win this bet battle, I'm going to repair the damage to the Roar with the money I get from killing you guys. You should have just surrendered when I gave you the chance!"

Tyler cursed as he continued fumbling with his controls.

Julian streaked forward, his sword held tightly in his hand. He spammed his revolver with the other, sending out ineffective shot after ineffective shot.

Even at this range, he couldn't pierce Liquid State Eternium. Liefield didn't even bother turning around.

Julian leaped into the air to add force to his strike then brought his sword down on the Boxer's head. The Eternium was so blinding that Julian could hardly see.

There was a loud clang. For one hopeful moment, Julian thought he'd gotten him, but then he saw the truth.

The blade shattered against the enhanced armor. Liefield giggled as he continued slamming blow after blow into the Cerberus Roar.

The health of its limbs continued dropping as Tyler fumbled through page after page on the control panel. The two kids chattered in his ear, giving him contradictory instructions as they tried to remember where to find it.

Julian did the only thing he could think of.

He grabbed the Heaven's Boxer tight with both hands, wrapping his useless Grunt's arms around it.

"Get him! Get him!"

Liefield let out a choked cry.

"What the hell?"

"What's wrong with you?"

Julian yanked the Boxer away from Tyler's machine. A furious elbow crushed Julian's cockpit, killing him and ending the fight, but his Mech's corpse remained in place. The metal on the Boxer fizzled as it attempted to warp away, but the Reality Step failed with another machine draped over its shoulders.

Julian let out a long sigh of relief.

He hadn't known that it'd work that way. They got lucky.

Liefield let out a frightened cry as he pushed Julian's machine away, but it was already too late.

Tyler stopped fumbling for the boost.

Instead, he yanked the massive Pride's Sword out of his machine's chest and swung it forward in a ludicrously wide arc, putting the whole force of his mighty Mech behind the blow. The Heaven's Boxer was cut clean in two.

VICTORY!

As soon as Liefield lost, he went straight back to begging.

"I'm so sorry for the trouble I caused you! I'll just be on my way now. I hope you got a valuable lesson from our match, new guy!"

But there was nothing he could do. He was the one who'd set up the bet battle, and now that the match was over, the Overdrive systems would take over.

Liefield chuckled nervously.

"Come on, I was just joking around anyways. Don't take the Boxer from me. Be the bigger man and give it back after, alright? It's just a game!"

None of them bothered to respond. They just wanted Liefield to shut up and let the game give them the stolen Boxer.

As the Victory sign faded away, Liefield and his machine suddenly vanished from existence. There was a loud pop and then a staticky sound.

Julian scoffed.

A forced log-out was a common trick unscrupulous players often attempted to avoid paying the price for losing a bet battle. The administration had patched out the cheap exploit over two years ago. Even though his opponent had disconnected, the game would detect it and then transfer the Mech to Julian. He'd won the Starlight R in a similar fashion.

Julian pulled up his inventory, then frowned.

The Heaven's Boxer wasn't there.

He refreshed.

Still nothing.

He turned to the others.

"Hey guys, check your inventories."

The game wouldn't have known that the machine was promised to Julian. It could have been transferred to any of them. Tyler needed a bit of help, but before long, all of them had their inventories open.

The Heaven's Boxer wasn't in any of them.

Julian's heart promptly sank.

The Heaven's Boxer had been one of the most amazing Mechs he'd ever seen. Their team had rightfully won it. In fact, they'd rightfully earned it from the mission until Liefield shot them in the back to steal it. The whiny pilot hadn't done anything during the Raid on Colony Seven.

The disconnect cheat didn't work anymore.

So, where was the machine?

TiggerLuvr888 frowned.

"That seems wrong. They should have patched the disconnect bug out."

Robby nodded.

"Yeah! I had someone pull that on me a few days ago, and it didn't work. Let's refresh again."

It wasn't there. This time, the two boys couldn't keep quiet. They'd remained professional throughout the game, but now they were just a pair of frustrated kids.

"Wait. That's so unfair!"

"Are you telling me the jerk got to keep his machine?"

"Dad! You can't let this happen! You need to report him!"

Julian took a long breath.

He knew exactly how the kids felt.

Liefield had acted in such a scummy way. He'd stolen the Boxer and then challenged them to a battle he'd carefully designed to exploit the fact that Tyler hadn't played before. They'd won anyway—and now they weren't going to be rewarded for it?

Liefield was just going to keep his stolen machine?

That was so unfair!

Julian pulled up his screen and sent a report to the administration. The two sons joined him. Tyler peered over Julian's shoulder. Although bystanders couldn't read the details of your status screen unless you allowed them too, everyone could see the box pop up.

"What are you guys doing?"

"The Mech should have been ours. He used a bug so he'd get to keep it. We're sending in a report to the administration along with information about our match. They'll be able to look at the recording and notice it was a bet battle."

Tyler pulled up his own status screen.

"Alright, help me send one too when you're done."

TiggerLuvr888 finished on his screen and then helped Tyler. When they finished, the older man smiled. Despite what had happened, he remembered calm and unbothered.

"Julian, don't worry about that machine. In addition to the report, I sent in a note to my friend in the administration. You'll have it as soon as I hear back."

Then he pointed at the broken machines around them.

"Let's pick up these frames. We wrecked them, but we'll still be able to get them repaired. Maybe one of you guys can grab the Spell Titan? Ice Mechs are pretty rare."

Out of the machines that had spawned, the cyromancer was

the rarest. Julian added it to his inventory. If Tyler wanted it, Julian would hand it over later. He focused on melee machines anyways.

Julian frowned and shook his head.

After this match, he couldn't just dismiss ranged Mechs anymore, nor could he dismiss Grunts. They'd won this match because of Tigger's kids, even after one of them got eliminated right off the bat. The knowledge of how far Julian had to go before he could consider himself skilled was like a slap to the face.

Tigger then pointed at the slaughtered Hemoborn Grunts.

"Oh, and don't forget about the Grunts. Tyler, I would grab one of each. You want to collect as many Grunt frames as possible. It's important to be able to fit in with any team."

He smiled kindly. Despite Liefield's cheating and the disappointing ending of their fight, TiggerLuvr888 still kept his cool, just like he always did on stream.

Tyler grabbed one of each, and then Julian did too. Unlike the other classes, which had been reduced to shattered parts, the Hemoborn revived in his inventory with a single hit point. He didn't have either of those dinosaur types.

When Tyler finished taking those machines—he ended up selecting the bomber out of the five Mechs available—he offered the Cerberus Roar back to Tigger.

The Mech hovered above his head, indicating that he was willing to transfer it back. Julian smiled. The Roar was such an amazing machine. Even though Tyler hadn't figured out how to activate the Overdrive, it'd saved the day with sheer force.

As soon as they logged off, Julian couldn't wait to tell his friend what an honor it'd been for him to sit in a World Championship-level Mech's cockpit. Tyler still didn't know who TiggerLuvr888 was.

But to Julian's shock, Tigger waved Tyler off.

"You should keep it. It's not my usual style. I only built it for the tournament anyway. I think it fits you better."

Julian gaped.

Tigger was giving away a priceless treasure without any hesitation. His kids were laughing about it!

"Yeah, dad likes fast machines."

"He said he only built this one because he needed brute force to win."

Robby shot his dad a playful look.

"It's because the other guy was better."

Tigger just laughed.

"Hey! Knowing when the other guy is better is a skill too!"

Tyler grinned delightedly as he dismissed the trade notification. He reached out a hand to Tigger, and they shook.

"Thank you very much! I will, uh, use it honorably!"

Despite his awe and jealousy, Julian laughed at his friend's attempt to sound cool.

Tigger just flashed a thumbs up.

"Consider that machine yours now. I'm sorry you had such a lousy starting experience, but your fight was incredible. You've got lots of potential. Please train hard! New players are the lifeblood of this game!"

With the mission completed—after a fashion—and the loot collected, their hastily-formed party exited the Raid on Colony Seven. The ruined battlefield around them vanished, and the five of them reappeared in the friendly main lobby.

TiggerLuvr888 and his sons had regained their privacy armor, but Tyler was back in his street clothes. Julian had his own piloting suit on, an orange and gold standard-type that he'd custom colored.

Tigger laughed.

"You're a real beginner kid—you need to start buying some gear with the Credits you won!"

"Dad, that mission doesn't award any credits."

"Oh, right!"

The award of the Raid on Colony Seven was simply the Mech you stole. Fortunately, Julian had about 30,000 Credits. He was going to use most of it to upgrade his Defender Mk. II and purchase other Frames—which usually cost between five to ten thousand Credits—but he could easily spot Tyler some money for a standard pilot's uniform.

Julian waved Tigger off before he could give Tyler Credits.

"Don't worry about it. I'll front him."

The big man sounded like he was grinning again.

"Sounds good! Well, I'd prefer it if you guys kept it secret, but I would be honored to friend you guys. That was an incredibly fun mission. And don't worry about that Mech. Once I get it, I'll be sure to send it to your inventory Julian."

When the friend request popped onto his screen, Julian practically fell over himself accepting. TiggerLuvr888 was just as awesome and kind as he'd seemed on stream. Julian knew several streamers who acted cool for the cameras but were secretly enormous jerks.

After they accepted, Tigger turned back to them and beamed.

"Well, we should definitely play again sometime. It was nice to meet you both—and best of luck in your Overdrive journey. New players are the lifeblood of this game!"

He and his sons disappeared as he logged out.

Tyler stretched and yawned lazily.

"Man. That was a lot of fun. I think I'm done for tonight, though."

Julian suddenly realized that he was exhausted. He peaked at the time and gasped.

It'd already been four hours since they'd logged on. They'd accomplished a lot tonight. Although it had only seemed like a single mission, they'd essentially played through three campaigns. The two friends had played through the actual raid, fought Liefield's army, and then battled Liefield himself.

Tyler faded away, and soon he heard a loud knocking at the door. Julian's best friend had a huge grin on his face.

"Yo, that was awesome! We need to play again."

Even though Tyler didn't like most games, it was impossible to deny how fun Overdrive could be.

Julian grinned back.

"Yeah, of course! Let me know when you get back from class tomorrow. Let's do this!"

[11]

Julian and Tyler lounged in their dirty living room with an open box of pepperoni pizza between them. Tyler folded his slices into halves and jammed them into his mouth, munching happily as Julian slowly worked on his second slice. The usual split between them was a 70-30% ratio.

"So, did you hear back from Tigger yet?"

"No, unfortunately not."

After they'd logged off, Julian had explained to Tyler just who Tigger was. They were going to watch the replay of his World Championship match against Brandon before logging in for the night.

Julian pulled out his phone and pulled up the Overdrive app. He'd downloaded it entirely on a whim a few years ago.

It was a wonder he hadn't deleted it yet.

The app was pretty useless.

You couldn't play Overdrive on your phone. All it let you do was scroll through various community-related databases and chat. There were only a few Overdrive players he regularly talked to, and Julian usually waited until he was back at his computer to talk to them. His closer friends, like Felix or Captain Maxwell, had his phone number.

But today, he'd checked the app nonstop. He hadn't paid attention in any of his three classes. He just kept refreshing his messages screen in the hopes of seeing something from TiggerLuvr888. Julian couldn't stop thinking about the Heaven's Boxer. It was the coolest Mech he'd ever seen, and the abilities were ideal for a close combat machine. The Heaven's Boxer would almost certainly guarantee that Julian made the Selection.

Even going beyond the Mech's strengths, Julian simply wanted it.

It was an ultra-rare drop that rightfully should have been his. They'd beaten the mission, no thanks to Liefield, and then they'd defeated him in battle. Liefield shouldn't have been able to disconnect to keep the machine. The bug had been written out of the game a long time ago, and Julian hadn't seen a single person complaining about it. Something strange must have happened, perhaps a bug associated with the Challenge System.

Julian had little faith that the game administration paid attention to the average report. There were millions of players, and every day, there were probably thousands who misbehaved. On top of that, fake reporting was a big problem. People would lie to try to get back Mechs they'd lost in bet battles. Sometimes they'd say the other player cheated. Otherwise, they might blame the servers and say that their poor performance was due to lag or bugs.

There were even people who tried getting innocent players banned for no reason.

In all likelihood, Julian's report had done nothing. But TiggerLuvr888 was very different. Not only did he have a direct line to the administration, but he was also a famous pilot who everyone respected because of his honesty. In this case, he wasn't even advocating for himself to receive the Mech. He was trying to give it to Julian.

Julian pushed back his chair and started nervously pacing back and forth. His thoughts turned back and forth in his mind. He angrily clenched his teeth. He couldn't believe what Liefield had done. The rude pilot had spent the entire mission hiding and whining. Then he'd literally shot them in the back to get the machine. But even that wasn't enough for Liefield. He'd then challenged them to a rigged battle with parts on the line—only to cheat again when he lost.

It was a masterpiece of unpleasantness.

Tyler looked down at him curiously.

"What are you doing?"

Julian shook his head. He just realized he'd been stomping back and forth. His slice of pizza had nearly fallen out of his hand.

"Never mind."

His friend laughed.

"You're still mad about that guy, right?"

Tyler knew him way too well.

"You know that driving yourself crazy isn't going to do anything, right? It's out of our hands now! I want us to get that Mech just as much as anyone, but freaking out about it won't do anything. We just need to wait and hear back from that Tigger guy. He knows what he's doing, right?"

Tyler smirked.

"You were fanboying pretty hard for him."

Julian blushed a little, but he knew Tyler didn't think he'd been acting dumb.

"Yeah, he's great. He's probably my favorite streamer—and even better, he's a cool guy."

"Yeah, I thought it was pretty cool how he played with his

kids. Kind of like my dad dragging me to the gym when I was growing up."

Julian beamed.

He'd tried explaining to Tyler why video games were cool before, but it was nothing like experiencing it. To Julian, playing Overdrive was a lot like Tyler heading to the park to play basketball. Julian still kept in touch with his close friends from home by chatting as they played through missions. He'd even met some new friends like Captain Maxwell and his band of stunt pilots, the Forever Brothers. Even Dynamic was a pretty cool guy, even though he'd eliminated Julian from Selection contention.

Julian grabbed another slice and started chewing.

Tyler smiled.

"We should play with him again. He sounded pretty excited to get another round in with us."

"Oh man, that would be nice. But I'm afraid to ask. I mean, he's rich and famous—he's probably got better things to do, you know. Like it was already an honor."

"But he friended us! And he said we fought a good fight."

"I mean, yeah, but it would be like if Steph Curry played a couple of games with you at the gym, you know. You wouldn't ask him to come back again tomorrow. You'd feel super lucky and tell your friends about it."

Julian had already told Felix and Edwin—his two closest friends from back home—about it. They'd both been insanely jealous, and that was before they found out about the Roar.

Tyler shrugged.

"Yeah, I suppose so."

He pulled up his Overdrive app and took a look at his friend list.

"Looks like he's busy anyway. It says he's streaming the game."

Tyler fiddled with the controls for a bit. It'd just been one day, but Tyler was quickly becoming a deft hand at managing the status screen. He'd also tracked down the hidden Overdrive mechanic and added it to his main piloting settings.

Julian did want to play with Tigger again, but their one match with him hadn't just been an honor. It'd been a valuable lesson.

Tigger's kids—and Tigger himself—were always thinking.

That was how they could defeat an army of enemy Mechs without taking any damage. Julian had focused too much on raw strength without considering the boundless strategies of Overdrive. He'd observed his weakness before, but he'd ignored it because it seemed too difficult. But outwitting Liefield yesterday had felt so incredible, and now, he couldn't wait to do it again.

Tyler grinned after he found the recording of Brandon's battle with Tigger.

"This is pretty cool. When I finally get good enough to battle Brandon, this is going to be a rematch of that famous battle—the Roar against a Patchwork Grunt."

He pumped his fist.

"It's got me hyped up. It's the perfect storyline."

Julian smiled. He got most of his stories from anime or video games. Tyler usually talked about stuff he'd read off of ESPN, but both of them were on the same page with this. Tyler had a long way to go, but Julian wanted him to get his rematch.

The match recording started playing as Tyler connected his phone to the TV he'd put in the living room. Even though it'd been the World Championship semifinals, only the final match had been a best of five. This battle was still a best of one. It was another example of how the Overdrive Corporation still struggled to keep up with the game's massive popularity. They'd planned for a shorter tournament because they hadn't realized that so many people wanted to watch Overdrive matches. By the time they cut a new deal with the event owners, it'd already been the finals.

The announcer excitedly rattled off the introductions.

"On the left side, we've got Ray "TiggerLuvr888" Chung. TiggerLuvr888 is one of the most popular Overdrive streamers around, and he had a former career as a professional first-person shooter player during his childhood in Hong Kong. Rather than his usual Nimbus Slash, Tigger has built a new Mech for the world championships, the Cerberus Roar, which places a premium on firepower rather than speed. After his upset against Lilac in the last round, it's looking like he may be the favorite to win the whole tournament!"

Julian blinked.

He'd forgotten about the narratives at the time.

After vermillionangel won, everyone sort of just assumed that the current Champion had been the favorite all along. But immediately after his defeat of a highly mobile and skilled pilot in Lilac, most fans and analysts had named Tigger the likely frontrunner. After all, his strategy had already overcome one offensively-focused pilot with excellent control skills. What were two more?

The familiar red and yellow machine roared. Julian opened up the stat screen just to check, but the information was identical to what he and Tyler had seen yesterday. It was really hard to tell whether he was more excited or jealous of Tyler's luck. The Cerberus Roar was a Mech specially designed to win a World Championship.

"The Cerberus Roar is backed up by three variants of the Defender Mk. III, with all three Mechs focused on playing a supportive artillery role!"

The Defender Mk. III was the upgraded version of Julian's usual Defender Mk. II. The fact that he was still using the Mk. II was a painful reminder of how weak his Grunt play was. After last year's World Championships, the designer who'd created the

Mk. III had already moved onto the Mk. V. Julian was three versions behind.

"In the red, we have Song Duos. In the white, we have Song Lucifer. And in the green, we have Song Crabby."

Beneath the screen, the subtitles showed the proper spelling of the names. Although Duos and Crabby had spelled their names normally, LuC1Fer's was in the classic mix of upper and lower case letters that had already become popular in other games. Tigger was a ringer who'd ended up partnering with three substitute players from the Song clan. Ironically, Tigger's team had gotten much further than the main Song squad, which had lost in the second round.

"On the right side, we have the miracle rookie—Brandon "Cal Sweetshot303" Cole. Mr. Cole is a college student who only started playing Overdrive this year! His previous experience with competitive basketball and his incredible game knowledge have made him one of the few players who can star in the often-over-looked Support role. His underdog team has won battle after battle, leaving a long trail of defeated favorites behind him. So far, he and his teammates haven't lost a single Mech this entire tournament! Welcome, Sweetshot and his aptly named Mech, the Patchwork!"

Brandon had eagerly embraced the fan-given name, adding it to all his designs.

Despite his crafting skills, he paid little attention to the all-important Cohesion and Maneuverability categories. Instead, he jam-packed his machines with as many items as possible, maximizing his raw strength and abilities over creating a balanced design. He often replaced parts in the actual frames, bringing in new limbs with built-in weapons to circumvent the Credit cap.

- General Data -
Pilot: Cal Sweetshot303

Machine: Defender Mk. III Patchwork
Class: Kingbreaker
Sub-class: Support
Designation: Grunt Unit

- Statistics -
Melee: S-tier
Shooting: A-tier
Speed: A-tier
Maneuverability: C-tier
Defense: B-tier
Cohesion: D-tier

- Weapons -
Smoke Grenade Cannon [x2]
Beam Spray Cannon [x2]
Grappling/Bombardment Arm (Full Custom) [x1]
Reinforced Steel Knife [x1]
Mine-Laying Shield
Foot-Mounted Beam Blade (Full Custom) [x2]

- Abilities -
N/A [Kingbreaker Class]

The Smoke Grenade and Beam Spray cannons were attached to the Mech's back. The items allowed the Defender Mk. III Patchwork to support either ranged or melee assaults. The Mine Laying Shield was another Sweetshot signature. By incorporating mine-laying abilities into his shield, he could include both weapons inside the points cap.

The machine's most bizarre characteristics were the awkward Grappling/Bombardment Arm and the Foot-Mounted Beam Blades. Because the parts were incorporated into the frame, they allowed Sweetshot to circumvent the Points cap and focus on supportive items.

The strange white, teal, and pink Mech was an absolute nightmare to handle. Every single one of Brandon's Mechs was an asymmetrical and clunky mess. Julian remembered a charity event when Sweetshot had challenged other players to try and drive his machines. None of them succeeded.

But Brandon had no problem with the machine's drawback, and he relished the additional stopping power.

Even though he played the Support role, he frequently scored the most kills on his team. During the tournament, the casters had noticed a particularly unfortunate trend. Unlike every other squad, Caliber Gaming's performance actually dramatically increased after Brandon's teammates died. It turned out that looking after his team was holding him back.

By the round of four, Brandon had become one of the darlings of the tournament. He was the only Grunt user who the announcers listed first in their team's order of battle.

"Behind Brandon, we've got the three other members of Caliber Gaming! The nominal Ace of their team, Cal Sleigh, uses an Ace Unit focused on inflicting damage from all ranges. His unit is a well-designed and reliable machine that's consistently scored the second-most kills on his squad. Behind him, we have Cal Ryu and Cal Atlas. This reliable pair focuses on long-range artillery bombardment. Unlike Sweetshot, neither of them are using adjusted arm and leg parts. Instead, their machines are standard Defender Mk. III-type Frames."

Tyler paused the screen.

"What's up with the Cal? Brandon didn't have that in front of his name in the crafter's exhibition."

"Alright, so basically, Cal is their gamer tag. It's short for Caliber Gaming, their full name. There are basically a few different ways that Overdrive is organized, but a lot of pilots have grouped up into these clans. They are pretty popular because it's almost kind of like a screening—even if you don't know them personally yet, you know you'll be playing with other Clan members, so they tend to be better or at least better-mannered than the average player. A guy like Liefield would never make it into a clan."

"Oh, that's interesting. So why aren't you in a clan?"

Tyler pulled up his Status screen and scrolled.

"It looks like Brandon's not in one anymore, either."

"Yeah, so being in a Clan can also come with some weird drama. Like some Clans will tax their members for rare parts—which sucks, but they can do that if it's like a new guy who wouldn't be able to finish a difficult mission otherwise. Another issue is the competitive team side. Like even though a Clan can have hundreds of members, only four are going to make their A-team. Basically, what happened was that Brandon was so good that he got on their A-team right away, so there already were people upset about that. Like they'd been playing with Caliber for a long time and were hoping to go to the World Championships."

Tyler nodded.

"Yeah, that makes sense. It sounds kind of awkward, right? Like if you're not on the main squad, it isn't like you get to ride the bench or anything. You just don't get to participate."

"Yeah, exactly. And on top of that, the trio of Sleigh, Ryu, and Atlas had been playing together for a really long time. So when they got to the World Championships, they wanted to be the stars."

They were kind of like Julian, Felix, and Edwin. The three friends had tried to make the World Championships last year too, but they'd gotten crushed repeatedly by the Fortress Masters. They just weren't good enough. Julian doubted they would have made it even if they'd lucked into getting a superstar like Brandon for their fourth slot. Julian was only in the top 500, and Edwin, while a decent marksman, was unranked. The only competitive player on their team was Felix, who was in the top 200.

After leaving their squad, Felix had managed to qualify, but he'd gotten cut by his team after they beat the Fortress Masters.

It was pretty ridiculous.

Julian had helped his friend write an appeal to the game administration, but there was nothing they could do. It turned out that when you beat a Fortress, only the team's captain qualified. Technically, they were free to pick the other three players. The other three had removed Felix and replaced him with a higher-ranked player with better control skills.

Tyler frowned.

"What does that matter that they've been playing together? Shouldn't they be grateful they got carried to the World Top 4?"

Julian shrugged.

"Yeah, you'd think so. But instead, they just blamed Brandon for taking the spotlight. The casters noticed that Brandon played way better after his teammates went down and had to stop worrying about supporting them. So the three of them—and the rest of Caliber Gaming—kind of just made up rumors that he was letting them go down on purpose."

"Wow, that's dumb."

"Yeah, so he ended up leaving the clan. That's fine, though. I mean, everyone knows he was the star of the World Championships. He's probably got tons of offers for the next tournament, and if he wants to, there's a spot in the Selection waiting for them."

The Cerberus Roar immediately cried out as Tyler restarted the clip. The gold lightning streaked toward Caliber Gaming's encampment.

Sweetshot was the only one who reacted in time. He grabbed his nearest ally and then jumped into the air, spewing out smoke grenade canisters to obscure the Roar's vision.

There was a tremendous explosion, and a storm of dismembered parts flew into the air. Sleigh and Atlas died instantly.

Sweetshot landed and set his sole remaining teammate down.

The Bombardment Cannon thudded, and one of the Song team's units crashed to the ground. It was an instant kill—a heavy blow right to the cockpit.

Julian couldn't help but feel bad for Crabby. Unlike Brandon's teammates, Crabby was actually good. The top 100 ranked pilot had trained all year only to get instantly downed in this match. There was a lot of variance to a game of Overdrive. Despite Sweetshot's incredible skill, even a slight shift would have made him hit the head instead. It was why most pro players preferred best of five matches.

The Bombardment Cannon and artillery pack fired again and again, shelling the smoked area. Flames and dark black smoke billowed as some of the shots struck home. As they fired, Brandon continued moving around so that the enemy squad couldn't discern his position. The smoke cannons still obscured the battlefield, but they'd run out of ammunition soon. He had to make a decisive attack as soon as possible.

Ryu didn't flee. He stayed in place, firing shot after shot. Eventually, they triangulated his position and returned fire through the smoke. He died.

The casters went on about what a big mistake it was, but Julian couldn't condemn Ryu. The other three Caliber players were all ranked in the top five hundred, about the same tier as Julian himself. Although Julian noticed outside of the battle that Ryu obviously should have moved, he wasn't sure he'd remember the same thing inside the game.

Julian had choked plenty of winnable matches before.

Julian nodded as he realized something very important. Things that seemed evident out of the game weren't always evident in the game. In the middle of the action, he needed to keep using his spectator thinking.

Once again, it was a difference between a pilot with good control skills and a pilot destined to battle on the World Championship stage. Julian had a lot of work to do before he could get to the latter category.

Sweetshot flew closer and closer, strafing the confused enemy units.

When the smoke finally cleared, the Patchwork had its massive cannon right in front of the Roar's head. The two surviving Grunts swiveled and fired, but not before Brandon had obliterated the Roar's eye cameras. Unfortunately for Brandon, the Roar had four heads. Even after losing the main cameras, there were still the big cats in the arms and chest.

On his way out, Sweetshot surprised one of the Grunts with a slanting kick. The beam saber went straight through the waist, bisecting the machine and causing it to crash helplessly to the floor. Moments later, the pilot died in the explosion.

The Roar sent blast after blast of golden lightning towards the swerving Patchwork. Sweetshot avoided the first barrage, but he'd failed to account for the enemy Mech's power.

The red and yellow machine slowly drew its hands across the battlefield as it continued the rate of fire. The enormous blasts of electricity had become a pair of gigantic swords.

The sudden motion caught the Patchwork off guard. The gangly machine ducked to the side, but it was too late for the massive grappling arm. It was cut off entirely at the elbow.

The casters gasped.

"Despite his incredible play earlier, the Patchwork is now at a severe disadvantage! The bombardment and grappling arm is the Patchwork's most powerful weapon by far!"

The Cerberus Roar slashed with the makeshift swords again.

Tyler paused the screen.

"Should I use a similar move?"

Julian shrugged.

"You can do that too, but it's a risk."

He pointed to the side of the screen, which indicated the power left in TiggerLuvr's machine. Although he'd lost the head unit, almost everything else was still functional.

"Look at his remaining energy. He's using up a lot of his power right now to try and end the battle quickly."

"Brandon is going to try and close the distance here. He has to. Otherwise, the Roar will blow him to pieces. This strategy of using your beam cannons like they are swords isn't very effective at close range."

He pointed to the arm.

"Look at how slowly the arms move when you're constantly firing. It's powerful from long range, but up close, you should just use a regular sword."

Julian hit play again. He couldn't actually remember how Brandon had won. It looked like a horrible situation.

The Patchwork streaked forward. To Julian's surprise, Sweetshot raised his shield and started blasting mines at the enemy Mech. When the last remaining Grunt moved to intercept, Brandon almost contemptuously flicked his knife at him.

Another direct hit to the cockpit.

Another instant kill.

Aces had far more firepower, but you didn't need raw strength if you had preternatural accuracy. It was Brandon's third direct cockpit kill of the match. He'd done the same thing during the exhibition with his repeated headshots on the Zombie Grunts.

The Patchwork twisted again and avoided the Roar's cannons.

Tigger drew his composite rifle, haphazardly spraying to try and halt the approach. Brandon twisted and threw his shield, which still had a pair of mines inside. There was an enormous explosion, and both parts—the rifle and the shield—were instantly incinerated.

The Cerberus Roar drew the enormous sword from its chest.

The bright yellow and red letters flashed across the screen.

OVERDRIVE: LIQUID STATE ETERNIUM

The metal bubbled, and the lunging swing nearly took off the Patchwork's head. The Patchwork's elongated limbs gave it an advantage in close combat, but the increased height also made it more susceptible to high strikes.

The Patchwork turned and directed a vicious kick straight to the cockpit. The Roar raised its arm to block. The tiger head deflected the first strike, then the second. When the Patchwork stabbed forward, the head bit down, chomping around the blade.

Julian's eyes widened as he finally remembered what had happened.

If it'd been Julian there, he would have lost. After getting your leg bitten, the instinctive thing was to pull back. But Brandon had seen that the only way to win was pushing forward.

Brandon relentlessly continued his kick, jamming the blade deep into the tiger's maw and straight through the arm.

There was a tremendous bang, and the Patchwork was flung to the ground. The leg had snapped off at the knee, but the Cerberus Roar was in far worse condition.

The beam sword had melted the internal circuitry completely. The left arm's explosion had rattled the Mech so hard that the cockpit had cracked open.

The chest head was a mangled ruin. There were still a few sparks in the liger cannon, but at this point, firing the chest cannon would likely incinerate the cockpit.

Julian paused the video.

"Tigger got kind of unlucky here that the explosion spread to the chest cannon. That's the weird thing about chest cannons. It's a great place to store some firepower, but you have a risk if it gets damaged. It's the same for cannons in the head—a good place to get some more firepower, but also a good chance someone can take advantage of the situation to blow up the cannon and destroy your eye cameras."

Cannons in the chest and head were almost like the long-range version of a generator-mounted beam sword.

Abnormal power came at an abnormal cost.

Brandon recognized that better than anyone.

Nobody knew that better than the crafter who turned every single one of his Grunts into highly volatile Patchwork units.

Tigger swung the massive sword again, but the Patchwork slipped away. Sweetshot blasted away with his back-mounted beam spray cannons. At the beginning of the fight, they'd been utterly ineffective, but now he was at zero range, and the Cerberus Roar's once-mighty armor was reduced to a sordid state.

More and more bits of liquid-like armor splashed off the Mech, but the Cerberus Roar was gaining. Soon it would be close enough to strike. The Patchwork's remaining leg beam sword flared to life. Tigger swiped once, then twice.

Brandon parried both blows, but when he tried blocking for a third time, the Roar's sword cut clean through the blade. The difference in strength between a Grunt and an Ace was too vast. Tigger hacked upward, aiming to bisect his gangly opponent.

Brandon countered with a reverse somersault.

"Oh my god."

Tyler had only played a single battle, but even he could tell what a masterful move that was.

His right leg lashed out. The beam emerged again and severed the sword at the hilt.

The Cerberus Roar countered with a grab and a throw, slamming the gangly Patchwork to the ground.

The Cerberus Roar barreled forward, activating its Finisher.

FINISHER: CERBERUS SOUL CANNON

The Cerberus Roar's Liquid State Eternium vaporized, starting at the legs.

The Patchwork shifted and avoided the beam, but the heat was intense enough to melt the gangly machine's legs and incinerate the backpack. Although Brandon had survived the attack, the Patchwork had no more weapons.

Tigger had only sacrificed his legs. He had several more Soul Cannon-level blasts prepared.

The Cerberus Roar lumbered forward. The Patchwork pushed itself off the ground.

It was over in moments.

The devastated Patchwork headbutted the cockpit, goring TiggerLuvr888 against his machine's communications antenna.

WINNER: Sweetshot303—Kingbreaker Patchwork

Tyler let out a long breath.

"Oh, man. What a fight."

He pulled up his status screen and marveled at the Roar.

"This thing is so strong. And the Tigger guy was so good. But he lost."

Tyler clapped his hands together.

"Alright man. Let's get back into the server. I've got a lot of work to do."

[12]

The two friends logged onto Overdrive and entered the brightly lit lobby. A wide variety of fellow pilots surrounded them. The majority of them were wearing the same default piloting suit as Tyler.

A customized pilot suit was a special privilege you had to earn. Julian had received his for breaking into the top 2000 ranks. There were a few other ways to get custom suits—like training a lot of beginners or becoming an accomplished PvE grinder—but in general, a custom suit told everyone that you were a pilot to be respected.

Most of the players around them were comparing Mechs. Images of their selected Ace and Grunt units hovered above their heads. If Julian wanted to, he could walk closer to get a better look at their individual statistics.

Some of them looked exceptionally interesting.

There was a Hemoborn-type that looked just like a giant samurai. Creating a Hemoborn that looked just like a human was a common project that only a few managed to accomplish. There was no default "human" frame. The closest were the giant or zombie types, neither of which resembled actual humans.

Another pilot had a Mech modeled after the Vermillion Flier. The phoenix was silver instead of red, and although the parts clearly were lower quality, this unit was capable of shifting between the standard Wild form and a humanoid Attacker form.

Tyler noticed that Mech too.

"Dang. That looks cool. How strong do you think it is?"

"It's hard to say. Most Mechs that look good tend to be really strong—like if someone is good enough at crafting to build a beautiful Mech, they usually have the fundamental skills they need to make it powerful. But every once in a while, you see one that's just a paper tiger."

Behind the crowd were the three large mission boards.

The first was exclusively for official Overdrive missions. Those were the missions created by either the game administration or the game-affiliated Fortress Masters.

That was where they'd accepted the Raid on Colony Seven mission last night. If you picked a mission from the first board without a team, you'd get filled into a random lobby.

The second board was for player conversations. Most of them were looking for a team or clan to join. Some players didn't feel comfortable just jumping into the random queues and preferred selecting others to play with before entering. The second board's most prominent benefit was that it allowed you to align your Mech with the rest of the squad.

Of course, the board didn't only have players looking to play regular missions.

There were also various player-assigned tasks. For example, some players were wealthy but didn't have the time to grind for valuable prizes. They could ask willing bounty hunters to pursue various parts or frames in exchange for in-game currency.

Some players wanted other pilots to join their custom maps. Overdrive had a sandbox mode that allowed anyone to play at being a Fortress Master. Some of the fan-made stages boasted uniquely difficult tasks that Fortress Masters weren't allowed to feature. A few rare maps even exceeded the official options in terms of their quality. They were run by aspiring Fortress Masters who wanted fame or attention. Unofficial maps had blown up in popularity after the last Selection. Two of the Fortress Grunts had been selected after they designed unofficial challenges that went viral on various pro player streams. Although they lacked the control skills of other Fortress Grunts, their creativity more than made up for it.

But despite the intrigue of player-created maps, they were pretty unpopular with the community. Player-created missions didn't grant Credits, although you could still get parts and other bonuses.

The third board was for accepting ranked challenges. There were three different queues available, and your overall ranking was a weighted average of the three. The first was individual one-on-one battles, which weighed the lowest. The second was the constructed team ranking, which let you bring a four-person team into the match. Although that was the competitive standard, it only had the second-highest effect on your ranking. The last was the random queue, which put you on a team with four players of about the same skill level. It was up to you to figure out what roles everyone would play. Although the random queue was probably the most unlike competitive play, where you played a consistent position and entered the match knowing what you were going to do, it had the largest weight in your ranking.

It was a point of contention among one-trick ponies like Julian, but the unfortunate truth was that there weren't enough players who could build consistent four-person teams to compete. To keep Overdrive accessible, the random queue was given the highest importance. Julian himself failed to consistently put up a four-person squad. He, Felix, and Edwin were only three players, and Edwin was playing less and less these days now that he'd become a high school teacher.

Julian wasn't sure what option would be best. He wanted to find something that could help him practice the lessons he'd learned yesterday from Tigger's two sons.

After Julian explained to Tyler what the three boards did, his friend opened up the shop again instead of immediately deciding what sort of mission to play.

Tyler frowned as he scrolled through the parts.

"So Tigger said to consider the Mech mine now, and I think that means I need to customize it, right? I mean, it's a great Mech, but I need to build it to fit my own style."

"Yeah, exactly! Like everyone has a different specialty."

Julian caught himself.

That wasn't true.

He would consider himself a close-combat specialist, but not everyone had a specialty. The best players could play all roles.

"Let me change what I said there. What I mean is that every pilot has their own preferences. Like take Brandon's transforming arm. He tends to use it on all of his Mechs—he even built a modified rig for his animal-type machine's tails. But that's more of a signature weapon or style, not necessarily a specialty. The coolest thing about the game is just finding out what parts work for you."

Customization was the best part of Overdrive. It what Tigger-Luvr888 had meant when he'd given Tyler the machine—consider this Mech yours now. Figure out what you need to do to make it the strongest for you.

Instead of buying any parts, Tyler just continued window shopping.

"So I don't know what I'm going to be buying yet—I mean, I don't even know how I want to play, but I'm going to just familiarize myself with all the different parts and weapons. I want to at least know what's possible and what I'll be going for. Do you mind giving me a bit of time here? Maybe you can pick a good mission for us to get started with."

"Yeah, of course! I have some mail I need to check anyways.

Julian pulled up his messages tab as he walked over to the bulletin boards. Three messages were waiting for him.

The first was from Felix, his friend from junior high who was trying to become a professional Overdrive player. Julian, Felix, and Edwin had all joined early enough to receive their given names as screen names, but Felix was the only one who'd taken advantage of the countless hours they'd poured into Overdrive. Felix was famous throughout the server for his solid gameplay and extensive game knowledge. He'd qualified for the last two Selections and was planning on attending this time too. However, he was also considering offers from teams competing for the two million prize pool at the second World Championship.

The second message was from TiggerLuvr888.

Julian forgot about Felix's message entirely. Fortunately, the status screen was just a virtual projection. Otherwise, it definitely would have cracked because of how hard he hit the open button.

TigerLuvr888: Hey, Julian. I wanted to give you a quick update on the Heaven's Boxer. My contact at the administration has messaged me back, and he says he is looking into it now. I should expect to get a result in two days at most. I'm going to get that machine back for you, so don't worry about it too much and keep training hard. Let's play again soon. I'm doing a charity stream for the next week, and I'm going out of town after for my anniversary, but I'll message you as soon as I'm free. Hope you and your friend keep growing. Let's fight against each other soon! The kids are really looking forward to it. They loved some of the great calls you made at the end of the game.

By then, Tyler had caught up to him at the board. Julian showed Tyler TiggerLuvr's message, and his friend grinned.

"Nice! We need to get good—want to show him how much I've improved with the Roar. Where are we going today?"

"Hang on, I got some more messages to look through."

Felix: Hey! I'm grinding for some more loot right now. Looking to get some more upgrades before I duck into the ranked queues. I was wondering if you wanted to come in. Let's both become Fortress Masters this time! (:

Julian wanted to play with him, but Felix took grinding very seriously. Julian's childhood friend would be happy to play with Tyler during one of his break days, but Felix usually just tried clearing missions as fast as possible.

Julian: Yeah! I'd love to. I'm teaching Tyler to play right now, though. Not sure if you're taking a break or anything.

Felix had met Tyler a number of times before. Julian's old friend tried making the trip from San Francisco to Chicago at least once a year. But even though Felix liked Tyler, he'd probably turn down the chance to play with him. Felix wasn't a rager or anything, but he'd be annoyed if Julian slowed them down by explaining everything to a new player. Felix was trying everything to become a pro and didn't want to play with anyone who wasn't serious.

Felix: Ah, got it. I don't mind playing with him normally, but I'm pretty focused on grinding right now. Maybe in a couple of months after the ladder update? To be honest dude, you should probably wait a few months to teach him too. I want us both to be Fortress Masters.

Under regular circumstances, Felix would have been right, but playing with Tyler was precisely what Julian needed. Tyler's dedication to getting better was already rubbing off on Julian, who also suspected that explaining complex game mechanics to his friend would help him better understand them for himself. Felix had already hit the cap in terms of his control skills and mental abilities. Julian had broken into the top 500 while playing only a single style. That meant he had a lot to go before he maxed out.

He quickly typed out his response.

Julian: Actually, I think this is working well for me. Just needed a new perspective.

Felix: Got it, got it. Well, best of luck and keep me posted. I'll be watching your ranking man, let's get this! Let me know if you have any free time—I'll always check in before filling up my lobbies.

Julian: Thanks, good luck to you too!

Julian popped open his Status screen and swapped from the Starlight R to his Grunt unit, the Defender Mk. II Julian Custom. It was time to improve his Grunt play.

When Julian saw the third message, he turned to Tyler and grinned. It was just what he was looking for.

"Alright, man. The best way to figure out what kind of machine to use is to train. The good news is that one of my buddies has the perfect stage for it."

They went to the second bulletin board. Julian scrolled down, trying to find the offering from Captain Maxwell.

The first three posted missions were nearly identical.

"Help out new players."

"New players guide."

"Mission for beginners."

There were a lot of veteran pilots that liked playing with beginners to help them get started. TiggerLuvr888 did that all the time. In a way, he'd fulfilled the same role for Tyler, although giving him a god-like Mech went way beyond what most beginner guides did.

The fourth mission was the one Julian was looking for.

"Forever Fortress—now debuting! Looking for both attackers and defenders. This is going to be a battle between armies!"

It was a Custom Map that one of the clans he'd played with

before—a group of former stunt pilots—had created themselves. The premise was essentially an unlimited battle you could always play on. Like many custom Fortresses, it broke certain rules. In this case, the Forever Brothers had removed the limit on how many people you could play with.

The max for official Fortresses was four with only one Ace— the competitive standard. The average PVE mission allowed you to bring anyone from four to fifteen players. But the Forever Fortress let you have an infinite number of players on your team.

The Forever Brothers wanted their whole clan to play. You could battle each other or their planned endless store of NPCs.

He got Tyler's attention and highlighted the mission.

"This is going to be a good one. It's the guys I mentioned earlier. It's going to be a big map—lots of chances to train on different terrain."

They created a Party and then clicked accept.

A familiar voice excitedly called him over.

"Julian! Julian! What's up, man! Good to see you! Nice to see you've brought a friend. It's an honor to have you test our map!"

[13]

The Forever Fortress was the sort of map where you didn't automatically start inside your machine. Instead, they landed on a massive balcony accompanied by a set of catapults. From the viewing platform, you could summon your Mech and ride into a battle.

A handful of other wide-eyed pilots stood beside them, gaping at the vibrant scene unfolding around them.

The parade of flamboyantly-colored Mechs swirled and dove like a living rainbow. Every so often, bolts of energy streaked back and forth between the enemy units. A pilot like Brandon used the most efficient movements possible. He only pulled off a move like a somersault when he had no other option. As Tyler and Julian stared at the cloud of machines above them, they must have seen at least four somersaults in two minutes. The Forever Brothers relished using the most complex maneuvers possible.

"Woah!"

That'd been Julian's first reaction to seeing the Forever Brothers too.

The Forever Brothers were infamous for their love of flashy Mechs. Maxwell and some of his fellow pilots had served in the

Air Force together before becoming stunt pilots in the entertainment sector. There were several military-related clans in the Overdrive community, and most of them preferred to use fighter jets or tanks similar to Lilac's machines. Most of them even stuck to weapons that existed in real life, like machineguns or smart missiles.

The Forever Brothers were the exact opposite.

Maxwell and his friends used designs that had nothing to do with their time on the battlefield. Their Mechs were all painted in flagrantly bright colors, and their weapons were the height of whimsy. Maxwell himself preferred the tricky beam whip. The pilots they attracted to their clan were the ones who wanted to have the most fun. The Forever Brothers had little interest in competitive strategies or optimal play.

It was such a stark departure from Maxwell himself. Julian had gotten to know him pretty well during their time playing together, and from what he could gather, the former captain had remained an intensely disciplined man in his regular day-to-day life.

Julian had first met the Forever Brothers after meeting Captain Maxwell in a random queue game. That time, Felix and Julian had been lucky enough to land on a random queue team where everyone naturally played their favored role. The two friends had matched up with Maxwell and his fellow stunt pilot, who'd also been a fighter plane ace in the military. With Felix and Mabry watching their backs, Captain Maxwell and Julian had dominated the front lines. Since that day, Julian and Maxwell had become fast friends. Although Julian was often too unmotivated to follow his sound advice, the older man was a great mentor.

A thunderbolt suddenly crackled towards him. The shot was aimed straight at the stage.

Julian jerked up, but there was nowhere for him to go.

Tyler swore and instinctively tried to run, but the bolt was huge.

There was a loud crackle. The bolt became strangely blurry, and then it fizzled away about seven feet before it reached them.

Julian blinked. There was some sort of barrier above the balcony.

Maxwell let out a delighted laugh.

"What do you think of our viewing platform?"

"Dang. How did you guys figure that one out?"

To a beginner like Tyler, the attack-nullifying properties of the viewing platform must have seemed obvious. He'd been startled at first, but in hindsight, it made sense that you wouldn't be allowed to shoot spectators.

Only a veteran like Julian knew how impressive it was. The lack of an anti-aggression barrier for player-created maps had been a longstanding gripe with the game administration. It was obvious that the technology existed. After all, the overall Overdrive lobby was a non-aggression zone, as were the stands for virtual exhibitions. However, the Overdrive Corporation hadn't granted the same privilege to player-created maps.

The Forever Brothers' electric barrier was an excellent innovation. The problem with most fan-made attempts was that it blocked off the view. The stage must have had a complicated sensor system as well as an advanced near-invisible forcefield.

The barrier wasn't the only significant change. The Captain's machine had evolved. The last time he'd played with Julian, Maxwell had used a royal blue Kingbreaker class whose hand had been replaced by a beam whip generator. This new machine was much taller with lanky limbs and an angular head that looked a little alien. The wide eye cameras peered down at Julian and Tyler.

Rather than merely replacing the hand, the coiling beam whip now swallowed up the entire arm. As always, Maxwell only used a single weapon, a restriction to make his battles more exciting.

Julian had seen Maxwell fight seriously before. He wasn't quite as good as Brandon or Tigger, but he was incredibly close. If he wanted to, the Captain would easily qualify for the Selection.

The sharp shoulders immediately gave away the Mech's Class. They were Mana Gatherer Spikes, the hallmark of a Spell Titan. Strangely enough, there were only two of them. Most Ace units could hold up to eight. A few had up to ten. Even the default Cyromancer frame Julian had captured the other day had six.

Julian pulled up the new report.

- General Data -
Pilot: Maxwell2
Machine: SPG-1 Caster—Maxwell2 Custom
Class: Spell Titan
Sub-class: Attacker
Designation: Grunt Unit

- Statistics -
Melee: S-tier
Shooting: C-tier
Speed: B-tier
Maneuverability: B-tier
Defense: C-tier
Cohesion: A-tier

- Weapons -
Mana Gatherer Spike [x2]
Mana Dispersal Finger [x5]
Laser Whip "Franklin" (Full Custom) [x1]

- Abilities -
Thunderbolt
Static Freeze
Storm Surge

No wonder it only had two Spikes. It was a Grunt. In addition to the 10,000 Points cap, Grunt frames had additional restrictions that prevented them from equipping powerful built-in weapons without destroying their Cohesion stats. Mana Gatherer Spikes were expensive and unwieldy. If someone used Brandon's Patchwork strategy to forcibly equip them, their Mech would quickly fall to the C or D tier.

Previous Grunt models only carried a single Mana Gatherer Spike. Competitive teams used them exclusively for ambush strategies where you needed as much initial force as possible. Otherwise, their frailty and low stamina made them inferior to their Kingbreaker or Hemoborn counterparts.

Yet this Mech's parts were near-perfectly integrated. The shoulders and upper arms were elegantly fused with the Mana Gatherer Spikes, granting the machine a strange and somewhat feral appearance. The powerful generators were completely balanced with the rest of the Mech, ensuring that none of the statistics suffered abnormal decreases. With two Spikes, the new design had twice as much fighting strength as the older models.

Julian wondered who had created the design. Maxwell was a decent but uninspiring crafter. This was beyond his abilities. The SPG Caster was the first Grunt with an S-tier statistic—other than Cohesion—that Julian had seen outside of the Patchwork models.

Maxwell laughed boisterously.

"Pretty cool, huh? I bet you didn't expect us to finally put one of these together."

Between their bright colors and flashy spells, the eccentric

Spell Titan Grunts were the perfect fit for the Forever Brothers' flashy and flamboyant playstyle.

Maxwell had been trying to create Spell Titan Grunts for a while, but his designs had been weak and clunky.

Maxwell raised an eyebrow when he scanned Julian's selected unit. The orange Defender Mk. II was a far cry from his powerful Starlight R.

"What happened to the Starlight R? Are you going all Grunt like us now too?"

Maxwell had always mocked Julian as a snob for only using Ace units. The Captain preferred playing with Grunts, explaining that it meant everyone could participate. After all, you rarely ran into a lobby where none of the players liked using Ace units.

"Yeah, you know what? I've realized I really need to raise my Grunt play."

Maxwell beamed.

"Well, the Forever Fortress is the perfect place for it. And we're finally open!"

Julian and Tyler walked over to the catapults and summoned their Mechs. The machines materialized around them and the Overdrive servers comfortably placed them inside the cockpits. The stars streaked behind them as their units launched into the massive Forever Fortress. There were a few startled cries from the balcony as Tyler entered the famous Roar, but everyone else was too busy with their intense battles.

Maxwell wasn't surprised to see the powerful machine. Julian had already told him what'd happened.

The bright blue machine led the way as its coiling whip trailed behind it. Although the Forever Fortress name suggested only a single map, there were really dozens of them, each surrounded by their own obstacles. There were even planets, moons, and space colonies.

Maxwell grinned impishly.

"Watch this."

He pulled up his status screen and pressed a few buttons. A storm of parts flew toward them, assembling bit by bit as the machine slowly reached them. By the time it arrived next to Maxwell, there was a complete white and olive green Grunt unit. The plain Mech carried a machinegun, a shield, and a beam sword. The armament and design were similar to an enemy from a mid-tier mission.

"How did you do that?"

Maxwell pressed at his screen a few more times, and more units spawned.

To Julian's surprise, the Mech had its own status screen as well. Typically, Grunts only had a basic description.

- General Data -
Pilot: Forever Fortress AI
Machine: FFAI Grunt
Class: Kingbreaker
Sub-class: Attacker
Designation: Grunt Unit

- Statistics -
Melee: B-tier
Shooting: B-tier
Speed: B-tier
Maneuverability: B-tier
Defense: B-tier
Cohesion: B-tier

- Weapons -
Beam Sword
Machinegun
Shield

- Abilities -

N/A [Kingbreaker Class]

Maxwell shrugged.

"Not sure why the report is so extensive. I thought it should have just been a basic thing, but it's treating it like a player-created Ace. It's probably just a bug. The good news is it lets you check out that quality!"

The Mech was built out of incredibly cheap parts. Julian recognized the look of salvaged and reformed metal. As he carefully turned from Grunt to Grunt, he noticed they had different arm and leg parts. The one on the farthest right had repainted legs from the Defender series, which were thicker than the standard. The one next to it had the same spindly legs as the spherical Guardian models. There was a specialized attachment at the hips to allow them to connect to a humanoid rather than a spherical torso.

But despite the mismatched appearances, this was the kind of Mech a Fortress Master would be lucky to command. You rarely saw base Grunt units with such reliable statistics. The actual strength and value of the machines had no correlation with their mediocre appearance.

"Where did you find these things? How did you even get it to launch and assemble like that?"

The strange parts catapult meant that the Forever Fortress players could summon their Grunts anywhere they wanted. As Julian looked around the map, he saw other players hailing Grunts of their own. Even better, the AI was smart enough to dodge mid-air if you tried attacking the parts as they started forming.

Before Maxwell could answer, a ray of bright blue light streaked through the dark sea of space.

Moments later, two of the units Maxwell had summoned

exploded. The sniper had blasted through both of the heads at the same time.

Julian blinked.

What a shot!

Maxwell beamed and pointed.

"My daughter helped me out! She's always been good at stuff like this. Only just got her into playing! Wish we figured it out how to get her on here earlier—it would have taken us years to figure everything out on our without Emma."

Julian turned. Whereas Maxwell's machine was a royal blue melee unit, his daughter's was a much more brightly colored neon blue and optimized for long-range combat.

There was a special sniper's helmet over the angular head. The long fin at the top granted the pilot exceptional sensor capabilities. Although the masklike device only enhanced visual abilities, the high quality meant it cost 3,000 Credits. To compensate for the expensive equipment, the Mech only carried one other weapon. It was the most beautiful rifle Julian had ever seen and clearly a Full Custom.

The long twisting sniper rifle was royal blue and gold. Lightning crackled along the barrel, which had been built to look like a magician's staff. Just looking at it made Julian feel like the pilot could perform miracles. He pulled up the Mech's characteristics.

- General Data -
Pilot: Guest 146
Machine: SPG-1 Caster—Emma Custom
Class: Spell Titan
Sub-class: Artillery
Designation: Grunt Unit

- Statistics -
Melee: C-tier

Shooting: S-tier
Speed: B-tier
Maneuverability: C-tier
Defense: C-tier
Cohesion: A-tier

- Weapons -
Scope Visor [x1]
Enhanced Mana Gatherer Spike [x2]
Mana Dispersal Finger [x10]
Boom Staff (Full Custom) [x1]

- Abilities -
Thunderbolt
Static Freeze
Storm Surge

As he expected, the Abilities were standardized, as was the need for Gatherer Spikes and Dispersal Fingers. Of course, the weapons itself provided the difference when it came to using Abilities. When coming from the Emma Custom, the Thunderbolt probably did far more damage than it would from a typical SPG-1 Caster. Based on the name of the frame, Emma was either a fan of Vile—or the popular Gundam anime series, which was where Vile had drawn the inspiration to use abbreviations and numerical codenames for her designs.

The blue sniper raised its staff again, which glinted with menacing beauty. When Julian zoomed in for a closer look, he realized that there was a port to connect the rifle directly to the arm. The closer proximity to the Mana Gatherer Spike meant the Mech would fire even more powerful attacks.

Yet another shot of blue lightning crackled out, streaking straight at Maxwell.

"Hey!"

He twisted and raised his hand, casting a zero range Storm Surge to cancel out the blast and protect himself.

Julian smiled. He remembered talking to Maxwell about her daughter before. If Julian remembered right, she was a few years older than he was. It was great that she'd finally started playing. He knew how hard the Captain had been trying to get her to log on.

From what he'd mentioned, she was wary of the game's body scan. As a result, she was currently using a Guest account, which meant that Overdrive wouldn't scan her before letting her into the server. Julian had used a Guest account too until he'd gotten tired of the inconvenience.

Guest accounts had a puny inventory, and they lost everything after logging out. She probably gave her Credits and Mech back to her dad at the end of every fight. Felix and Edwin had performed a similar banking service for Julian back in the day.

She raised the staff again and fired off another shot.

This time, she destroyed three units in a row up, clearing out the Grunts charging alongside her father. Usually, such an impressive display of skill would have merited a combo kill notification and an additional Credit reward. However, like all player-made maps, the Forever Fortress couldn't award Credits for kills.

Julian gaped at the flawless triple kill. It was clear that Emma had inherited her father's flair, but she was even more skilled than Maxwell. Her talent for trick shots was unlike anything he'd ever seen before.

Maxwell summoned a new force of machines and then charged for the attack.

The sniper snapped its fingers, and its own AI Grunts appeared. Her units focused on setting up a perimeter and defending her position. When Maxwell finally reached her, the defenders shifted to protect her. The beautiful sniper rifle released blast after blast of blue lightning.

"Tyler, you notice that?"

"Yeah, that's cool."

"Using bodyguards alongside a sniping unit is a pretty conventional strategy. The point is basically to let your sniper free-fire for a while. It's also a good way to use a machine that's a Grunt unit but give it Ace-level abilities. Like all you need to have a sniper is a good rifle—you can equip any old machine with that."

"That's what Brandon did too, right? Like he was able to carry the games from the Ace position."

"Yeah, there were a few matches where he played a sniper role. Using the sniper in conjunction with the bombardment arm made for a menacing Mech."

"Still can't believe that the Cal guys kicked him off his team. What a dumb move. Honestly, if they couldn't win with Brandon, they probably just suck. When I played with Brandon in high school, he was just able to elevate everyone's game. I never felt so good dunking as when I caught a pass from Brandon. It was crazy."

Julian agreed that Caliber Gaming had made a massive mistake, but the truth was that Brandon probably wanted to find a better team anyways. They'd been the ones holding them back.

Tyler cursed.

"Man, it's going to be tough for me to beat Brandon, especially if he finds a good Ace to pair up with. I know he wouldn't have any problem figuring out how to optimize everything. He made so many different players work. Back in high school, he could play with any four players and have them humming in just a few minutes. In our sophomore year, we had a transfer student who came in as a senior, and he was used to having the ball all the time. Everyone thought it'd be a problem, but Brandon just figured it out."

Someone laughed behind them.

"Hey, didn't you know it's rude to talk about people behind their backs?"

Tyler jerked around at the sound. His face immediately erupted into a massive grin.

"Hey, man! It's good to see you!"

A friend request popped up on their screens.

SWEETSHOT303 WOULD LIKE TO BE YOUR FRIEND!

When Julian accepted, Tyler's handsome friend smirked at the side of their screen.

"Hey! And I thought it was just the Brothers who were always talking about old times."

[14]

Julian hadn't paid too much attention to Brandon's appearances in exhibitions. If he had, he would have recognized him already. Although he'd changed a good deal since his high school basketball days, he still greatly resembled the boy in Tyler's photos.

He was very tall—not quite as tall as Tyler but still just under six and a half feet. He'd gained a good deal of weight, including a broad stomach that pressed against his pilot's suit. His face had widened a good deal too, filling out his cheeks, but it'd only made him look even more charmingly handsome. His grin went from ear to ear. Even after moving from basketball to video games, his strength was still apparent.

In the pictures, Brandon had been lean and muscular. Now, he looked like an incredibly tough bouncer who could stop trouble at a bar with a single word.

The Mech he'd brought today had only a passing resemblance to the one he'd used at the World Championships.

Unlike his previous close-combat Mech, this one was outfitted for long-range artillery support. It maintained the same bombardment arm and supportive back cannons, but it held a bazooka in the right hand rather than a shield, and a strange UFO-like disk had replaced its legs.

The hover plate was a unique item designed to improve firing accuracy. Under usual circumstances, it would be extremely irresponsible to use an explosive weapon like a bazooka for long-range support. You had about an equal chance of hitting your teammates as you did hitting the enemy.

The hover plate allowed your Mech to aim as if it were standing still even as you were moving. Despite that benefit, it was one of the cheapest items in the shop—only 1,000 Credits—because you had to forfeit your legs to equip it.

The general consensus was that it wasn't worth using a hover plate on stages with gravity. Because you couldn't stand or walk, your Mech would almost certainly run out of power before the end of the battle.

The hover plate was more useful in space, but even space stages had obstacles like asteroids, moons, or space stations. On top of that, the Mech was poorly balanced and top-heavy.

But in addition to equipping the hover plate, Brandon had also swapped his frame, trading in the Defender Mk. III for the state-of-the-art Guardian X. The hover plate looked extremely strange on the spherical Mech. It trailed down like it was a skirt.

The frame was a better fit for Brandon's current role. The Defender had initially been built as a frontline skirmisher. Another critical advantage of Grunt frames was that you could carry an infinite number of them. Naturally, the Master of Minions knew to switch up his weapons and frame for each perfect situation. That kind of strategy required overwhelming game knowledge.

It was another thing Julian needed to consider.

"What are you doing here? I'm glad I got to see you!"

"Yeah, sorry for putting it off. I don't have a lot of time. I was just here to drop by and congratulate the Captain. I've got some offers I'm looking through. Just trying to be more selective this time."

He shook his head wryly.

"Last group I signed with were just terrible people all-around."

Julian cut in excitedly. As a fan of Overdrive, he wanted to see the legendary Master of Minions on a top-tier team.

"Are you thinking of pairing up with someone from the exhibition?"

Brandon had even managed to overcome Vile's ingenious Zombie tunneling strategy. He'd clutched a two against one ambush before losing to the impossibly powerful Hyde. If Brandon went from supporting a mediocre team like Caliber Gaming to playing alongside someone like vermillionangel or TiggerLuvr, that team would easily be the favorite to win the Championship.

And with a new Selection coming up, Brandon wasn't restricted to playing for a World Championship contending team. He could just join up with a Fortress and take a steady paycheck. Any Fortress would want to sign him on as a Grunt. So far, nobody had beaten Vile's Fortress team yet. A Sweetshot303-led team would be just as unbeatable.

Brandon just shrugged.

"Ah, I'm not sure yet. Like I said, I've got a ton of offers."

It took a beat for Julian to realize why Brandon might be guarded.

Brandon didn't want anyone spreading rumors. He might have signed with a team already, one that was secretly practicing for the Championship. Pros were extremely aggressive about researching enemy rosters. Alternatively, Brandon might have been saving the announcement for his stream to try and get a big publicity boost. After his strong play at the World Championships, Brandon was building a pretty significant following.

To Brandon, Julian was just a random guy who couldn't be trusted. And in this case, Brandon was right. If Julian knew where Sweetshot was going, there was no way he wouldn't tell Felix or Edwin.

Brandon hastily changed the subject.

"Tyler mentioned you're trying to go for the Selection, right? How's that been going so far?"

"Oh, well, I just found out about it after the exhibition. It's going alright. I think I need to train a lot more before heading back into ranked games. Last time I fell out of the top 500 because I wasn't ready."

Brandon nodded seriously.

"Yeah, that's a good idea. If you're not where you need to be yet, you'll just be flailing around."

He pulled up Julian's status card, which showed that he was ranked 524th. Julian took the time to pull up Brandon's own profile and admire his sterling ranking. Brandon was currently the 3rd highest-ranking player on the server, which was incredibly impressive for a pro. Most of them only took the time to get into the top 500 to remain eligible for Selection. They preferred to practice with their team or grinding for rare equipment. Top-tier pros already spent hours each day scrimmaging other competitive rosters in custom games. Whenever a new map released or a Fortress was adjusted, pros played it over and over again to discover every hidden secret or exclusive part. That left little time for ranked play.

Yet Brandon had the time to scrimmage, grind, and play ranked games at the same time. That was a crazy amount of Overdrive.

"You're probably about three or five games from the top 500. Honestly, you could do that in a single day or maybe a week. If you beat someone in the top three hundred, you'll climb up all the slots at once."

Julian winced inwardly as he thought of his invite from Dynamic. He had a long way to go before he could beat the skilled sharpshooter.

"You've got a lot of time. Honestly, you might be good enough already. It's not hard to climb thirty spots if you go on a hot streak. What are you trying to work on?"

Even though they'd just met, Brandon acted like Julian making the Selection was the most important thing in the world. It was just like Tyler said. Brandon had a magnetic personality. He was a leader people liked hearing from.

"I think I need to improve my Grunt play. I really let it fall by the wayside. And then…"

Julian trailed off.

He'd sound like an idiot if he just said he needed to work on thinking in the middle of the game. He didn't want Sweetshot303 to think he was dumb.

Then he shrugged. Brandon was Tyler's friend. He could still say it, just reworded a little bit.

"Just like keeping good habits and stuff and staying cognizant of the game. Sometimes I know how to do something or that I need to do something in X situation, but then I don't actually do it in the game. You know what I mean?"

"Yeah, absolutely! That happens to me all the time too. "

Brandon smiled.

"We're only human you know? There's a ton of matches where I regret my play. Sometimes it's just luck—you might narrowly lose a shooting duel—but usually there's something better you can do. What angle should I have approached from? What equipment should I have given my Mech? Stuff like that. Honestly man, those are probably the two biggest things. Figuring out how to be a reliable Grunt and then thinking through your moves. That totally makes sense."

Brandon pulled up something on his status screen and

frowned thoughtfully for a moment before dismissing it. It was probably just some random message.

"By the way, Tyler. I heard you have the Cerberus Roar now. How did that happen? Is Tigger selling Mechs?"

Like most pilots, Brandon preferred turning his Mech in a specific direction when he was having a casual conversation. It was strange—after all, you were talking into your camera chat, not actually talking from your Mech's speakers—but it was a habit that'd become second nature among the Overdrive community.

"Actually, he gave it to me!"

"Wait, what? How did you pull that one off?"

Tyler told his friend about the mission they did together and the missing Heaven's Boxer.

Brandon's first response was to grin when he heard about how Tigger gave away the Roar.

"It doesn't surprise me. That guy is incredibly generous. Every time I talk to him, he's just like 'hey man it's just a game, why not pass it on?'"

He shook his head.

"What a good dude."

But when Julian asked Brandon if he knew anything about Liefield or the Heaven's Boxer, the handsome man grew serious.

"I haven't heard of this Liefield guy—seems like he's not a particularly notable pilot. But yeah, I definitely know his type. He probably would have fit in pretty well on Cal Gaming."

Brandon's frown grew deeper.

"The thing is, I don't know how come you guys didn't get the Mech. They removed the forced log-out bug a while ago. I don't think he'd be able to take advantage of that."

Julian cut in.

"Tigger said it might have been a bugged due to the Challenge System."

Brandon wrinkled his forehead.

"Maybe. The Challenge System sounds like a headache to make work on the backend. You said it didn't let you log out after he started the challenge, right?"

"Yeah."

Brandon pulled up yet another document on his status screen. He scanned it for a moment, then turned it over so Julian and Tyler could see it.

"There's a chance the Mech was just deleted."

"Huh? What do you mean?"

Julian winced. He'd responded a little too hastily. It made him sound like an idiot. But he'd been thinking of the Heaven's Boxer all day. It was the coolest Mech he'd ever seen. How could it have been deleted?

Brandon ignored Julian's obvious overexcitement.

"It might have been a bug that the machine appeared in the first place. Look at this. I don't think the Reality Shapers were released. I actually remember it was a big scandal a while back—people weren't happy to hear about them. People thought it was important to respect fundamental game mechanics. Look at what that Liefield guy did, just using the Boxer to bully new players. I remember another unit called the Critical Snipe—or something like it—that was a sniper that could only hit cockpit shots."

Julian seemed to remember hearing about something like that. If he remembered correctly, there was another unit that had cloning abilities. Even disregarding the Challenge System, the Heaven's Boxer was definitely overpowered. The Mech's Reality Step let it completely ignore the typical weaknesses of melee units. If he had the Boxer, beating Dynamic would be a piece of cake. He'd just teleport in and smash the Self-Supporting Sniper to pieces.

Julian looked at the article Brandon sent over to him.

PATCH UPDATE: REALITY SHAPER SERIES CANCELLED

It was dated over four months ago.

"The one you guys saw was probably a drop possibility that the Overdrive Corporation forgot to remove. Like it vanished not because Liefield stole it but because the game did an inventory check after you left."

Overdrive factored in difficulty and party size into missions. For example, you could deliberately equip your Mech with weak parts to trigger scenarios that led to exclusive drop rates. As a result, each map had countless different drop possibilities. That meant that it'd be easy to overlook a line of code that dropped a defunct machine.

Julian sighed.

"Hopefully not."

Brandon's explanation made sense, but he didn't want to give up the hope of getting the Boxer. Besides, Tigger had expedited the issue to the game administration. They should hear back soon.

Tyler sighed.

"Man. I was hoping to get that machine for you too. Even a total beginner like me could tell that was a nice Mech. Hey, maybe they'll give you something else nice to compensate."

The game admin was generous with awards when players caught bugs. Mechs could sell for over a thousand dollars, but in-game content didn't actually cost the Overdrive Corporation any money to distribute.

"Yeah, maybe."

Brandon pointed out to the battlefield.

"I wouldn't worry too much about that Mech for now. Based on what you said earlier, I think you've got a good idea of what you need to improve. Your mental play is more important than any Mech."

"Yeah, I suppose."

Julian was still feeling worried, but Tyler could hardly hide his excitement.

"Yo, Brandon, are you free for the next ten minutes or so?"

"Yeah, I just have something at 7."

"How about a quick battle? I've been watching your clips, but I want to see it in action."

"Okay! That sounds great!"

Julian was surprised that Brandon accepted. It was probably just because they were such good friends. A battle between an expert and a total newbie wouldn't teach anyone anything.

But then Julian got a battle invite too.

"How about this? Two against one. No restrictions. If you guys want, you can both use Ace units."

[15]

Julian was already surprised by Brandon's confidence. Yes, the Master of Grunts had clutched countless two against one battles before. He'd even won in four against one situations. But all of them knew the strength of the Cerberus Roar, and despite his imperfect crafting, Julian's Starlight R was still a powerful Ace-level Mech.

Not only that, but Brandon seemed to be under the impression that he could win before 7. Instead of a drawn-out battle where he picked them off one by one, but it sounded like he was planning a head-on assault.

Before Julian could respond, Brandon started waving Maxwell over.

"Captain! Captain! I was just about to battle these two. I was wondering if you wanted to join in?"

Maxwell just laughed.

"No thanks! I think Emma might be interested, though. You'll have a handful with her."

The sniper drifted back towards them, and then Emma flickered on the side of their screen. Guest armor worked a lot like privacy armor. It was white instead of black and provided no additional statistics, but it still completely obscured the user's face.

"Yeah, I would love to join in. Is this going to be a two on two? I'd like to fight against Sweetshot if I can."

Brandon shook his head.

"No. You three against me. Bring an Ace unit too, if you want."

"What?! You think you can beat all three of us?"

"I'm not sure, but I'd like to try."

Oh.

Now Julian understood. Brandon sounded completely earnest about his doubt.

Earlier, Julian had thought Brandon simply had a dim view of their skills. Julian couldn't have blamed him. He was the star player of the second-finishing team in the World Championships. Brandon was the Master of Minions, the best Grunt pilot who'd ever logged into Overdrive.

But this was just how the ferocious pilot continually improved his skills. He flung himself headfirst into difficult challenges he wasn't sure if he could conquer. When Brandon had first started leveling up his account, he'd used the default Paragon Grunt—the weakest Mech in the game—until splurging on machines for the World Championship. It was only at the championship that he diversified his play, wowing the crowd with innovative selections like the awkwardly-shaped Brontosaurus Gunner or the swift but fragile Katana 4.

The invitation popped up on Julian's screen.

CHALLENGE: SWEETSHOT303 WANTS TO BATTLE!
ALLIES: TYLERFORD21, GUEST 146

Julian and Tyler immediately hit Accept, but Emma paused before confirming. It sounded like she was frowning.

"Can we do a regular battle if we win?"

"Of course!"

Julian immediately decided that he liked Emma.

She wanted to beat Brandon in a fair battle. Emma had the competitive edge that her father lacked. Julian knew the former stunt pilot had incredible skills, but the captain just wasn't interested in seriously playing Overdrive. He wondered just how good Emma was.

Although she'd just loaded in with a guest account, her earlier moves were nothing like a beginner's.

After they accepted, the four of them instantly teleported to a faraway planet. The Forever Fortress featured independent maps. The battlefield was a crumbling European castle instead of a standard competitive stage.

The hangar arms popped up so Julian and his team could pick their Mechs and equipment.

Across the field from them, the Guardian X's profile was immediately shrouded in shadows. In exchange for their weaker frames and low points limits, Grunts were allowed to adjust their weapons before every battle. It was hard to say what weapons Brandon was equipping. Considering that they were fighting on a planet, there was very little chance he'd bring the hover plate.

Julian and Tyler instantly locked in the Cerberus Roar and the Starlight R. Because they were Ace units, Brandon could see all their parts and details. He'd already battled the Roar during the World Championship, and Julian's Starlight R was built from a fairly common frame. Only newly created Ace frames like the Heaven's Boxer could hide their statistics at the beginning of a battle.

That meant that Brandon had the advantage when it came to customization.

Beside them, Emma selected the same SPG Caster she'd previously played. Julian and Tyler could clearly see the parts, but

Brandon would have seen a dark shroud just like the one that obscured his own machine.

"Sorry guys, but I don't have an Ace unit."

"Do you want one of mine? I've got some nice Spell Titans."

Considering Emma's skill with her rifle, she could probably work wonders with an Ace-level Mech.

"No, thanks. This is the frame I designed, so I like to stick to it."

That made sense. Some pilots insisted that crafting your own Mech and then piloting it were the crux of Overdrive. For skilled builders like Emma, that went down to the machine's very frame.

Julian took another admiring look at the special sniper's visor and the beautiful staff-like rifle. It was amazing how smoothly Emma had integrated the Mana Gatherer Spikes with the arms.

"It's a beautiful Mech."

"Thank you!"

Tyler turned towards him.

"What do you think we should do? What's our game plan?"

Julian bit his lip.

There was still some time left before the match started.

Julian had to formulate a strategy. That was what he was trying to work on, and considering how hard it was to think in the middle of a match, it'd be best for them to enter the game well-prepared.

The only problem was, he had no idea what equipment Brandon was going to use.

Julian groaned.

"I mean, I don't know what he's trying to go for. Considering that he said he's going to try and win before his event at 7, I think it's going to be a head-on attack? But I'm not sure what kind of attack he'll use."

An aerial bombardment and a spear charge were both direct attacks, but the two had completely different counterstrategies.

"Emma, do you have any ideas?"

"Um, well, I mean, if he charges at me, it's going to be tough. I'll need you guys to batter him away. If he does something else..."

She trailed off.

There was no way to plan for that. Brandon could use whatever strategy he wanted.

During a competitive match, the design of the enemy's Ace usually gave Julian a good idea of the other team's overall team composition. Even though the Grunt equipment was hidden, virtually every team built around their Ace unit. However, Brandon was able to play at an Ace pilot's level without giving away his equipment information. It was an incredible advantage. In general, you knew that Brandon would try and bring his Bombardment/Grappling arm, but that didn't actually tell you anything. The weapon was extremely versatile and designed to be used at all ranges.

Julian couldn't imagine how overpowered it would be if your Ace could hide their equipment before a battle. It would turn every match into a guessing game. Dominating the game with a 10,000 Credit cap instead of a 50,000 Credit cap was an enormous advantage.

He shook his head as he realized the truth. When he responded to Emma, he was much more confident than before. This was the way to go.

"Oh, I know. We should just play to our strengths. Like we don't know what Mech he's going to use, but we know what we have. Between you and Tyler, that's a lot of firepower. He won't be able to trade with us if we keep him far away, especially because his machines have low Cohesion."

"Oh, I like that. That sounds good."

Julian groaned.

"I should probably change my Mech for this, but I didn't assemble anything yet."

He'd switched to the Defender Mk. II so he could practice, but he'd carelessly forgotten to upgrade the parts. Although there were benefits to using a weaker Mech for training purposes, this wasn't the time to train.

He shook his head.

"My Grunt isn't strong enough. I need to stick with the Starlight R."

He had a few shields he could equip in his inventory, but it wouldn't do him too much good. The broadly armored Defender Mk. II might look a lot tankier than the Starlight R, but the unfortunate reality was that the quality and maintenance of the parts were too low. Even if he raised his nominal defense to an A, Brandon could still defeat him in a single shot by shooting around the shield. It was another example of how the stats could sometimes be misleading.

Besides, it wasn't worth the offensive trade-off. Julian made a mental note to buy better parts as soon as the match ended. He'd already been planning to, but the missing Heaven's Boxer had been such a distraction.

"It's fine. Just use the stronger Mech. We'll overwhelm him with stats."

"Yeah."

Their massive advantage in raw strength was undeniable. They had three Mechs with two Ace units.

The remaining timer ticked away, and then the battle started.

The shroud of smoke around Brandon's machine vanished, and his design was revealed.

To Julian's shock, the Master of Minions was still using the hover plate. The cannons at the back thundered as the Mech streaked towards them. The Guardian X raised its unwieldy bombardment arm and unleashed a massive missile. This was no support machine. This was a Patchwork unit built entirely for brutal firepower. Brandon was looking to win the battle in a single decisive move.

Tyler and Emma returned fire, but Brandon dodged.

And then he was on them.

Too late, Julian realized their mistake. Saying that they would protect their long-range shooters was one thing, but a detailed plan was quite another. They hadn't coordinated what they'd do if things went off track. Brandon's ferocious attack sent the three of them scattering to separate parts of the castle. Tyler dashed to the right just as Julian veered left. Emma leaped off the castle walls, landing inside the shadowy interior.

Within mere seconds of the battle beginning, their formation had split apart like a broken set of billiards.

[16]

The Guardian X hovered in the air, spraying a relentless stream of gunfire at Julian. The orange Starlight R sprinted furiously along the base of the tower. Whenever Brandon's bullets destroyed the ground beneath Julian's feet, Julian briefly flew before shifting back to a walk as soon as he landed safely. He felt hyperaware of the energy meter at the bottom right of his screen. Using a hover plate on a stage with gravity was very inadvisable. They might be able to defeat Brandon simply because he ran out of energy.

On the other side of the castle, Tyler released volley after volley of golden light. Brandon jerked back and forth with a strange elegance as he dodged every shot. His current Mech looked almost impossible to pilot. The massive bombardment arm must have taken up at least a third of the Mech's weight. There was a second set of massive cannons at the back. Julian recognized the artillery pack as costing 8,500 Credits. The combination of an artillery pack with a hover plate was a niche customization set. Julian had seen it used on Kingbreakers before. The pilots usually amplified their Mech's high base stats with a defensive shield.

Instead of taking a shield, Brandon had topped off his equipment with a flamethrower. The machine was a complete glass cannon.

A single blow would destroy his Mech, and the hover plate meant his Mech wobbled awkwardly back and forth. The bombardment arm forced it to lean to the left. Yet whenever Brandon raised his guns, the skirt-like thrusters would forcibly stabilize his position. Oftentimes, Brandon would raise his bombardment arm just to stop his flight, even when he had no intention to fire.

Tyler had no idea how to deal with the bizarre movements. He couldn't land a single hit.

Julian's eyes widened as he realized what was happening. He'd never seen anything like it before.

Brandon was using the plate's stabilizing properties in a way the game designers had never intended. His machine was a highly mobile attacker instead of a sturdy long-range gunner.

Julian quickly pulled up the status information.

- General Data -
Pilot: Sweetshot303
Machine: Guardian X Patchwork
Class: Kingbreaker
Sub-class: Artillery
Designation: Grunt Unit

- Statistics -
Melee: C-tier
Shooting: S-tier
Speed: A-tier
Maneuverability: C-tier
Defense: B-tier
Cohesion: C-tier
Special: N/A [Kingbreaker Class]

- Weapons -
Shelling Cannon [x2]
Full Shifter Grappling/Bombardment Arm (Full Custom)
[x1]
Flamethrower [x1]
Hover Plate

- Abilities -
N/A [Kingbreaker Class]

The Mech had Brandon's typical skewed statistics, similar to Emma's hyperspecialized SPG Caster. The back cannons were conventional artillery tools and presented an intriguing synergy with the hover plate. Brandon could use them to stop anytime he wanted, and the plate allowed him to hit opponents from virtually any angle at the expense of meager operating time.

Julian felt another stab of jealousy and admiration. These weren't adjustments that could be made in a single day. Brandon must have had countless pre-set Patchwork models ready to ride into battle. He must have spent countless hours discovering powerful synergies.

Tyler continued blasting over and over again, but to no avail.

Julian raised his arms and tried locking the Patchwork in place with his machine cannons, but as soon as he stopped to aim, a great gout of flame nearly knocked him from the castle walls. Julian cursed. Both his arms had been reduced to 40% health.

The frustrated pilot raised his shield and then slashed with the Starlight R's massive beam broadsword, but Brandon halted mere inches before it would hit him. The Patchwork fired another round of shells then jerked backward to avoid Tyler's retort. Thus far, all of Brandon's concentration had been on Julian. It seemed like he was saving the Roar for last.

Julian considered diving down to join Emma, and then

thought better of it. Their team should have all entered the castle. Emma had the right idea. It'd be harder for Brandon to use his strange stop-start movements inside a building with tons of walls. But now, if Julian dove inside, he'd only be leading them straight to Emma. Julian had no doubt that the skillful sniper was waiting for the perfect shot. He had to keep her safe.

As soon as he thought of her, Julian kicked himself for not communicating. Brandon was relentlessly chasing him. Although the seasoned pro must have been watching for a sudden attack from below, he wouldn't be able to pay attention to everything at once. If he led Brandon into Emma's path, that'd make things way easier.

"Where should I lead him?"

"Oh!"

Emma started as if she too had just realized that they should have been coordinating from the start.

"Left! Left! I'll be able to get a good shot to the left."

"Tyler, can you push him left too?"

Brandon was just using a single Grunt. They should be able to coordinate and pin him down.

"Should I activate my Overdrive?"

That could be a good idea. If Tyler used his Overdrive, Brandon would be extremely hard-pressed to dodge. The flimsy Guardian X looked like it could fall apart in a few strong hits. It was only in the B-tier for Defense. It was even possible that a lucky blast from the Roar could just instantly incinerate it. It had a C in Cohesion.

Julian was just about to agree when a new thought stopped the words in his throat. Overdrive boosts, especially Liquid State Eternium, also expanded a lot of energy. They were just trading blows with Brandon's Mech. If Julian had to estimate it, the other machine had likely spent over a fifth of its energy by now. Couldn't they just wait it out?

The two factors battled furiously in his mind. Before, he'd charged in without thinking. But now, Julian realized that thinking was pretty hard too.

"Uh, Julian? What should I do?"

His friend's question jerked him out of his silent musings.

"Yes! Yes! Do it!"

Emma ended up making the call.

"I can hit him! If I hit him, we'll win!"

Julian hastily agreed.

"Okay. Okay. That sounds good."

Building around their long-range Mechs had already been their pre-discussed victory condition. Their best bet was to stick to their initial plan.

"Alright, then."

The yellow and red flared across the screen.

OVERDRIVE: LIQUID STATE ETERNIUM

Tyler fired. The beams were even larger and faster than before. Julian sprinted left, continuing to shoot his machine cannons. The last time he'd turned, Brandon had immediately moved in to shoot him.

This time, Brandon didn't pursue Julian. He focused on dodging Tyler's shots. Brandon didn't ignore Julian's submachinegun cannons, but nor did he foolishly fly into Tyler's lethal attacks. Whenever he couldn't dodge, Brandon would simply raise the arm that held his flamethrower and tank Julian's attacks. Soon the limb was smoking.

Emma groaned.

"Ugh. So close. Just a little more. Just a little."

He was just at the edge of her shooting range.

Brandon twisted just a tiny bit to the right.

None of them saw it coming.

If Brandon had thrown the flamethrower, Julian would have called for Emma to run. But throwing the flamethrower at Emma was the kind of a move a fairly clever player would make. It would have been a strong surprise attack, especially because Julian's team wasn't sure if Brandon knew Emma's position.

But Brandon wasn't just a fairly clever player. He was the best.

The bombardment arm fired, and the entire left side castle wall collapsed. Brandon had hit a low point that brought the whole structure tumbling down. The sudden strike also jerked Tyler off balance. The golden lightning streaked upward, granting Brandon a brief reprieve.

And instead of throwing his flamethrower, he ejected his entire smoking arm. The purge command forcibly removed a limb from your machine. It was typically used to escape from grabs or traps. Losing a healthy limb was a significant sacrifice, but not if you'd die otherwise.

Julian hadn't seen someone purge offensively before.

The sparking arm soon ignited the flamethrower's canister. Emma had just battled out from beneath the wall when the dropped limb exploded in her face, immediately eliminating her from the fight.

PLAYER 3 ELIMINATED

"How did you know I was there?"

Brandon flickered onto their screens, a big grin on his face.

"I took a look at the castle and figured out where the different chambers were. It was clear you guys were trying to drive me left, and I saw Emma jump inside. Considering the walls, there was only one place she could be."

Dang.

He was good.

The castle wasn't even a standard map. He'd figured it all out in the middle of the battle.

Brandon canceled the communication wire, and the battle continued.

By then, Tyler had recovered. His empowered Mech continued firing at Brandon. Eventually, he started using the same "sword-cannon" arrangement Tigger had used in the World Championships. The massive beams chased the one-armed Mech all around the map. Brandon flew further and further, eventually diving into the castle. Tyler continued blasting, sending clouds of rubble high into the air. The bubbling on his Paragon's metal was getting slower and slower. Soon he'd revert to his normal state.

Julian wished his Ace unit was a little more balanced. His most potent ranged weapons were the arm-mounted submachine-guns, which were only effective from medium range.

He was just about to fly inside when Emma called for him to stay.

"Wait. Wait. This isn't the end of the world. Don't chase him."

"Why not? I need to hold him in place for Tyler."

"Nah, he's running away from you guys. He can't duel the Roar from long-range, and he's going to run out of power soon. Even if Tyler runs out, we still have you. You running in won't do anything—you'll just get in Tyler's way."

"Right!"

They were probably around 40 or 50% away from the enemy Mech losing power. Julian understood why Brandon was so keen on using the hover plate—it helped compensate for his low mobility while also boosting his speed—but there was still a reason why nobody used it on gravity stages.

Julian took a deep breath and then just hid. They could win by waiting out the battle.

The Guardian X's cannons thundered, obliterating the wall

that Julian had been standing on. Before Julian could activate his thrusters, a giant arm grabbed him from underneath.

Tyler let out a cry of frustration.

"I can't get a free shot!"

Before Julian could respond, the grappling arm crunched, and his sword clattered uselessly to the floor. Despite the large and unwieldy weapon, Brandon's move had been almost surgical. He'd grabbed the joint at his elbow and then excised the Starlight R's arm as it'd never been there. Julian raised his other hand and slammed his arm forward for a point-blank blast.

To his surprise, Brandon leaned into it, wrapping his massive arm around Julian's machine. Julian fired right into the shoulder. The armor exploded, but it was only the surface layer. He hadn't even done enough damage to expose the vulnerable joint.

Julian cursed.

A good weapon could have broken through and destroyed the heavy grappler arm.

Then he realized the truth. Brandon had recognized that the weapon was weak. It'd only taken him a glance at his Stats sheet to know that he could successfully tank it without losing or taking a risk with his Mech's low Cohesion. Now, with his enormous arm wrapped around Julian's machine, Brandon was at an indisputable advantage. He'd given Julian that seeming opportunity on purpose to encourage him to lean in.

The grappling arm crushed the Starlight R's shoulder, and Julian's other arm fell to the floor before he could attack again.

Tyler cursed again.

"Agh! I can't land a hit!"

The three mouth cannons were open, but there was nowhere to aim.

Julian's eyes widened.

Brandon was using him for cover.

There was just so much to consider—so much he hadn't even thought about.

Inspiration struck moments later.

He could use the same technique he'd used to beat Liefield.

Julian wrapped his legs around the Patchwork's cockpit. Then he accelerated and slammed his machine into the ground, burying both of them into the wall. The Patchwork's weaknesses included its lightweight and low maneuverability.

"Tyler! Get him! Get him!"

His friend drew his sword and charged forward.

Julian slowly inched closer, slamming the stubs of his shoulders over the Patchwork's thrusters to hinder any escape. It was a dirty trick to use a suicide tactic in a two-on-one battle, but he had to do what worked. Brandon was just too good!

There was a tremendous bang.

The two machines went spinning out of the wall, and Julian slammed to the floor. The massive grappler arm reached into the cockpit and crushed him like he was a grape.

He respawned in the loser's lobby, the white room with screens to watch his teammates fighting through their camera perspective. Emma turned to him and shook her head.

"Did you see what he did there?"

Julian hadn't. One moment, he'd been grabbing Brandon. The next, there was a bang, and he'd fallen out of his pilot chair. Mere milliseconds later, he was dead.

Julian pulled up the replay. Brandon had fired the massive shelling cannons without anchoring himself with the plate. Naturally, his lightweight machine went spinning away. He'd used the massive kickback to free himself from Julian's trap.

Not anticipating the sudden movement, Tyler had overswung.

The Patchwork slipped around Tyler's Mech and grabbed the Roar by the waist. The two Mechs struggled furiously together. As soon as the Roar ran out of Liquid State Eternium, Brandon smoothly shifted the claw into bombardment mode and fired at zero range. The Cerberus Roar was torn clean in half.

WINNER: SWEETSHOT303

As the four of them respawned on the lobby, all Julian, Emma, and Tyler could do was shake their heads in amazement.

Brandon had beaten them three against one with an experimental machine.

[17]

Brandon eagerly embraced Tyler.

"I should come up to Chicago sometime and visit you guys."

"Yeah, that'd be great! What do you think I can do better?"

Tyler was serious about eventually getting to compete against Brandon, who eagerly anticipated a real challenge. It was clear how much Brandon loved the game. After all, he was the only pro who still found time to grind out the ranked ladder even after spending hours scrimmaging and hunting for the best loot.

"Well, you're pretty new. So the biggest thing is just figuring out all the game mechanics and items. You don't even know your own Mech yet."

Brandon smirked.

"You were kinda just blasting randomly out there."

Tyler laughed.

"Yeah."

"Well, that was the right strategy, but you need to get the specifics down."

Brandon called up an image of his latest Mech, having it hover over his head just like all the other players showing off their designs did. He started tapping at it, manipulating the joints on the strange spherical design.

"I'm still learning the full limits of this one, but look at this."

He shifted the bombardment arm.

"On this Mech, I know that can move the limb up all the way here in less than a second. In terms of the maximum length it can stretch..."

He pushed a little more. Because of the Guardian X's stubby joints, it could only go a little further. It would have been much further on a typical machine.

"It can only go here. So I know exactly where I need to be before I can move."

With a tap, Brandon transformed the bombardment arm.

"I have this much time before I can switch from shooting mode to grappling mode."

He simulated a flight then halted it with the hover plate.

"I'm sure you noticed me using the plate to stop on a dime. That took a lot of practice, and it isn't actually instantaneous. I need to enter the command about half a second before I intend to stop. But because I anticipate that, it seems to you like I can stop immediately."

Brandon dismissed the machine.

"It's stuff like that. You need to move the Mech like it's your own body. What's the maximum speed? If you need to escape, what's the farthest you can run? Exactly how many blasts can you use before you run out of power? Energy weapons are tricky— that's why I usually prefer solid weapons and the ammunition system."

Brandon went on and on, listing all sorts of essential statistics. These were things that came up every single battle, yet although Julian had used his Starlight R for years, he wasn't sure if he could answer even a quarter of those questions.

Julian pulled up his status screen and got to work. He had an instinctual knowledge of how far the Starlight R could stretch, but he didn't know the precise amount.

Tyler nodded thoughtfully. He immediately summoned the Roar above his head and started moving the model around, but Brandon stopped him.

"Do that in your spare time. You're in the Forever Fortress! You should just find out in action!"

Brandon pulled up his status screen and frowned.

"Uh, how do I call Grunts again?"

Emma hastily pulled up her screen.

"Ah, I need to give you guys permission. Hang on."

Moments later, the CALL GRUNTS option appeared in the bottom corner of all their screens. Julian grinned. Ordinarily, CALL GRUNTS was a command only available to official Fortress Masters. Emma's innovation of a parts launcher was incredible.

"The best way to do this is just to practice on the Forever Fortress! Call up some Grunts here and try these drills on them. I just transferred you a list of training exercises. Start simple at first and then build up from there."

Tyler summoned a line of opponents then flew off to battle them.

Before Brandon could leave, Emma hastily stepped forward.

"What about me? What do you think I can improve on? I need to get better at the movement knowledge stuff you mentioned too. I was just wondering if there was anything else."

Brandon grinned.

"Yeah, I'd be happy to help!"

Julian stood there awkwardly. He wanted to ask Brandon for help too, but he didn't want to interrupt Emma. It felt like waiting outside a teacher's office. When would be a good time to ask? Should he just say that he also wanted advice?

"I would say the biggest thing is communication. You were

right that with your team composition, the best bet was to go inside and start shooting. If I wanted to chase you, I would have had to funnel myself into the castle walls. If I didn't chase, I would have run out of energy. But I won because your team split."

He smiled.

"If I know Tyler, the reason he didn't go that way is that you didn't tell him to beforehand. There's no way he wouldn't want to support a teammate."

"Yeah, I didn't."

"Yeah! Like it's great to be able to recognize stuff like that. It's a big strength. The most important thing is just making sure your team knows too. That's especially true with a specialized role like sniping. You just train yourself to see stuff most people don't."

Brandon walked to the edge of the viewing platform and then zoomed in on the castle. As soon as they'd left, the same kind of white and olive green Grunts Maxwell summoned earlier had started repairing the walls. Julian wasn't sure where the parts to build these Grunts were coming from. He'd have to check in with Emma after Brandon finished explaining everything.

"The other thing is that you need to be more cognizant of your set-ups. That one was just too obvious. It's not just about hitting the perfect shot. You also need to think about what the other player is seeing too. In that case, you made a sudden move to drive me to the left. Based on where I was standing, there was only one place you could be."

He pointed at the wall.

"You see what I mean?"

Julian and Emma immediately saw it. Brandon was an outstanding teacher. Tyler used to always rave about what a good teammate and captain Brandon was. Now, Julian knew exactly what his best friend had been talking about.

"I doubt could have hit a shot from that angle. It was really impressive to identify it. But it wasn't a good spot because it told me exactly where you had to be. That's the other big thing to keep in mind, just think of what your opponent is thinking."

"Got it, got it."

"And get an Ace unit when you can—it doesn't matter too much since Grunts are more flexible, but it's nice to have."

Then he turned to Julian.

"Do you mind if I give you some advice too?"

"Yeah, of course!"

"Have you taken a look at your report recently?"

"The what?"

"The report in the Database! You've reached a top 2,000 ranking before, so you're in it."

Brandon smiled.

"I mean actually, you usually land in it once you're in the top 5,000 or so. There's a lot of people aspiring to get ranked who write out reports of everyone else floating around the area."

"I haven't. Should I look now?"

The Database was a community record which reported on previously played matches. Overdrive players could also detail information about their fellow opponents or teammates. It included a profile of strengths and weaknesses along with a list of commonly used Mechs. Julian had heard about it, but he'd never taken it seriously.

He didn't get the point of looking people up before games.

Some pilots swore by it, though. There was always a guy every two to three matches who would read up on everyone in the Database before playing.

Usually, it was just to get a better sense of their teammates and adjust to their strategies to fit their team. But there were players who could be pretty irritating about it. They'd get mad if the Database told them that their teammates wouldn't be able to play their preferred style. It was sort of like how Liefield spent all his time moaning before The Raid on Colony Seven about being paired up with two kids.

Julian wasn't surprised that Brandon liked using it. Tyler and Brandon were very alike, and Julian's roommate was a fiend for game film.

"Yeah, it's always worth a glance."

Julian started pulling up his report.

"Did you take a look at mine before the match?"

"Yeah, I peeked at it again before our match just to check and see what strategy to use, but I've read it a few times. I mean, you were almost in the Selection last time, so I wanted to keep an eye out for you."

It was pretty amazing.

Julian was a decent pilot, but he was barely outside the top 500 on Overdrive. Even though Julian followed the pro scene, he couldn't tell you who was on every top team. He also wouldn't be able to name every member of every Fortress. But even though Julian was just a nobody, Brandon knew who he was.

"The biggest thing is to take it with a grain of salt. I've noticed that people tend to remember the bad more than the good. I think my page is just members of the Cal clan complaining about me."

Brandon laughed, but it was clear that he was still irritated. Julian doubted Caliber Gaming would make the World Championships without their superstar Grunt player, but if they did, Brandon would relish eliminating them.

"I'd ignore some of the harsher comments, but I think they generally make some good points. I was able to get a lot out of reading mine. For you, I do think you need to work on your game knowledge and overall preparation. You guys were going for a long-ranged strategy, but you used your typical Mech instead of an escort-type unit. Ideally, Emma would have gone for the Ace, and you would have adjusted your Mech for her. Even though she couldn't, it still would have made sense to change your machine."

Julian nodded. Tigger's younger son—Robby—had been able to carry them while playing as a support. It was essential to put your teammate in the perfect position.

"Frankly, your control skills are a lot better than someone who is just in the top 500. I think you could go pretty high if you trained. For a while there, I thought you might have outshot me. You just needed a better gun."

"Thank you."

Julian wasn't sure if he could have outdueled Brandon, but it was still an incredible compliment. And for all he knew, he really could have won. The arm-mounted submachineguns were only there to ward off missiles or hold enemies in place for his sword. They weren't a primary range weapon.

"Anyways, take a look. Look at your last few matches, and see if you notice any prevailing trends. That's the best way to improve. Like you actually already have the control skills, you just need to improve your strategic skills. Like you said, habits and thinking."

Tigger had almost certainly taught his kids the same thing. It all went back to thinking.

Perhaps Julian could beat Dynamic if he improved his strategic thinking. According to Brandon, Julian was already there in terms of his control skills.

"Again, I'd take the comment with a grain of salt, though. Most of the people who update the Database are butthurt about a recent loss and want to blame people."

That meant that Julian's report was almost certainly terrible. He took a deep breath and steeled himself. From what Brandon said, the star player's report wasn't much better. That meant that Julian shouldn't beat himself too much about his.

Pilot Name: Julian
Main Unit: Starlight R (Click for Information)
Strengths: Close Combat, Control Skills (Click for Team-
mate Comments)
Weaknesses: Can't Play Grunts, Easily Discouraged, Not a
Team Player, Bad Game Knowledge (Click for Teammate
Comments)

Julian felt particularly offended by the middle two weaknesses. Sure, he couldn't play Grunt units, but he wasn't more
easily discouraged than the people who would quit trying in the
middle of the game. And he was definitely a team player.

Brandon noticed that Julian was feeling down.

"Hey, it's not everything. Like I said, most of the people who
update the Database are just mad. But look. If you can figure out
which of the criticisms are real, and then improve on it, that's how
you become the best. And not just that."

He raised a finger.

"You can use the Database offensively too. Sure, you can't see
who your opponents are before the match starts, but based on the
Mechs they are using you might figure out at least who the Ace is.
If you study the Database, then you'll have a big leg up ahead of
time. You'll know how to attack them."

Huh.

Julian hadn't thought about it that way before. He scrolled
back and forth, flipping to the players above and ahead of them.
Even the pilots he recognized as good players had a long list of
weaknesses. Perhaps he could learn to exploit them. The one-on-
one battle system seemed like a particularly easy way to attack
the ladder and quickly rank up. Most pilots who challenged you to
one-on-ones only did it because they were confident they could
beat you.

Julian took another look at the invite. Dynamic was ranked

around the 280s, and he'd already beaten Julian twice before. Even a single win against someone of Dynamic's caliber would propel Julian to the top five hundred.

Could he turn the tables with the Database? What were Dynamic's weaknesses?

"So first, I'd fix what you think are the biggest problems listed for yourself, and then research people around you. That's part of how I climbed up so quickly. Do you have anything else you want to ask about?"

"No, not at all. Thank you so much."

It was such an honor. Brandon had not only battled them but then provided individual tips and suggestions. It wasn't every day you could get coached by a World Championship finalist.

"No problem. Now, if you don't mind, I want to shoot down a few of these things before my meeting."

Brandon's grin went from ear to ear as he summoned a different Guardian Patchwork. This new unit was a mass-fire type. It retained the same hover plate and backpack cannons, but a two-barreled bazooka had replaced the flamethrower and Bombardment Arm. The explosive weapon required both hands to hold, meaning that Brandon couldn't use his typical grafted attachment.

It was the perfect set-up for killing a bunch of Grunts at once. Mass-fire units were a vital part of any party looking to grind through as many missions as possible. Instantly evaporating enemy Grunt units with strong area of effect attacks meant that you could efficiently clear maps.

However, they were near worthless in competitive play, so seeing a superstar level player with one was rare. They couldn't compete with more specialized Artillery units that also allocated Credits to shields or close-combat weapons. Spraying and praying was ineffective when most of your opponents had top-tier stats in Defense and Mobility. You either needed concentrated blasts from a sniper or a more well-rounded unit that could contribute additional benefits. Typically, if you saw a mass-fire Mech in a competitive match, it was a beginner who was just starting to move from missions to player vs. player battles.

But Brandon always did what was optimal, even if he didn't need to. He'd thrown away his signature Bombardment Arm just to do a better job of killing AI Grunts.

Seeing Brandon's flexibility forced Julian to take a much harsher look at his own play.

As Brandon said, the comments could be harsh, but you had to decide for yourself what to keep. Julian got pretty discouraged at times. He wouldn't curse out his teammates or anything, but he often shut down in the middle of a discouraging battle. And although his teammates on the server wouldn't know, he frequently gave up entirely and logged off after a tough loss.

As for his teamplay, he was a one-dimensional player. Although he always tried his best, his Starlight R could only be used for a single purpose, and he had no Grunt experience at all. If someone looked at him in an unflattering light, it could seem like he wasn't trying to cooperate.

He clicked the In-Depth Report, which featured several detailed discussions from players who'd played with him. As Brandon said, it was full of critical comments.

"This guy cost me my game to get into the top five hundred!"

"Said he had to play the Ace, but couldn't carry us."

"Kept swerving in front of me and making it hard to shoot."

The first two comments were fair—he probably had made mistakes—but the last comment stuck with him. He'd made that same mistake when playing with Tigger's kids. Julian was really spoiled. When he'd played with Felix and Edwin, his friends just wordlessly adjusted for him.

Although the page was mostly complaints, there were compliments praising his control skills and mastery of the broadsword. He took another look at those and smiled.

He had a strong base to build on. He was relearning the game with Tyler, and Brandon thought he was skilled enough to contend for a Fortress position. If he beat himself up, he'd only fall into the problems the scouting report listed.

Emma called out from behind him. To Julian's surprise, she hadn't gone back to grinding.

"Don't beat yourself up too hard. Don't get easily discouraged."

Although she wore a helmet, it was clear she was smirking.

"I read your report too."

"Oh, why?"

She shrugged.

"I knew you were dad's friend, and I thought this game was cool. I actually spent a lot of time reading about it without playing it. Is that weird?"

Julian thought for a moment then shook his head.

"Not at all."

Overdrive was cool.

There were so many different frames, parts, and weapons. It was easy to get lost in the Overdrive Wiki. Julian should have gotten lost in it more often. He had to work on his game knowledge. If Julian had known the strengths of Brandon's Bombardment Arm vs. the Starlight R's submachineguns, he would never have made that mistake.

"Yeah, but I followed the game for a long time. I didn't log in because of the scan stuff."

Oh.

That explained why she was using a Guest Account. Julian smiled.

"Yeah! I was the same way. I actually played with a Guest Account until halfway through high school."

He made a face.

"Honestly, the whole scan thing is pretty weird. Like that's probably one of the most awkward parts about the game, I wish they'd just let you make an avatar like every other game. And the Privacy Armor costs so much!"

Emma snickered.

"I read that it's because the game owner got catfished a couple times."

Julian laughed too. He'd heard a similar rumor. It could get pretty tricky during online games. Julian himself had a pretty embarrassing story from high school.

But at any rate, the lack of custom avatars was one of the weird things that The Mechanical King was obsessively adamant about. Half the time The Mechanical King insisted on adding something to the game over the fanbase's criticisms, it led to disastrous balance patches. During the Item Mech saga, the game's board of directors had to personally interfere. It sounded like a similar thing might have happened with the Reality Shapers too.

"I'm guessing it took you a while to figure out about the Guest Accounts?"

"Yeah."

The Guest Accounts were a hidden feature that was extremely difficult to access. There wasn't even a log-in as a Guest option on the log-in screen. Instead, you had to create a Guest Account on the more or less defunct Overdrive website, which would spit out a random code for you to enter in the Password Section.

Julian had only known about it because all beta testers had initially used Guest accounts. When the game launched, he'd been delighted to discover that it still worked.

"Ah man, I wish the Captain had told me about that problem. I could have just told him about my own Guest days."

"That was a nice fight earlier."

"Yeah, it was. I think we might have gotten him with tighter play. It seemed like we only needed a single hit."

He grimaced.

"I should have followed you down to the castle."

"Nah, Sweetshot was right. I should have told you about it. It's hard in the middle of a tense fight."

"You can say that again. I've been playing for a while, and I still shut down. Still, it was clear that you went in the right direction. I've been playing for a long time, I should have known."

It felt pretty bad to be outdone by someone with a Guest account.

"I need to get better at thinking. I can't run around like an idiot after playing for so long."

She shook her head.

"Hey, but you haven't been practicing it, right? Now that you're starting to think and stuff, you'll improve really quickly. Read the report! Don't get easily discouraged."

Once again, it sounded like she was smirking. It was just so hard to tell behind the helmet. He grinned back.

"Thanks for the match. Next time we play, the report is going to be totally different!"

He sent Tyler a message letting him know that he was logging off for now.

He removed his headset then pulled up the Wiki and Database on his phone. Getting good wasn't just about playing. You had to think and study too.

[18]

Julian spent the entire night scrolling through the Database, slowly moving from his place at 524 to the mid-400s. As soon as he woke up the next day, Julian kept on researching. After hours of research, he reached the top three hundred, which was the edge of the players he'd commonly match with. As a player in the top 600, Julian could only match with players ranked at 250 or below. In the past, he thought that rule seemed pretty unfair. After all, he usually fended for himself when he had pro players in his lobbies. It was only after his match with Brandon that Julian realized just how steep the skill curve really was. Getting lucky in a few matches was different from consistently competing.

At the same time, reading through the Database gave Julian a new appreciation of his high standing in the world of Overdrive. Yes, he wasn't a superstar professional player, but skilled players surrounded him. They all had their weaknesses, but there were no bad pilots here.

Even if Julian didn't recognize someone by their name, he knew who they were as soon as he saw their preferred Mech. The pilots who had made it up to the top five hundred had the resources to customize their Mechs however they pleased. Only a few rare players like Felix didn't use custom colors.

Every five or so minutes, Julian peeked to make sure that nobody noticed that he wasn't paying attention. He was actually in the middle of an online class, but as long as he didn't overtly goof off on camera, his professor would think that everything was alright. It was later in the semester now, and he wasn't calling on people nearly as often. Most people who didn't care for the class had dropped out in the first two weeks.

It turned out that studying the Database was just as challenging as studying for school.

In hindsight, Julian shouldn't have been surprised. Both involved absorbing as much knowledge as possible, and his upcoming battles were essentially tests. Julian remembered Tyler explaining that NBA teams had a whole stable of assistant coaches and videographers who scouted teams and helped develop strategies. Of course, the competitive Overdrive ecosystem wasn't nearly as advanced. There was a chance some of the Fortresses had analysts, but otherwise, players scouted for themselves.

The next player on the list was a support-oriented pilot named Alt3ration. Julian grinned. He liked Alt3ration. Like Felix, Alt3ration was a supportive Grunt pilot. Although he lacked control skills, his strong game knowledge and steady thinking under pressure meant that Julian usually won when they matched together.

Pilot Name: Alt3ration
Main Unit: CWT-141 Zombie Grunt—Steroids Type
Strengths: Close Combat, Strategic Knowledge, Grunt Player, Great Teammate (Click for In-Depth Report)
Weaknesses: Weak Aim, Low Control Skills (Click for In-Depth Report)

According to the match history, Alt3ration had played his last seven games in a row using the CWT-141 Zombie Grunt. It seemed like the reliable Mech was quickly becoming a new competitive standard unit, much like the Defender or Guardian lineages. The only time Alt3ration played as the Ace was when he landed in a lobby with three other Grunt users. It was rare, but not unknown, for you to end up with a team where nobody was an Acer user. As you got higher up in the ladder, more and more players focused on using Grunts because it was the fastest way to increase your rank. After all, three out of four players had to use Grunts, and there was no guarantee on the random ladder.

When Julian hovered over the Main Unit, a separate graphic popped up to showcase Alt3ration's Mech. The unit was identical to the one from the Exhibition, save for the enormous metal fists. Much like how Brandon had his Bombardment Arm and signature Patchwork designation, Alt3ration added his Engorged Gauntlets to all his machines. The Fists were a much smaller adjustment than the extensively grafted Arm, resulting in only a small hit to his Cohesion.

- General Data -
Pilot: Alt3ration
Machine: CWT-141 Zombie Grunt Steroids Type
Class: Hemoborn
Sub-class: Attacker
Designation: Grunt Unit

- Statistics -
Melee: A-tier
Shooting: C-tier
Speed: B-tier
Maneuverability: B-tier
Dcfcnsc: A-ticr

Cohesion: A-tier

- Weapons -
Engorged Gauntlet—Crusher Type (Full Custom) [x1]
Engorged Gauntlet—Hammer Arm Type (Full Custom)
[x1]
Zombie Vulcan [x8]

- Abilities -
Relentless Level 8
Bloodlust Level 8
Stench Level 3

Although the game had classified Alt3ration's Mech as an Attacker, his play was support oriented. He loved soaking up damage for his teammates and disrupting enemy formations.

Julian flipped to Alt3ration's team reports and clicked through them. Almost everyone felt the same way Julian did—Alt3ration and his Steroids machines were always a welcome sight on your team.

Dynamic had actually written two consecutive entries under Alt3ration's comments. During Dynamic's first match, when he'd fought alongside Alt3ration, the Steroids Mech had been the perfect bodyguard. Dynamic had landed all four kills and the win. Unfortunately, when they were placed on different teams for the subsequent match, Alt3ration led his squad cleanly through Dynamic's blind spot and stole the win.

Julian gulped. He had far better control skills than Alt3ration. If the support pilot could defeat Dynamic, why couldn't Julian?

It was well-known that Alt3ration's biggest weakness was that he just didn't have the control skills to execute his strategies consistently. In particular, he struggled with weapon usage. No wonder he preferred to use his fists.

Alt3ration's reliance on hand-to-hand combat reminded Julian of the Heaven's Boxer. A sour smile crossed his face. He still hadn't heard back from Tigger, and he was reluctant to bother him. Brandon was likely right. The Boxer was probably a deleted bug. There was no time to worry about it. His best bet was to focus on what he could actually control.

After finishing his notes on Alt3ration, it was time to start researching for his match against Dynamic. He was just putting it off by studying the other players in the Database.

Julian jotted his observations on Alt3ration down in his notebook and smiled to himself. Some of his college professors had been extremely strict about Julian's lack of notetaking. He'd always blown it off, but now he acknowledged that they were right. There were just too many entries in the Database. He'd played with most of these guys, and he still couldn't remember all their characteristics.

"Alright, so I'll put this guy as a Type 3."

All the pilots ranked around the top 500 range were good. You didn't end up in the top 500 out of over 3 million players—the top 0.01%—without skills. But there was a reason why the top players like vermillionangel or Brandon could wreck players of Julian's level. Almost everyone he'd encountered so far suffered from one or more key weaknesses.

Julian had developed a rough classification system to best identify how to counter foes and accompany allies.

Type 1 was for players like Julian.

They were players who'd climbed to the top 500 off the backs of a single transcendent skill. There was a decent chance that Julian's mastery of close combat approached a World Championship contender's, but that didn't do him any good when he was weak at everything else. Overdrive matches were about more than just control skills. You had to have game knowledge to know what weapons would win in a clash. You had to be crafty about your approaches and retreats.

Type 2 players had attitude or communication problems.

Playing on any team—either a constructed team or a random one—was about communicating with your teammates without bringing them down. There were a fair number of obnoxious pilots who lost their cool at even the slightest mistakes by their teammates. That kind of attitude made it harder—though not impossible—to rank up. On top of that, players with attitude problems only ended up on top-tier teams after everyone else of their skill level had already been chosen. Focusing fire on an enemy Type 2 was an excellent way to disrupt opposing squads. On the other hand, Julian knew he had to manage his own Type 2s with extreme care.

Type 3 were guys like Alt3ration or Julian's friend Felix.

Both players had a wealth of game knowledge and stayed cool under pressure. They were great communicators and strong team players. Like Brandon, Felix probably could name the Mechs of the top 1,000 pilots on the server. Unfortunately, they just weren't that good at piloting compared to their rivals.

Felix had bounced back and forth between several Constructed teams, usually filling whatever role they needed. Although Felix preferred to play as a pure support—using items like smoke grenades or scouter drones—he could also serve as a frontline tank like Alt3ration. At times, he even accepted a damage-dealing role. Felix had defeated a Fortress Team to qualify for the World Championships as a spearman. Unlike Julian, who realized every day how much farther he had to go, Felix had already maxed out his abilities. Felix spent about 8-10 hours a day playing Overdrive. Instead of going to college, he'd stayed at home and worked odd jobs to sponsor his ambitions. Felix grinded as hard as he could to continue improving, but there was nothing else he could do. He'd hit his skill cap.

And unfortunately, that meant his teams almost always cut him when they thought they had room to improve their control skills. That was how he'd lost his spot in the World Championships after qualifying with his team. In Julian's opinion, that was a mistake. Even if you improved your overall control skills, losing Felix's game knowledge and strategic mastery was a significant cost.

Julian scrolled to the next screen and grimaced. Of course, there was a 4th type too—an obvious cheater. After several years of mediocre performance—not even landing in the top 10,000 players, this player had suddenly been elevated into the top 300. It looked like he was on a 50 game winning streak.

A few of the players who abruptly climbed the ranks were genuine rising stars. When Brandon first debuted, he'd soared up the rankings so quickly that everyone thought he was a professional player playing on someone else's account.

It was impossible to tell for sure, but Julian suspected that wasn't the case here. The poor prior play was just a little too suspicious.

It was difficult, but not impossible, to get someone to play on your account. There'd been a spate of similar incidents in the last two Selections. It was mostly just rich kids who wanted to go to the Selection to meet their favorite players or show off the exclusive gear you got from qualifying.

There were a few ways to trick the full-body scan. Some players hacked the game code and allowed other pilots to control their account remotely. They would log in and then leave their gaming rig. The hacked console would then move according to the commands of the player they'd hired. That was the easiest way to boost someone's rank, but it was also the easiest for the game administration to detect.

It was also possible to change rigs in person after both pilots logged on. Once Overdrive captured your vital statistics, it operated everything based on the pilot inside. Julian and Tyler could do it if they wanted to. The problem with that method was availability. If you didn't live near an elite player, you couldn't use the rig switch. There were only so many elite players who could reliably put someone into the top 500. Despite Julian's skills, there was a huge gap between him and someone like Brandon. Every so often, vermillionangel would reset his account to stream his climb back to the top of the standings. He'd win game after game without even trying. There was no way Julian could do the same.

The most disturbing and bizarre cheat was the motion suit. The motion suit was a complex system involving two different sets of clothes connected over the internet. The drawings Julian had seen resembled an astronaut outfit. The rank booster could use the motion suit to pilot the other person's body. When the experienced player inputted demands, the motion suit would move the receiver's body in perfect synchronization. Naturally, it was impossible to get caught using that configuration. The game would only see a pilot moving their arms regularly. People joked about it whenever someone had a particularly good performance, but Julian doubted it was real. It sounded like an urban legend.

Of course, nobody had ever gotten caught using it, so how could you know for sure?

Selection boosting was a big problem. Last time, thirty players were caught after investigations and permanently banned from the game. Considering Julian's spot as the 524th player, he technically would have qualified if it weren't for the cheaters. But The Mechanical King didn't go down the list to find more players after removing the cheaters.

When Julian complained to his old friend Felix about it, he'd ignored Julian's message on Overdrive.

Instead, Felix had texted Julian back on his cell phone. Felix's meticulous preparation extended to the messages he sent on the in-game client. Felix thought that The Mechanical King checked chat logs for criticisms and that it had an impact on whether or not you were selected to be a Fortress Master.

Julian smiled when he remembered Felix's conspiracy theory. His friend was totally paranoid. Everyone knew The Mechanical King could be a real pain, but he had a company to run. He couldn't just sit at the screen and stop people from making fun of him.

Julian took another look at the likely cheater's profile. Many of the boosted players used the same build—a spearman Grunt. Perhaps it was the same player playing on all the accounts, but more likely than not, it was just a red herring. Getting caught ended your career. Nobody would be dumb enough to use a Mech similar to their primary unit.

It was likely someone with excellent skills but a low streaming presence trying to make more money. Julian thought the rates for boosting accounts were obscene. There were a lot of rich people who wanted to brag about their Overdrive ranking. Julian had even thought about doing it himself. He wouldn't be able to carry anyone into the top 500, but he could definitely get an account ranked. Breaking the top 2,000 wouldn't be much of a problem for Julian. It was cheating, and it sucked for people you played against, but money was money.

Julian shook his head. He shouldn't worry about boosting when there was an opportunity to make the Selection right in front of him. He had to stop stalling and get to work studying Dynamic.

He switched over to his rival's profile before pausing and looking back at the class to see if anyone had asked him a question. The screen was completely black. He'd spent all his time preparing and hadn't even noticed that the class was over. Julian smiled. He hadn't known that studying could be so engrossing.

He went back to Dynamic's profile and took a meticulous look. Dynamic's Mech was named the Self-Supporting Sniper.

Although most Sniper units were vulnerable to a head-on assault, the Ace machine's high mobility and robust artillery package flipped the matchup. Julian had already lost twice to him.

Julian pulled up the shop on his Overdrive app and carefully studied all the parts Dynamic used, noting their damage output and durability. Then he returned and scrolled through the comments.

To Julian's surprise, Dynamic's weaknesses were very similar to Julian's own. He was a one-dimensional player who struggled with thinking on his feet. He was a Type 1 especially vulnerable to counter-strategies. That meant that Julian's plan would be even more effective than he'd hoped.

Most interestingly, Dynamic's biggest weakness was his tendency to panic when things didn't proceed as expected. It was a very atypical vulnerability for a sniper, but Julian supposed that was why Dynamic's Mech also boasted high-mobility. He'd built the Self-Supporting Sniper to compensate for his unusual weakness. Reading the reports brought a smile to Julian's face.

When he battled against Dynamic, the talented sniper had seemed invincible. But things would go very differently if Julian approached the match strategically.

The last Selection, he'd spent his time turtling, hoping to simply keep his spot in the top 500. That had only allowed people to climb past him for free.

He couldn't let it happen this time. It was time to go on the offensive.

If he beat Dynamic, he'd break into the top 500. After that, Julian could keep using the Database to climb higher and higher.

When he'd gone through all of Dynamic's parts three times over, Julian had a rough idea of what he needed to do to win. But then he remembered yet another takeaway from their three-on-one match against Brandon. It was easy to come up with a generic plan like "hit him from long range." But if you wanted to win, you had to know precisely what you were doing. You had to practice.

Even if he knew Dynamic's weaknesses in theory, Julian had to do much more. Julian sent Maxwell a message. He would have preferred to mail Emma directly, but that was one of the many downsides to using a Guest account.

"Hey! I have an upcoming match against a sniper soon. I was wondering if Emma would be interested in helping me practice?"

He got the reply moments later.

"Of course! She'd be more than happy to."

[19]

"Captain!"

"Hey, how's it going, Julian!"

The Forever Fortress had expanded even further. They were adding a space colony at the edge of the second planet's orbit. Judging from the vast array of shining lights streaking across the stage, the Brothers had also attracted many more players.

"Good! Good! How's everything going for you?"

Maxwell smiled.

"Well, the good news is, we've got a lot of new players. I think the Fortress is definitely catching on. We even got a shoutout on Brandon's stream the other day. However, we still don't have a lot of new players. I was hoping they could use this as a training ground, but I think they're worried because there's no level restriction on this map."

Julian took a closer look at the mass of new Mechs. Most of them seemed pretty advanced. There were only a few beginners' machines.

"Yeah, that makes sense. It'll probably just take some time for the good word to get around!"

"Yeah, of course."

Deliberate bullying of new players had been a pretty big problem in the Overdrive community before it got patched out. In the past, you could repeatedly kill beginners to farm them for parts and Credits. Honest pilots strayed away from those bullying tactics, but a veteran who was determined to kill beginners could take down dozens in a single session. It was what Liefield had been planning to do with the Heaven's Boxer.

Nowadays, you could only kill other players in official battles or on specialized custom maps like the Forever Fortress. Because custom maps had no Credits incentive, there was no reason to teamkill. Unscrupulous pilots could still be jerks, but guys like Maxwell usually kept things in line.

"Is Emma online yet? I was hoping we could get some practice for my match."

"Ah, not yet! I'll log off and go grab her."

Maxwell flickered and then disappeared.

Julian pulled up his friend list just to check on what everyone was doing.

Felix was grinding a PvE mission. Although his friend had hit his skill cap, the parts cap on Overdrive was effectively infinite. New frames and weapons entered the game every month. Fresh parts were not only intriguing in and of themselves; they sometimes had powerful synergies with previous releases. To succeed, Felix constantly innovated new strategies.

To Julian's pleasant surprise, Tyler was already logged inside the Forever Fortress. He'd taken Brandon's words to heart. Julian scanned the skies, but he saw no hint of the Cerberus Roar. It was only after using Tyler's beacon—a friend list feature that allowed you to track allies on the same map as you —that he realized what his friend was doing. He'd built a Grunt Mech focused on durability and long-range bombardment. The machine was a weaker version of the Cerberus Roar. More likely than not, Tyler hoped that practicing on a similar but weaker Mech would give him an even stronger mastery of his Ace unit. That was a smart idea. It was like training with weights.

To his surprise, Brandon and TiggerLuvr were currently playing together. It might have been for some sort of celebrity stream.

A notification popped up in the right corner of his screen. GUEST198 wants to add you!

That was yet another annoying feature of Guest Accounts. There was no stable guest number, and you had to re-add your friends every time.

Moments later, someone tapped Julian on the shoulder. He turned and smiled.

"Hey! Thank you so much for agreeing to help me!"

"Hi, that's not a problem."

Julian felt shy asking Emma for help. Although they'd played a very enjoyable game together yesterday, they'd only just met. But he needed to learn how to craft a counterstrategy and figure out a way to deal with Dynamic's Mech, the Self-Supporting Sniper. He couldn't think of anyone better than Emma to teach him. In a way, she was also the queen of preparation. She'd studied the game for years without playing!

"Honestly, this sounds like it'll be a fun project. I've been hoping to learn more about the competitive side of the game anyways. I don't think most top five hundred players would let me just tag along in their preparation."

Julian sighed.

"To be fair, I doubt most top five hundred players would even need help on their preparation. That's why I'm not quite in the top 500 yet."

Dynamic's current ranking was 287. If Julian beat him, he'd be past the cut-off mark for the Selection. However, Julian intended to keep aggressively playing even if he won. He wanted to be a safe choice, not just a guy waiting until the last day to find out whether they'd gotten in.

"Don't worry about it. We're going to win this. I did some research, take a look, and let me know what you think."

Like Julian, Emma had searched up Dynamic on the Database and highlighted the efficacy of his parts. She'd also looked into his past games and constructed a profile of his strengths and weaknesses. The two forwarded each other the documents and began comparing notes.

Emma's research contained insights Julian couldn't have known by himself. Emma noted that Dynamic had an unfortunate habit of dipping his barrel when he fired upward. She'd watched some of his past games, and it looked like the stats bore out the results. If you approached Dynamic from above, his shooting dropped 10%. It was a small gap, but enough to make a critical difference.

Julian smiled. That was another reason why he had to diversify his game. He hadn't used a sniper rifle since he was in high school. His form was awful. He'd never notice if someone else were making a minor mistake. By diversifying his weapons, he would also broaden his perspective and discover how to best counter his opponents.

When the two finished reviewing, Emma circled back to her critical insight.

"Did you notice the thing about upward angles?"

"Yeah, thanks a lot for that. I could never have picked it up."

He smiled.

"I need to watch you shoot more."

Emma's dad had been in the Air Force. Maybe that was why she was so good at shooting.

Julian shook his head. That couldn't possibly be it. Usually, shooting in Overdrive and shooting a firearm in real life were two totally different things.

Emma only acknowledged his compliment with a gentle nod before going straight back to business.

"Alright, for the first part, I don't get why you think this guy has an advantage against you. You said he's already beaten you twice, right?"

Julian winced.

"Yeah—I've paired with and against him in random queues before in addition to one on one. He's almost always beaten me...I mean he's about 200 ranks higher than me, right? So he's probably just better. Last Selection we played one-on-one twice. I thought that I'd win because of the favorable matchup, but he got me both times. Now he's re-challenged me for this Selection. He seems to think I'm a free win."

The mask covered her face, but it sounded like Emma was frowning.

"Taking a look at his Mech, I'm not sure why that's happening. Your Starlight R seems like it's good against it. Getting to use an Ace unit gives him some advantages, but the matchup fundamentals aren't changing. He's still slower than you, meaning your melee machine should beat his fragile long-range machine. In general, sniper-type Aces aren't competitively viable, right?"

"Yeah, usually. Dynamic is the highest-ranked Ace sniper. Usually, it's not worth spending all the extra points on a sniper since all you need is a high-quality rifle. That extra mobility and stuff make it a pain to deal with, though. I think the main problem is its bombardment. He's able to blow me out of my position and flip the matchup."

Typically, a sniper unit needed a well-constructed team composition to succeed. You needed a bombardment unit to flush out enemies and a bodyguard to keep the frail Mech safe. Dynamic's Self-Supporting Sniper was a highly mobile Mech that brought its own artillery to the fight.

"I'm not sure about that. Based on the speed and mobility

scores, you should be able to charge him and win. How did the last two matches go? Was there a map problem?"

One of the problems with one-on-one battles—and best of one matches in general—was the random map selection. Some maps rendered certainly matchups unwinnable. For example, a sniping unit would almost certainly lose to a close combat Mech on the Void stage, which was black space utterly devoid of obstacles. Despite requests by competitive Overdrive players, The Mechanical King insisted on keeping the maps randomly selected. Other esports usually allowed a pick and ban process for stages, ensuring that no one team got a dominant random advantage.

"No, the maps were fine."

Both times, they'd fought on balanced maps that didn't do much to shift the matchup.

"Let's go through what happened?"

It'd been half a year ago, but Julian still remembered his defeats pretty clearly. After all, that'd been the beginning of his downfall from the next hundred.

"So the first battle he hit a lucky snipe on me as soon as the match started. He blew off part of my back thrusters, making it harder for me to fly to him. I ducked around cover to try to get to him, but I wasn't able to make it before he took me out. After damaging my thrusters, he was too fast for me to catch him. He just kept flying backward and shooting me over and over again. He even shifted his sniper rifle into a rapid-fire mode. He just needed to spray out shots."

Dynamic's machine used a more expensive variant of the Roar's composite rifle. The rapid-fire mode was practically a Gatling cannon.

"So I thought he beat me by getting lucky, you know? After all, the first shot had been blind. Later on, I also found out that he was an expert on the Cityscape stage. So when he re-challenged me a week later, I accepted it. Didn't think he would get lucky again."

He smiled ruefully.

"Of course, he was the one who challenged me again, which means he probably thought he beat me with skill. And I think the next match showed he was right. He didn't hit any early snipes, but he flushed me out with an artillery barrage. It crumpled the rock I hid behind and battered my Mech too. When I tried moving to another bit of cover, he just blew me apart. After he challenged me a third time, I spectated some of his games. It looked like it was the same with his other matchups. Dynamic either hit a good shot at the beginning and switched over to running and gunning, or he would flush people out with his artillery. That was when I decided that I couldn't beat him."

"Hm."

Emma took another look at her profile of the Self-Supporting Sniper, where she'd carefully marked up all the parts to indicate how much damage they'd do per shot. She'd done the same thing with the various limbs to calculate how long it'd take for Julian to defeat it. Next to that profile, she'd done the same thing with a chart of the Starlight R.

"I still don't see it. How about we take a look at the film?"

"Oh right, good idea!"

Julian felt a little embarrassed to bring up videos of his defeat, but this was the only way to get better. He bet guys like Brandon studied film all the time. It took Julian a while to flick through his archive to find the appropriate video. He'd played a lot of matches. Scrolling through them made Julian wonder if there were any hidden reasons for his other defeats. He'd thought he'd lost to Dynamic because of an unfavorable matchup, but based on Emma's knowledge of parts and sniping, Julian should have won.

He hit play on the first video.

As he remembered, the first fight had started with Dynamic

hitting a great shot. Julian hadn't rewatched the video before, but looking at it now, it was almost like Dynamic had bent the bullet. The repeat films could be seen from all camera angles—his, his opponents, and several overall map views which showed both units.

Emma immediately paused.

"Look here."

"Hm?"

Julian didn't know what she was pointing out.

"What do you mean?"

She flickered to Dynamic's point of view.

"Look at this. You had a bad launch."

She pointed at where Julian had entered the map. He'd aimed for a spot behind the city's tower to give himself coverage. It was one of the best spots on Cityscape—one of the few places where your Mech was hidden even if it was standing. That gave you a huge advantage when you started moving.

It'd been a smart idea for Julian to launch behind the tower, but Emma was right. Julian had made a mistake and missed his launch by several degrees. His thruster was clearly visible. The bright orange wing immediately betrayed his position.

She pressed play again. This time, Julian noticed another problem.

"He wasn't even fast enough to shoot after the bad launch. It was only after I shifted again!"

"Oh. Good catch."

Emma replayed the video from Dynamic's perspective.

"Yeah—this guy seems good, but not great. In addition to the overhead shots thing I mentioned earlier, I think he struggles with immediately shooting."

An immediate shot—sometimes called a no-scope—was an essential part of any sniper's toolkit. The shots were much more difficult than ones where your rifle was already trained, but nothing was more satisfying than hitting an opponent right after launch or when you were technically on the move.

"He's outstanding once he's set up, though. You showed just a sliver of your thruster that second time."

Emma played the video again. Even after getting hit, Julian still poked out for a third time.

Emma paused and turned to him.

"What were you trying to do?"

Julian frowned and swapped back to his view. Why had he moved? It was obvious he needed to stay still. It was only when he looked at his control inputs that he saw it. He groaned.

His mom was always making fun of him for fidgeting. He lifted his hands off the control board. Although he hadn't realized it, he'd been doing the same thing even while watching the match. Out of his Mech, the game had dismissed his movements as white noise, nothing more than inputs without a corresponding in-game command. But when he was inside the cockpit, unnecessary movements instantly betrayed his position.

Julian groaned.

He'd been playing for so long.

How had he failed to realize this?

Emma was quick to console him.

"Hey! It's like we said the other day. Better to know about a weakness than to just keep doing it."

Julian just shook his head.

"I'd seriously thought that all the snipers hitting me were just good. No wonder that dude thought I was a free win."

He paused. He didn't want to be easily discouraged.

"Hey, you're right. Better to figure this out now rather than later."

He moved to switch the video.

"Alright, so that's why I lost this game."

Emma stopped him before he could bring up the second match.

"No, hold it. This indeed put you at a disadvantage, but it didn't mean that you lost. Let's keep watching."

The sniper bullet tore through Julian's thruster. He groaned again just watching it. He remembered cursing himself for being so unlucky. After all, his game plan had been to move through cover until he was close enough for a straight charge. It turned out he hadn't been unlucky at all—just bad at Overdrive.

His Mech turned towards the direction of the bullet, then soared forward.

Emma paused the video again.

"You got lucky here. There was no guarantee he was actually in that direction. You were right, but let me show you what I mean."

She pulled out her own status screen and called up a map of Cityscape.

"Which variant were you guys on?"

Other than Void, each of the main maps had four variants, which reshuffled the various obstacles.

"Four."

A few taps later, and the map was open.

"Take a look at this."

She drew several lines across the buildings, which led back to Julian's line of sight.

"See? If you look at where the bullet traveled, it could have come from here or here."

She pointed to two further locations that were behind the building Dynamic had actually roosted in.

"If he hadn't been there, you would have given up your position for no reason."

She smirked.

"I would have taken the harder vantage point. It's a trickier shot, but the safety is greater. Although, as Brandon taught us, taking the hardest angle isn't always the best option. But anyway, the problem with staying behind cover is you get less info of where the sniper might be. You can only see the shots from one perspective. Imagine if the shot had come from this direction."

She labeled the map and graphed out a bullet coming from the southern side. The tower would have obscured most of his vision. As a result, there were a whole seven different places he could have fired from.

"This is where some better equipment can help you. Smokes or drones would make this way easier. I don't think his artillery flips the matchup per se, but it does make it harder for you, especially because it seems like you struggle with snipers to begin with. You need your own self-support items."

Drones and smokes were usually the responsibility of Support players. In team battles, where Julian knocked out snipers without a problem, he'd taken advantage of the powerful items without even thinking. But now he had to do it himself.

Julian had to build a new Grunt frame. If you changed your Ace unit after someone challenged you to a one-on-one fight, the invite would fizzle away. This prevented pilots using all 50,000 Credits to build a Mech that countered their opposition.

Emma played the video again.

"Look, the thing is, even after you decided to charge, you weren't doing it right. You're just running at him. Of course, he could keep his distance and shoot you down. What were you expecting?"

At the time, he'd thought that with himself injured, he had no choice but to dash straight ahead and hope for the best. In hindsight, that was a dumb thing to do. He'd just gotten discouraged —one of the big problems on his scouting report. If his machine was slower than the opponents, that just meant being all the more careful. He should have hidden behind cover. Instead, he'd just charged and hoped to luck out.

"Ah, I just panicked after he hit me. I shouldn't have done that."

Emma drew a squiggly path around the map.

"You need to have a plan on these approaches. Where are you going to come from? What are you going to do? You can't just run at people even if you have a speed advantage. This is kind of like our battle against Brandon. You had a good plan, but you didn't think it all the way through. It can't just be like 'I plan to charge' it has to be like 'I plan to charge in this direction—but if it doesn't work, I'll go this way.'"

When they finished analyzing the first film, they moved onto the second. Emma was a diligent and patient teacher, pointing out all of his mistakes and clearly indicating how he could get better. She was practically just telling him all of her own weaknesses.

"Snipers hate it when you do this."

"Snipers struggle if you come from this angle."

When they finished, Emma succinctly summed up his main problem.

"Alright. I would probably like to play against you, too, if I'm being honest. I agree with you that the level of his Ace Mech means you can't just use brute force, but the matchup is still in your favor. The big problem is that you're just weak against snipers. You're a great sword, but you suck at approaching by yourself. You're also not that good at quickly calculating all the factors. In the second match, your damage wasn't even that bad. It looked like the bombardment rattled you into leaving your cover."

Julian nodded.

It had rattled him.

"I have a similar weakness, honestly. I'm not too fond of close combat. It's scary with something coming at you quickly. Do you mind helping me with that after?"

Julian grinned.

"Of course! I'm not sure I'll be as good as teaching as you though."

If Julian were being honest, he wasn't good at thinking when things came quickly at him, either. He mostly succeeded at close combat because of his well-built instincts after playing the game for so long.

"Awesome, thank you."

It sounded like she was grinning again. The Guest Accounts were also a pain for communication. Back in high school, Felix and Edwin could only tell how he felt because they'd been friends for so long. It was harder with someone you'd just met.

"The good thing is, you should be able to beat him pretty easily with your close combat skills. Just build a Grunt Mech that's designed to make a good approach. As I mentioned, smoke grenades and drones will help. It's not bad to be weak against snipers. I would try to cut down on the fidgeting and stuff, but that's not going to go away in a week. The good thing is that you can just build something that compensates for your weaknesses."

Julian should have thought about that himself. Building a Mech to cover for his weaknesses was such a smart idea. It was what Tigger had done for the World Championships with the Cerberus Roar.

Emma stood up and dismissed her status screen.

"Alright. Let's start grinding for parts so we can set up a good practice. You need to buy some more parts too, right?"

Julian nodded. He needed to purchase all new armaments for his counter Mech. He'd never bought support items before. He'd always left that to Felix.

She pulled up the CALL GRUNT feature and pointed at the launcher.

"Besides, this thing doesn't pay for itself! We need to keep it loaded up with fresh parts. We'll need them to develop the Sniper-type Mechs I want you to practice on. Besides, you need to pay me for helping you!"

Ah.

That explained where the Grunts came from. By building a Mech that could reconstruct other Mechs, the Forever Brothers had fulfilled the promise of an ongoing battle.

"Of course! Let's get to grinding!"

Emma high-fived him.

"After we get back from grinding, I want to show you how to Craft, too. You're going to need it to build a new machine."

"Thank you!"

Julian was relieved.

Crafting wasn't something that you got good at just by doing it a bunch. You had to study it. That was why Emma could enter the game as a top-tier Crafter despite not having played before. It was also why Julian still sucked after playing for so long.

Emma and Julian exited the map and reappeared in the main lobby. Julian confidently walked over to the first Board and selected March of Grunts. The hard mode mission was the best for speedy grinding.

It was tough to fight an entire army, but the rewards were spectacular, and unlike other maps, there wasn't a penalty for being defeated. March of Grunts encouraged you to play until you were finally shot down.

"Alright. Let's do this!"

[20]

With the push of a button, Emma and Julian entered the lobby for March of Grunts. A notification appeared on Julian's visor to remind him of the mission restrictions.

MAX UNITS ALLOWED: 4
ACE RESTRICTIONS: NONE

You were allowed to bring up to four units, but like most AI missions, there were exclusive bonuses for taking on a more difficult challenge. For instance, clearing The Raid on Colony Seven with only one player let you take as many of the prizes as you could escape with. On one of Lilac's streams, she'd claimed all six units—hijacking one and dragging the rest behind her in a massive line.

March of Grunts was a little different. Pilots always fought the same army and claimed the same awards. It was only at the end of the mission that the team size and unit type bonuses multipliers kicked in. Playing the map with a single Grunt Mech gave you the highest multiplier—a whopping 8x increase to your Credits. Brandon had streamed several March of Grunt campaigns using a

Patchwork model. He currently held the server record at 467 Mechs destroyed using a solo Grunt. Vile had captured the overall single player record by destroying over a thousand enemies with the now-banned Moby Dick. Playing through the mission with two Grunts, or one Ace unit, unlocked a 4x Credit bonus.

Julian set the lobby to private, preventing other people from joining in without his permission.

After his last experience joining a random lobby, Julian was wary of playing with people he didn't know. The last thing he wanted was for another annoying experience with someone like Liefield. That was the unfortunate thing about randomly assigned games. The vast majority of Overdrive pilots were just regular people who wanted to grind out missions. There were a lot of really cool pilots, and letting a single negative experience stick with you was a mistake.

Despite Liefield stealing and possibly deleting the Heaven's Boxer, that mission had been an amazing experience overall. Julian hadn't only ended up in a lobby with his hero—he'd also gained invaluable insight from watching how TiggerLuvr888 and his kids approached the game. On top of that, Tyler had received an invaluable Mech.

However, recognizing a logical fallacy and stopping himself from acting on it were two different things. Especially for one of Emma's first missions, he wanted to play it safe and stay away from the random queue.

Emma turned.

"You think we can take this on with just us?"

"Yeah, probably. We have a pretty good set up here. I spent some of my Credits upgrading my Grunt frames too, so I'll be able to block for you this time around."

After his battle against Brandon, Julian had splurged on various Grunt upgrades. Battling with a weaker machine was a great way to train, but there were times when he needed a stronger Grunt. He was happy to take on a difficult challenge on his own, but he didn't want to drag down Emma with a weak machine.

"Would you be able to switch to a mass-fire version? I can play something tankier to protect you."

Emma groaned.

"Yeah, I suppose. I hate mass-fire. It just feels so inelegant."

Julian laughed.

"Oh. You're one of those pilots. A perfectionist."

Certain pilots could be very finicky about their skills. Julian stuck to swords because he wasn't as skilled at anything else, but he wasn't offended by learning new tactics. Pilots like Emma were different.

Vermillionangel was the most famous example. The champion hated getting hit, leading to some pretty amusing moments during Mech swap exhibitions. Even when the world champion switched from his highly mobile Mechs to one of Vile's titanic walking fortresses, the thought of getting hit by an enemy attack wounded his sensibilities.

"What the heck? What's wrong with being perfect?"

Emma sounded peeved.

It was a shame to take a brilliant sniper like Emma and move her to mass-fire duties. After around level 15, the AI spawned officer units that bolstered the enemy army's organization. A sniper was perfect against those high priority targets. Unfortunately, they wouldn't make it far enough into the map without a mass-fire machine. The best team composition with just two players was pretty obvious—a mass-fire unit and a bulky bodyguard.

Julian pulled up his messages tab.

"Let me see if Tyler wants to join us. Then he can play the mass-fire role."

Julian's roommate was still doing Brandon's drills on the

Forever Fortress. Tyler could probably do the same shooting drills on the March of Grunts map. If anything, it'd be an even better practice. From what Julian had noticed earlier, Tyler was still firing against targets that didn't shoot back. He'd set the Grunts to fly random paths so he could work on gunning them down. It'd be better in a live match.

Julian quickly typed out the message.

"Hey man—about to hop into a mission with Emma. You wanna join us?"

"What kind of mission?"

"March of Grunts."

He sent Tyler the description.

Mission: March of Grunts
Type: Survival
Creator: The Mechanical King

Although Julian had heard that this wasn't actually true, all the missions in Overdrive—other than those made by Fortress Masters—were listed as created by The Mechanical King.

Clicking the hyperlink on March of Grunts opened up a separate description tab.

"This is a special mission meant for farming parts and Credits! Grunts will charge at you endlessly until they finally bring you down! There is no time limit on March of Grunts. Instead, your only goal is to bring down as many of them as possible! Unlike other missions, there is no death penalty. You keep what you earn! Bonus multipliers are available for playing the map with fewer than the maximum strength required."

The two peculiar eccentricities of March of Grunts—the lack of a death penalty and the bonus multipliers—meant the best way to play the mission was to keep attacking. You could survive for much longer by running and hiding, but you wouldn't get any points for it.

After a while, Tyler responded.

"Hm, this seems too hard. I'm going to pass and stick with these drills."

"You sure? It might be easier to practice on live opponents!"

"I'm not ready yet. I need to make sure I do things right when they aren't firing. Don't want to develop bad habits."

"Alright."

That was a pretty weird way to look at it. Wasn't shooting at targets who wouldn't shoot back developing bad habits too?

Julian decided to ask Tyler more about it after they logged off for the night. Perhaps it was a training technique he and Brandon had picked up from basketball. Tyler shot a lot of baskets just by himself with no defenders.

"What do you think about this one?"

Emma sent over her modified design.

"Dang, that looks nice!"

Her new Mech was an adjusted version of her former Spell Titan. The sensor helmet had been removed, exposing the same spindly face that'd been on Captain Maxwell's Mech.

Instead of using her extremely expensive Sniper rifle, a Full Custom weapon that'd pushed Emma to the edge of the Credit limit, she'd split it into several cheaper parts. This new Mech had a pair of back-mounted beam cannons as well as a gigantic bazooka.

The bazooka was a particularly intriguing Full Custom. Julian had encountered firearms with under attachments before. Mounting a grenade launcher or shotgun beneath a rifle was one of the easiest ways to increase versatility without needing to switch weapons. But he'd never seen a bazooka with an attachment. The top barrel fired explosive rounds, and the bottom was a missile launcher.

Although the new machine looked significantly more frightening than Emma's sniper, it'd merely split her once formidable damage across several components. Both Mechs had an S rating in Shooting, but the sniper was the superior machine for competitive play. As menacing as the bazooka appeared, it was a conventional solid weapon that couldn't connect to the Mana Dispersal Domes. It probably only did about a third as much damage as the average sniper shot. However, dividing your firepower was optimal when you had to contend against hundreds of opponents instead of just four.

"What do you think about mine?"

Julian hastily assembled his Mech using the freshly bought parts in his inventory. After his match with Brandon, he'd purchased a variety of generic Grunt items.

He selected the Bronto Grunt he'd won in his mission with TiggerLuvr and attached weapons to the harnesses on its head and tail. Unlike most Hemoborn, attaching artillery to the brontosaurus's back was a mediocre proposition. The chest area was best suited for heavy armor. The machine's most critical advantage was its high and flexible firing angle.

- General Data -
Pilot: Julian
Machine: Bronto Grunt—Julian Custom
Class: Hemoborn
Sub-class: Wild
Designation: Grunt Unit

- Statistics -
Melee: C-tier
Shooting: B-tier
Speed: D-tier
Maneuverability: D-tier

Defense: A-tier
Cohesion: C-tier

- Weapons -
Head-Mounted Machinegun Turret
Neck Armor
Back Armor
Tail-Mounted Anti-Aircraft Turret

- Abilities -
Majesty Level 3

The Mech was indubitably a poorly created design. Julian had fallen to a C in Cohesion, and due to the mediocre quality of his gun turrets, he'd only managed a B in his primary offensive stat. The only good part about his build was the sturdy A in defense. It was hard to mess up throwing armor all over a dinosaur. The Majesty buff was essentially a reskinned version of Stench. Cool-looking Hemoborn got Majesty. Scary-looking ones got Stench.

To his relief, Emma didn't comment on her far superior crafting skills.

"Not bad. That's a nice complement to what I'm doing."

"Wish I was as good at this as you are."

"It's not as hard as you think it is. I'll help you out after this mission!"

Julian really had to work on crafting. Hopefully, he could pay her back with enough close-combat tips for all her help. She said that giving her some of the parts he won here would pay her back, but Julian didn't think that was good enough. Julian decided to give the Forever Fortress all his collected scrap metal. Just a few parts wouldn't be enough.

Now all he had to do was play well.

Unlike battles, missions loaded into the same map every time.

March of Grunts occurred on Scrapyard, a rusty grave where broken Mechs were laid to rest. Their two Mechs spawned at the top of a massive pile of devastated Grunts.

The enemies started at the bottom of the hill and would continually charge upward. Although the defenders began with a significant high ground advantage, it was impossible to stave off their relentless enemies forever. The March of Grunts had an infinite store of opponents.

"Let's do this."

"Yeah."

MISSION START

[21]

As soon as the battle started, Emma and Julian promptly launched an enormous barrage of bullets.

The first two Grunts in a row died, then the ones after them. Credit numbers flickered above the defeated Mechs to indicate their winnings.

Emma's bazooka repeatedly thumped as she destroyed opponent after opponent. Although she was using an inelegant weapon compared to her usual sniper rifle, her shots were always accurate.

She carefully timed her gunfire to maximize the chance of combo kills. Despite her newness to the actual game, she already knew how to capitalize on the terrain. She strategically collapsed portions of the walkway, forcing Grunts to fall to their deaths. Because this was just the first part of the mission, Emma refrained from her Special Attacks. A single Storm Surge would have instantly cleared the first wave, but the SPG Caster was restricted to only two spells every five minutes, which averaged out to about a spell a wave.

It was best to save her mana for more challenging opponents.

From his extremely high vantage point, Julian couldn't miss.

Although his machinegun turret was far weaker than Emma's bazooka, the odd angle was virtually impossible for the enemy Mechs to block. If the Grunts raised their shields, they'd only expose themselves to Emma's direct attacks. As a result, he effortlessly collapsed their cockpits from above, racking up kill after kill. He tried to keep his attacks to a minimum, only knocking out the few that Emma couldn't reach. Because it was difficult for a guard unit like Julian's to amass combo kills, it was most efficient to let your mass-fire ally defeat the Grunts.

The first part of the mission was extremely straightforward. The Grunts were all weak melee types charging up the hill, so there was no real threat. It was essentially a freeroll on collecting points. However, the upcoming waves rapidly ramped up the difficulty.

After they'd been blasting for about four minutes, the enemy wave had thinned to about a half dozen Mechs.

"Wait. I only have Credits showing up in my inventory, not parts."

"Ah yeah, you need to loot them."

"Oh, got it. The guide wasn't clear on that."

A lot of the guides were like that. They assumed you'd just know something automatically, which made things tough for beginners. Despite her research, Emma hadn't spent much time playing Overdrive. Stuff like looting parts seemed evident to Julian, but it made sense why she didn't know.

"Better to wait. You get some time between each wave to grab them."

"Oh, nice!"

You had about three to five minutes between each wave to gather up the fallen parts. Julian blasted another Grunt to pieces. Considering how simple the first wave was, the two comfortably chatted as they polished off the surviving units.

"Wait, so how exactly does the launcher work? I've never

seen anything like the universal CALL GRUNTS feature before. It seems pretty cool. You basically built a Mech that makes Mechs, right?"

"Yeah, exactly. Our Mechs are made of almost anything we can get. The good thing is that the design is really straightforward —I made it so that most of the parts and limbs are pretty much interchangeable. The only things we can't use are Wild types and Hemoborn. I'm working on making an easy-fit Wild-type Grunt, but as you can imagine, it's pretty hard."

"Yeah, that's awesome that you put all that together already. Those Grunts look pretty sturdy. Having a B in every category is nothing to sneeze at."

In comparison, the Grunts they were blasting through right now had a D in Defense.

Julian finished the last one off with a casual flick of his tail. The two climbed down from the mountain to gather up the lost parts, continuing their conversation they added items to their inventory. Fortunately for Julian, all you had to do to loot a defeated part or frame on March of Grunts was to tap it with your Mech. After that, it'd appear in the inventory. If it were a mission like The Raid on Colony Seven, it'd be difficult for Julian to try and grab and hold something with his Bronto Grunt.

"What do you guys do about Hemoborn parts?"

"Nothing—I try to stay away from those missions."

She shuddered in a familiar way that Julian recognized. He didn't like most Hemoborn, either.

"So the kind that you have, you know, the animal-types are pretty cool. But we won't be able to breed and then modify them fast enough on the map right. The only way to do Call Grunts for Hemoborn would be to use like a Zombie-type where you can just stitch all the flesh together."

She shook her head.

"I don't like Zombies."

"Yeah, same here. I like the live ones, though."

"Yeah, live ones are cool."

With their prizes gathered, the two climbed back up the hill. The first round had been melee Grunts climbing up the hill—an easy kill for even beginners. But the next round, the Grunts had guns, which meant they could attack before making it up to the top. The third round featured planes and other aerial units. Fortunately, Julian had chosen his Mech well. The Bronto Grunt countered most airborne attacks.

It was only during the fourth round, when the enemy Grunts started coordinating their attacks, that Julian and Emma began to struggle. Ground bound Grunts started riding the other aerial units. As the first team strafed them from above, a group of well-armed assault units began a furious charge from below.

Emma cursed but didn't say anything else.

After a moment of uncomfortable silence, Julian cleared his throat.

"You focus on keeping them off us from the ground. I'll guard the air."

"Got it."

During his usual matches with Felix and Edwin, Julian rarely spoke. They were more social than he was, and besides, Felix knew so much about Overdrive. It was easier to have his friends point him in the right direction.

But now, it was up to Julian to be the shotcaller. Perhaps because Emma and Tyler had just started, they both looked to him for instruction. Emma had already informed him that she didn't like thinking on her feet when enemies charged at her quickly. Right now, enemies were definitely charging at them quickly.

Emma activated Storm Surge, eviscerating half the wave before returning to her physical-based projectiles.

With Emma covering the ground units, Julian turned his focus to the air. The enormous neck meant that even though his enemies were flying, he was still shooting from a level playing field. He twisted the anti-aircraft battery on his tail around, and he blasted down the opposition.

Throughout his exchanges, Julian made sure to keep his Mech positioned in front of Emma's. He didn't want to make the same mistake he'd made when fighting Liefield's army. His well-armored unit needed to care for Emma's mass-firing glass cannon.

Julian focused on bringing down plane after plane. At this early stage, most of the machines couldn't fly under their own volition. That meant that destroying the support craft was already enough to cripple the Grunt riding it. If he got particularly lucky, they'd land on top of the others charging up the hill. After a few successful attacks, some of the ground-bound Grunts started firing at Julian instead. Although it worsened his firing angle— anti-aircraft guns performed the best while firing upward—he lifted his tail high off the air.

This would keep the distracted Grunts shooting at an angle where they had no chance of hitting Emma.

Julian grinned.

That was a good plot, and he hadn't struggled to come up with it. As soon as the AI Grunts changed their strategy, Julian had adjusted. Now that he was actively trying to think, he was getting better and better at that sort of thing. He hoped it would pay off in his fight against Dynamic.

Emma shot him a weird look. At least, Julian thought it was weird based on the tone of her voice.

"What the heck? You're actually pretty good at shooting."

He didn't get what she meant.

"Yeah, I mean, you just put the cursor over them and click. Why wouldn't I be? It's so easy."

"Why do you always use a sword then?"

"I'm better with a sword. See?"

He smirked and used his tail to whack the last aircraft,

sending the Grunt on top of it spinning high into the air. Emma took it out with a well-placed blast from her left side beam cannon.

The round ended, and the two left the hill to collect their prizes.

"You should try and shoot more too. You're good! I wouldn't say it's easy to hit some of those shots you made. It's hard to keep bringing down those planes."

Huh.

Julian had always dismissed shooting as too difficult—or not worth learning after he'd already mastered swords—but Felix had always been telling him to diversify his game too.

Julian should have listened to his childhood friend, and he should definitely listen to Emma now.

Getting complimented by someone as skilled as Emma felt good.

The fifth round was the same as the fourth but with higher quality Mechs. The repeat missions eventually turned pretty brutal, but Julian and Emma managed to survive through judicious use of her skills. The seventh round featured no aerial assault. Instead, their enemies used battering rams. Although it was meant to be a more difficult challenge, it was actually surprisingly easy for their composition. Julian's high angle more or less nullified the rams' advantage.

However, the eighth mission involved both rams and planes. With Julian forced back to anti-air duties, it was up to Emma to clean through the ground forces. That battle required both of her spell charges, putting them in a terrible position for the ninth round when their enemies wheeled out the heavy artillery.

Julian used his high firing angle to destroy the priority targets immediately. Artillery had no problem shooting enemies on a hill. Unfortunately, that forced Emma to focus on flying machines. It was possible because of her skills, but that took them out of contention for combo kills.

When the round finally ended, the two let out relieved sighs as they collected their prizes.

"Ah man, good job getting through that one. Loved your aim."

Emma tsked.

"Yeah, but we have a problem with the next match. I'm almost out of ammo."

Julian's stomach sank, and he sighed.

"That's probably the last round then."

Ammunition was another reason why the March of the Grunts mission never lasted particularly long. The best bet was to use a Kingbreaker that featured a mix of solid ammunition-based weapons and built-in beam weapons that ran off the internal generator.

That was how Brandon had set the Grunt record.

The Spell Titans were a particular problem. They weren't the best Mechs for this kind of mission since their reliance on mana meant that they ran out of power the fastest. The problem was exacerbated by the fact that Emma was using a Spell Titan Grunt. Even with her improvements, the Grunt still had far fewer Spikes than an Ace unit.

"Nah, it's on me. I should have switched my Mech. I just wanted to stick to my design."

"Nothing wrong with that! The design is awesome! Let's end this on a bang."

If Julian were playing a battle to qualify for the Selection, he'd be pretty annoyed by someone who wasn't using an optimal Mech. But Emma was a casual player. Most pilots stuck to the designs they created. Self-expression was one of the coolest things about Overdrive, and Julian would never begrudge them as long as their machine didn't negatively affect others. He'd played with a few jerks who used Mechs that leeched energy off their teammates before. That had been a real disaster.

The two of them climbed back up the hill.

The Grunts arrived.

To his surprise, Emma suddenly cried out. Her voice was bursting with excitement.

"This is it! Time for the last stand! Shoot until you have nothing left!"

Julian let out a surprised laugh. He hadn't known she was that into it.

The Grunts charged. Julian squared his guns and shot until he had nothing left.

[22]

Julian smiled happily as he looked through his prizes.

"Not bad. Not bad at all."

"Is 258 kills good?"

"Yeah, I'd say so. It's a lot more than what I've gotten with a solo Ace, that's for sure."

Julian pulled up his records and showed them to her.

"I was at 53 with just one Mech—mostly just the first three waves. The Starlight R wasn't built for killing a bunch of enemies at once."

"We had two people, though, so that's not a great comparison."

"I don't have anything to compare with! I've never done it with two Grunts before, so this is a new record for me. But hey— just look at the money!"

He grinned.

"That in and of itself tells us that we did a good job."

At a rate of 25 Credits per Grunt, they'd wound up with a very handsome total of 6,450 Credits. Once they added the combo bonus of 3,000 Credits, the two were up to 9,450.

The multiplier for two Grunts was 4x, bringing them up to 25,800.

"I'll take the 10,000 for Crafting, but you take the rest."

"You sure? You already gave me all the frames and parts!"

"Yeah. Most of those kills were yours anyways. I was just the bodyguard!"

On top of their Credits, they'd picked up eight different types of Grunts. Most of the frames were older models—Mechs like the Defender Mk. II or the Guardian IV. But frames were frames, and the parts would do well inside the Forever Fortress's launcher. At the push of a button, he transferred all the earned equipment to Captain Maxwell.

As a Guest Account, Emma needed her dad to keep hold of so much loot. She'd have to pass on her Credits before logging off too. Otherwise, they'd vanish.

"Besides, I've got enough Credits to buy a new frame myself."

Julian pulled up his status screen and moved to his inventory. He had just over 8,000 Credits already in his account, so taking 10,000 moved him past 18,000. He'd spent most of his money on upgrades and grabbing Tyler a new piloting suit. Pilots like Felix preferred saving up a giant stash of over a hundred thousand, so they could quickly respond to the metagame's adjustments.

Now that Julian planned on studying his opponents, he'd have to do the same. He pulled up his research notes to remind him of the specific parts he needed.

A model of Dynamic's Mech popped onto Julian's status screen. The camouflaged machine with the enhanced scope visor and massive drone backpack had been the bane of Julian's previous attempt to make the Selection.

- General Data -
Pilot: Dynamic

Machine: Self-Supporting Sniper
Class: Kingbreaker
Sub-class: Artillery
Designation: Ace Unit

- Statistics -
Melee: C-tier
Shooting: S-tier
Speed: A-tier
Maneuverability: B-tier
Defense: A-tier
Cohesion: S-tier

- Weapons -
Variable Sniper Rifle (Full Custom) [x1]
Combat Knife [x2]
Drone Boost Pack (Full Custom) [x1]
Boost Pack-Mounted 8-Tube Missile Launchers [x2]
Boost Pack—Beam Cannon [x2]

- Abilities -
N/A [Kingbreaker Class]

The Mech was a well-rounded machine with strong overall stats. Julian would have placed the awkwardly named Self-Supporting Sniper near the top of the S-tier for Shooting. It wasn't as strong as the Vermillion Flier, but it was pretty close.

The Self-Supporting Sniper was an example of how the Tier system didn't make a lot of sense. Either the Sniper Rifle—which could also shift to a rapid-fire mode—or the Drone Boost Pack, which mounted two beam cannons and two missile launchers, would have given a machine an S-tier rating in and of themselves.

The Drone Boost Pack was a particularly dangerous feature,

as it could either operate independently or provide Dynamic's Mech with a significant increase to its Speed.

It was difficult to calculate a Full Custom, but it was possible to loosely approximate the damage by looking at the base components in the shop. Using the resilient Guardian X as a basis, Emma and Julian had devised the following chart.

Variable Sniper Rifle: Arm Shot (60-100% Damage); Leg Shot (40-80% Damage); Cockpit (100% Damage); Head (100% Damage)

Missile Launchers: Arm Shot (30-60% Damage); Leg Shot (20-50% Damage); Cockpit (80% Damage); Head (70% Damage)

Beam Cannon: Arm Shot (45-70% Damage); Leg Shot (30-55% Damage); Cockpit (100% Damage); Head (100% Damage)

The combat knife was more or less irrelevant. Since Julian was planning on using a sword, the match would effectively end once he got into range.

"Not worth using a Guardian-type. Don't pick a Defender, either. Nothing tanky is going to work."

"Yeah."

The powerful Self-Supporting Sniper would destroy a tanky Grunt unit in only about three or four shots. A cockpit hit was an instant kill. Once again, there was a marked difference between Grunts and Aces. Although the Starlight R was optimized for offense, its parts survived three attacks from the Self-Supporting Sniper, including two cockpit shots.

Considering those results, they were best off relying on an all-out offense.

Because of the Self-Supporting Sniper's power, it wasn't a big sacrifice to give up some armor in exchange for strength and mobility. When your opponent was capable of rapid-fire attacks, the difference between surviving one shot and three shots was tiny. On the other hand, a more offensive Grunt could make all the difference. The key was for Julian to defeat Dynamic before he got to attack at all.

The first thing to do was to buy a new frame. Julian's current collection consisted entirely of tanky and defensive Grunts.

"Alright. Let's get shopping."

Julian pulled up the shop menu, hitting the share button so that Emma could see what he was looking at.

SHOP
- FRAMES
- WEAPONS
- ENHANCEMENTS

The three categories were all fairly self-explanatory. Frames were base units. Weapons were weapons. Enhancements were exclusive bonuses that varied from class to class. For instance, that was where you purchased buffs like Stench or Majesty. You could also scroll through a list of pre-created Finishers for Paragons, although most of the best Finisher results came from extensive crafting.

When Julian hit FRAMES, it divided into Aces and Grunts, along with the various classifications.

GRUNTS
- KINGBREAKER
- HEMOBORN
- SPELL TITAN

ACES
- KINGBREAKER
- HEMOBORN
- SPELL TITAN
- PARAGON

As always, the possibility of purchasing a Paragon as a Grunt flickered on and off. To qualify for the official shop, you needed a certain number of sales each week. The Overdrive game administration paid qualifying frames a share of Credits each week. If you failed to qualify, your item was removed, and you were stuck selling your parts independently until you qualified again.

Because Paragon Grunts couldn't use Finishers or Liquid State Eternium, there wasn't any reason to use them over Kingbreakers. On occasion, a Paragon Grunt made it into the shop for aesthetic purposes, but they usually fell back out of the rotation within a few weeks. Julian had no idea why people kept designing them.

Out of curiosity, he clicked the Spell Titan category under Grunts. To his surprise, Emma's Mech was the seventh-highest seller and still rapidly rising in popularity. That was seriously impressive. As powerful as the machine was, it was hard to succeed in the shop. You had to beat out a lot of entrenched designs.

"Wow! You got your build entered into the main shop? That's awesome!"

"Yeah—I had my dad enter it in for me. We've been putting the profits into the Forever Fortress."

That was yet another one of the negatives of using Guest Accounts. The Overdrive game administration heavily pressured Guests from all sides, but Julian understood Emma's reluctance. The body scan was weird.

He promptly purchased it.

"Wait, why did you buy it?"

She said it like he was an idiot.

He paused, looking for words.

"Um, I think it's cool! Plus, you know, I think it's a great fit for our strategy. Your Mech is super powerful and can do tons of damage. That's what we're looking for!"

He also wanted to support her. She was the first person he knew personally who'd managed to get a design in the shop, and the SPG Caster was amazing.

Julian loved the built-in Spikes in the shoulders and how smoothly integrated everything was.

Julian bit his lip.

He was worried that if he said he bought the Mech to support her, she'd think that he'd bought it just to make her feel good, not because he thought it was the best Mech possible.

It was both. He wanted to support her, and he wanted to use the best Mech possible.

Emma laughed.

"No, I know my Mech is good. But why would you buy it? I could have just given you one."

Oh.

Right.

"Well, I wanted to support the Forever Fortress."

"Then you could have bought it directly from me instead of giving the Shop a cut."

He had nothing to say to that one.

Julian shook his head.

"Okay. Yeah. I'm just dumb."

They laughed.

"Let's get to work designing. Tell me what to do! You're the expert here."

He pulled out the Spell Titan and applied his custom colors. The Mech went from a shining blue—Emma had used her personal colors as the default—to a vibrant orange and gold. Emma tilted her head to the side.

"Not bad. It looks pretty exciting. And I like the gold on a lightning Mech."

"Thank you!"

Julian was pretty proud of his custom colors. Light orange

was his favorite color, and after a few years of experimentation, he'd decided that gold was the perfect compliment.

Emma sighed.

"Well, I do think it's the best pick here—and not just because it's my Mech. But the damage calculations look tough. You're going to have to play really well."

Julian had already known that defense would be a problem, but it still shocked him to see the numbers.

The sniper rifle was guaranteed to punch off any part in a single shot. The beam cannons could destroy his arms in a single shot and his legs in two. The missile launchers would smash any part in two hits. A blow to the cockpit from any of those weapons would be an instant fatality.

The thin frames of Spell Titans meant they always faced a substantial trade-off. Even if Julian used the cyromancer Ace unit he'd picked up from his mission with TiggerLuvr888, he still would have been vulnerable to the Self-Supporting Sniper's long-range barrages. A well-built Spell Titan could either rank above the A-tier in Defense or Speed, but never both. Their gangly frames couldn't move quickly while holding a lot of armor.

Julian brushed the calculations aside.

"It's fine. It looks bad, but this is the best way."

It sounded like Emma was grinning under her helmet.

"I better do a good job of training you then. Let's start by building this machine and then figuring out what items you need."

Julian smiled back. He really hoped she was smiling. Otherwise, he'd look like a buffoon.

It'd feel good to use the Spell Titan. It was an absolute marvel of engineering, and he'd feel like he was representing the Forever Fortress while piloting it.

After purchasing the frame, Julian scrolled through the weapons, going down to the very bottom to look at the support items. Julian read through each one with keen interest. Because he'd never considered playing support before, he actually didn't know what every item did.

He'd gotten a general sense from fighting against them in his matches, and he'd developed some simple heuristics to avoid danger. Yet now that he was reading out the exact text, he realized that he'd been making some pretty damaging mistakes.

Julian scrolled through the Poseidon Net, one of the many available trap items. The net was modeled after a fisherman's and released a paralyzing electric shock whenever a Mech got too close. Since it stunned for thirty seconds, Julian instinctively avoided it whenever it appeared. Standing still for that long was death in Overdrive. Enemies would instantly crush your cockpit. But now that he took a closer look, he realized that avoidance wasn't the only option.

Poseidon Net
Cost: 3,000 Credits

Ability: Creates a net that walls off a specific area. Units that touch the Poseidon Net will be paralyzed for a thirty-second duration. This duration is divided by the number of units that trigger the net. The trap will last for a total of three minutes before dissipating.

It sounded like there were times when your team should trigger the net together.

Julian jotted down some notes, and then moved on. He wasn't looking to use the Poseidon Net today. That was a specialized weapon that countered melee units. It'd be useless against Dynamic.

He finally found what he was looking for.

Julian picked up two smoke grenades, and then he moved over to the drone section. There were a variety of drones available, but as a Grunt, Julian could only equip the cheapest ones.

Grunts couldn't use armed drones. Due to the low Credit cap, Julian couldn't build a drone that functioned as an independent Mech like Dynamic's.

"This looks like the one."

Julian selected the remote-controlled camera drone, one of the five available for a Grunt to purchase. He grabbed one before Emma stopped him.

"Wait. Why are you only getting one? You need at least three drones to monitor most map angles."

She took a closer look at his screen.

"And why did you only get two smokes? I would try to have four smokes."

Julian paused.

With three drones and four smokes—which would require its own canister—his Cohesion would take a beating.

But then Julian remembered that Emma was going to teach him how to craft.

"I'm going to need your help on this one. I suck at this."

"Of course! Just make sure you get the right parts."

She firmly repeated herself.

"Four smokes and three drones. Trust me."

He made the purchases, and then moved over to the close combat weapons section. On his way down, he saw a wide variety of melee weapons—broadswords, rapiers, axes, maces, and even eccentric items like morning stars or grappling hooks. Julian sighed. He was so proud of his close combat skills, but even in his specialty, he'd failed to learn Overdrive's true diversity.

He had the talent to be a much better fighter. He just hadn't used it yet!

She reached out a hand to stop him before he purchased yet another broadsword.

"I'll show you how to craft a sword. We'll build it up from cheaper ingredients. It's time to get your first Full Custom."

[23]

Crafting was weird. The intricacies had always eluded Julian, which was why he'd spent his Overdrive career repurposing parts and weapons he'd earned from drops. Of course, that was why his Mechs had such poor Cohesion.

Crafting was one of the most essential areas for him to improve if he wanted to make the Selection. Just like training his strategic thinking, crafting didn't come from spamming a lot of games.

As if to prove that point, Emma was one of the best crafters Julian had ever seen, and she'd technically only been playing for just over a month. Her long hours watching streams and studying the Overdrive Wiki had really paid off.

Julian handed over the parts then stepped back as Emma pulled up her Crafting Menu, creating a workshop both of them could participate in.

The crafting process involved manipulating a series of builder drones, floating pod-shaped workers that were only slightly larger than a person. Creating an all-new frame like the SPG Caster reminded Julian of building model mecha, just like those from the

Gundam universe. But adding parts to a frame was a lot more like surgery.

By maneuvering the various crafting drones around your Mech frame, you linked new weapons and parts to power spots and energy hubs. Overdrive crafting was all about manipulating the internal wiring. The power spots running through your machines were like organs. You had to connect them to your new weapons properly. Otherwise, you'd lose both Cohesion and offensive power.

Crafting was much easier with high-ranking parts, which had more abundant and forgiving power outlets. The arm on Julian's Starlight R had been a high-quality part designed for close combat. Mounting his generator-attached sword had been a relatively simple task. Crafting would have been even easier if he'd managed to capture the pristine Heaven's Boxer.

On the other hand, the SPG Caster was an extremely difficult Mech to craft with. The built-in Mana Gatherer Spikes at the shoulders severely restricted the available outlet space. The Spell Titan class's bizarre limbs only made things worse. Not only were the arms thin and gangly, but they also had to be completely hollow. Spell Titans needed an unimpeded Mana flow from their Gatherer Spikes to their Dispersal Finger. Clogging the arms rendered the Mech inoperable.

Emma seemed utterly undaunted. She took one look at the Mech's internal wiring then started jotting away at her notepad.

Like most experienced Crafters, Emma used a grid to track her total planned unit price. The total cost of a Grunt's add-ons had to come below 10,000 Credits, but that didn't include the weapons built into the frame.

Base Weaponry: Free
Mana Dispersal Finger [x10]

Mana Dispersal Fingers were a conduit for spells. Typically, the fingers were only used as a last resort. Ideally, they linked to various weapons like Emma's sniper rifle or Julian's planned beam sword.

Required Weapons:
Grenade Carrying Shield—2,000 Credits
Drones—4,500 Credits Total
Melee Weapons—??? Credits

"The Grenade Carry Shield is the best option here to hold your four grenades. The Grenades themselves already cost 500, right, so once you hit four, you might as well stick them in the shield. Normally, a solid shield goes for 2,000 Credits in and of itself."

"Yeah."

It was an interaction he'd seen before but hadn't actively remembered. It was sort of like the Poseidon Net. He saw the net and knew not to go near it, but because he hadn't explored the weapon, Julian hadn't realized there were alternative paths to defeating it. The round carrying shield was the same way. He saw it and assumed the guy was carrying grenades, but he hadn't realized it let Support units sneak past the Credit cap.

"Where am I going to put the drones?"

Emma laughed, flipped the shield upside down, and just put the drones on top of it.

"Wait, what? Don't I need a backpack or something?"

"You do if you plan on calling the drones back, but this isn't a long-term mission. It's just a one on one. Once you find the guy, you're good. You won't need to call the drones back to find someone else."

Julian grinned.

"Dang. That's smart."

Putting together some kind of drone pack would cost Credits. Recharging them with his ports would have damaged his Cohesion. But if he simply charged them up before the battle and brought them there, there would be no additional costs.

So far, Emma had managed to equip all the items without risking a single port. Neither the shield nor the carry-on drones needed to dock with the actual frame. The Cohesion remained at an undisturbed S.

Emma took the compliment in stride and went right back to business.

"Alright. How many swords do you think you'll need? I was thinking two. Just to have a backup."

"Wait, what? Wouldn't that bring the sword quality too low?"

Julian had believed Emma when she said she could attach the grenades and drones.

He hadn't studied crafting enough to figure it out, but it was still fundamentally a matter of following the rules. The Drones cost 1,500 each, and the Grenades were a measly 500. Put them all together, and that was just 6,500 Credits. Emma had integrated them exceptionally cleverly, but anyone could buy and attach the weapons.

The shield was a hidden game bonus, but Julian knew there weren't any such bonuses for swords.

Bringing in two good swords would shatter the 10,000 Point Cap.

Julian pulled up the shop again.

There were cheap items like low-quality short swords that cost fewer than 2,000 Credits. If Julian downgraded to knives and daggers, the weapons were even less expensive. A single throwing knife only cost 700, just a bit more than a grenade.

But it'd be better just to buy a single top quality blade. With 3,500 Credits available, Julian could afford to buy either a Great Broadsword for 3,000 or a Beam Broadsword for 3,500.

"Uh, Emma, I'm not sure I can pick up two swords. I'm more comfortable with broadswords, which are expensive. Just taking a look at the base costs, it doesn't seem possible."

She took a look.

"Which of the two were you thinking?"

"Probably the beam sword. I know it's possible to infuse mana into a solid blade, but from what I understand, it's a lot more reliable with beam-based weapons, right?"

He smiled bashfully. He didn't want it to sound like he was telling her about her own Mech. She knew far more about the SPG Caster—and more about Spell Titans in general—than Julian did.

She nodded.

"Yeah, I was thinking the same thing. A beam sword is smart. But considering the Self-Supporting Sniper's defensive stats, I don't think we need to upgrade the item in the shop. That sounds like total overkill. Instead, we should make a Full Custom to upgrade a weaker base item to help circumvent the Credit cap."

Oh.

"Dang. That's smart."

Julian hadn't thought about using a Full Custom for those purposes before. He'd only envisioned it as a way to maximize power, but there were other uses as well. Even though he could buy a Beam Broadsword from the Shop, Crafting his one would allow him to wield it for a significantly lower price.

It was similar to what Brandon did with his Patchwork models. Emma was right. A single high-quality sword was enough for him to defeat Dynamic, but he couldn't put all his eggs in one basket. Dynamic was crafty. If he saw that Julian only had a single sword, he'd focus his efforts on destroying it.

The strategy of crafting Full Customs for cost purposes explained a lot. Julian had beaten down enemies using Full Customs before and failed to understand why they'd seemed weak. He thought their pilots had only been Crafting for aesthetic purposes. Now he knew better.

It also explained why there was a strict Full Custom limit on Grunts. Otherwise, the professional players would use builds with all Full Custom items, essentially circumventing the Credit cap and using a Grunt with the equivalent of twenty or even thirty thousand Credits. If you wanted to cheat the Credit cap, you had to do it the hard way, like Brandon did.

Emma pulled up her own shop.

"Here's what I was thinking so far."

She ordered a pair of beam daggers, a cheap close-combat weapon that cost 1,250 Credits apiece, a full 550 more than the throwing knife. In general, beam variants of conventional weapons cost more, although the difference in actual combat effectiveness varied wildly depending on your opponent's armor type.

"The hilt is short, but you can add scrap metal onto that to extend it. That turns it into a full beam sword hilt."

She activated one of the drones, which used scrap metal to elongate the base and make it more appropriate for a sword. Then she took the dagger apart, removing the internal battery and exposing the inner workings. The tiny beam dagger carried an independent power source, but Emma planned on linking it directly to her Mana Dispersal Fingers. She created a series of ports then gently coaxed a set of connective wires into the handle. It seemed like a simple process, but Julian knew just how complicated it really was. One misstep with the cables and the whole thing would explode instead of activating.

He sighed.

She turned back at him. Although he couldn't see past her helmet, it felt like she was rolling her eyes.

"It's not as hard as you think it is, and even if it is hard, you won't get it if you don't practice. Just make sure you pay attention."

She went back to the wire. This time, she slowed down so he could see her every move.

"Look. Don't jam it. The key is not to get it done. You need to fly into battle with this thing."

The pincer of her drone inched the wire forward.

"Now, all you need to do is make sure it can extend into your machine."

She gently placed the modified dagger in the Mech's hand. The hilt looked just like a sword's now.

The item name hovered above the sword as the wires snaked into the fingers, and the blade flared to life.

Mana-Infused Beam Broad Sword (Full Custom) [x1]

There was a resonant hum as the beam emerged. Unlike his usual orange blade, this one was bright blue and infused with the electric-oriented mana gathered by the spikes on the shoulders.

Emma grinned.

She cleared her throat and called out to the drone. The Crafting Area's Trial Zone allowed you to see your Mech in action before bringing it to an actual fight.

"Cast Thunderbolt."

The sword swelled to enormous size. The heat from the blade turned everything around it into a dazzling blur.

Julian let out a cry of excitement.

"Yes! Yes!"

Julian could tell how powerful it was with just a glance.

Emma's craftsmanship was immaculate. The sword would be the strongest weapon he'd ever used. Even better, the strength came not from brute force, but from the synergy and interaction between the parts. It'd only cost 1,250 Credits, yet the elongated hilt and the access to Mana Gatherer Fingers granted the weapon undeniable strength. He couldn't wait to work on some top-quality Full Customs under the Ace Credit cap.

"Good. Now's your turn to try to build your own. I've got to work on an independent project for a bit."

She handed him the parts then kicked him out of her Crafting module. Even after equipping the second blade, he'd still have a few more points to go. He figured he'd go with a cheap ranged weapon like a 4-shot revolver. Unfortunately, Grunts were limited to only two Full Customs, which meant that he was stuck with a mediocre ranged weapon. That wasn't a problem for this battle. No matter how he spent the 10,000 Credits, he'd never beat the Self-Supporting Sniper at long range.

Julian entered his own Crafting Workshop, then pulled open the dagger and started emulating Emma's movements.

As he expected, removing all the parts was hard. He actually crushed a bit of the battery when trying to drag it out, and the dust stayed inside. He looked up, expecting Emma to laugh, but she was busy with her project. Because she'd set her Crafting module to private, he just saw her staring intensely at a screen.

He sighed and fiddled at the controls of the pod, bringing up a dusting component. He did his best to clear everything out, but part of the battery remained. He hefted the blade, hoping it wouldn't make too much of a difference in weight. The battery components wouldn't damage his Mech since he hadn't left any flammable components. The main issue was that it would impact his Cohesion.

He thought about starting over from the beginning and purchasing a new dagger, but he decided to see this one through. It was just like how Emma told him to keep watching the first match even after he got shot. If he didn't keep working, he wouldn't have any experience with creating the mana cables. If he restarted now but messed up again later, he'd have two wasted daggers.

Threading the wires through the hilt was a painstaking process. The good thing was that it was much harder to mess up than crushing the battery. The holes Julian punched were the precise size of the wires themselves, meaning he wouldn't damage the hilt so long as he gently inserted the cables.

Even if he messed up, it could only damage the soft wire, not the blade itself. That wasn't a problem. Overdrive provided you with an unlimited number of wires at no cost.

It took him almost two hours—and over a dozen discarded wires—but he finally got it.

"Yes! Yes! Yes!"

He placed the sword in his hand and activated the hilt. To his immense relief, there wasn't an explosion.

The blue blade flared out, but it was only about 50% of his other sword's length. Julian groaned when he realized what had happened.

He hadn't adjusted the hilt. The game still considered the sword a dagger, and the maximum output was restricted. Instead of a broadsword, he had an exceptionally thick knife. It looked like a cleaver.

Emma turned and laughed. She immediately knew what had gone wrong. She must have finished with her own crafting.

Julian was just about to discard the item and try again, but then she stopped him.

"Slash with it. Don't give up yet. It's pretty impressive you made something at all."

Julian didn't want to get discouraged. After all, he'd greatly improved his crafting. The item was still a Full Custom. He could consider the two and a half or so hours as training.

The item name flickered as he commanded the drone to swing the blade.

Mana-Infused Beam Cleaver (Full Custom) [x1]

He cast Thunderbolt then let out a surprised gasp. His disappointment vanished.

He could feel the heat of the sword from his place behind the glass of the Crafting Module.

When he cast Thunderbolt with his Cleaver, the blade didn't extend in length. Instead, all the power was concentrated at the very edge.

He flicked it.

It was just a casual cut, but he felt the power rushing through the air.

Emma smiled.

"I think this is for the best. It gives you some versatility. Either a giant blade or a concentrated strength that can blow through everything. I'd watch out, though. It looks like the edge of the Spike is sparking pretty dramatically."

Concentrating the charge was putting a significant toll on the shoulder. This wasn't a weapon with a long operating time, but it was perfect for this match. Up close, he would only have a few chances to destroy Dynamic's Self-Supporting Sniper.

"I did it! I did it! I'm a Crafting master!"

Emma laughed.

"Let's see it in action!"

She snapped her fingers, and Julian realized that he wasn't a Crafting master at all. He gawked at the new Mech Emma had created.

- General Data -
Pilot: Guest 198
Machine: Self-Supporting Sniper Copy
Class: Kingbreaker
Sub-class: Artillery
Designation: Ace Unit

- Statistics -
Melee: C-tier
Shooting: S-tier
Speed: A-tier
Maneuverability: B-tier
Defense: A-tier
Cohesion: S-tier

- Weapons -
Enhanced Scope Visor (Full Custom) [x1]
Variable Sniper Rifle (Full Custom [x1]
8-Tube Missile Launchers [x2]
Beam Cannon [x2]
Solo Boost Pack (Full Custom) [x1]

- Abilities -
N/A [Kingbreaker Class]

The listing of the items was a little different, but as far as Julian could tell, it was almost a perfect replica of Dynamic's machine. When Emma said she'd create sniper units for him to practice with, he hadn't known how far she'd go.

Julian let out a long breath.

He felt it now. After looking through the Database, he'd seen the possibility. But now, he knew.

If he practiced hard enough, he could beat an opponent two hundred ranks ahead of him and quality for the Selection.

Emma snickered.

"Alright. Stop gawking and let's get going. You have a match to win. Let's start practicing."

[24]

The two of them loaded into a casual one-on-one battle and examined the map. Both sides received a minute to adjust their machines, but neither needed it. Emma was using an Ace, and Julian was using a custom-built counter.

Julian grimaced.

Caverns was the best map for snipers. In general, Julian wanted there to be as few obstacles as possible. Stages in space or most underwater stages were particularly beneficial. They allowed the attacking unit to move in all three dimensions without providing adequate cover for the gunner.

Caverns was filled with caves atop high hills. This particular map was Cavern 3, one of the four different settings.

Julian took a deep breath and stopped thinking about how he wished it would be another map.

This was practice. It'd be best if Emma got the most favorable maps possible. He tried looking at the map like Brandon would. What were the key landmarks? Where were they likely to launch? Based on Emma's previous comments, Julian thought he had a pretty good grasp of her sniping style. She liked to pick spots that gave her the most options, even if it required exceptionally tricky shots. She was confident that her skill could carry the day.

Julian mused beneath his breath.

"Peak Cave is an option, especially since it's on the corner in this iteration."

The Peak Cave was simply a cave at the top of a peak. It was one of the highest vantage points for snipers to shoot from, but the slot was fool's gold on iterations 1 and 2. The cave was filled with openings, and there was no way to defend every assault. But on stages 3 and 4, the Peak Cave spawned in a corner, making it an invaluable option.

He ran his hand against the map, highlighting the various nooks and crannies on the walls.

The two Mechs would launch on two randomly selected spots opposite each other on the map, which meant Julian should figure out where Emma planned on running once the game started. The Peak Cave was an obvious option if she started on the northern side, but there were still three other areas to consider.

"There's a slit in the wall over there. She might go there."

It was too narrow for Dynamic, but it was the kind of crevice Emma loved shooting from.

"And then to the south…"

There weren't too many good places in the south. Emma would probably run for the narrow slot he'd picked out on the western side of the map.

The eastern corner was another troublesome spot. There was no singular location like the Peak Cave. Instead, countless holes perforated the canyon walls—players called it the Swiss Cheese Fortress. Both the Peak Cave and the Swiss Cheese Fortress were absolute nightmares. With the Peak Cave, you knew exactly where your enemy was, but high cavern was nearly impregnable. On the other hand, no one spot in the Swiss Cheese Fortress was comparable in quality to the Peak Cave. However, the sheer number of high-quality locations made it virtually impossible to root anybody out. Julian would have to search through every single area with his drones. Even if he did discover her, she could simply destroy the scouting camera and then reposition.

The game started.

To Julian's immense relief, he was given the eastern wall, the one with the Swiss Cheese Fortress. That meant that Emma was north, south, or west.

Julian aimed his launching cannon for the nearest cavern. Unlike Emma, Julian didn't need to worry about shooting angles. He just had to get under cover and start scouting.

Julian quietly set the drones to the cavern floor.

A moment later, he sent one to watch the slit in the wall. Based on his prediction, there should have been a two-in-three chance that Emma was headed there.

There weren't any good locations from the South. She wouldn't run all across the map to access the Peak Cave. The Boost Pack granted the Self-Supporting Sniper significant mobility, but soaring through the skies was a dead giveaway.

Julian made a mental note to study more of Dynamic's previous games. He needed to grasp his opponent's thinking. Although Emma and Dynamic were both snipers—and likely to make the same decisions—even a slight difference in their skills and mentality would lead them to different spots.

Study his opponents and study the map. There was so much more to winning at Overdrive than just having excellent control skills with a sword.

He sent another drone to peer at the cave. And then, just in case his hunch was right, Julian immediately started moving toward the western side of the map.

The odds favored him.

There!

The drone beeped, indicating that an enemy machine had just

crossed its line of sight.

To Julian's immense satisfaction, he saw Emma hustling up to the slit in the wall he'd picked out during his scan of the map. Rather than using the Boost Pack, she carefully clambered up in the shadow of the cliff.

Julian considered rushing, then thought better of it. She was still too far for a head-on charge to succeed. The Self-Supporting Sniper could easily reposition.

By the time he arrived, Emma had already climbed into the cave, but now that he knew where she was, finishing her off would be a piece of cake.

All he needed to do was throw the smoke grenade into the wall and then storm the cavern. Although the cave provided incredible cover, it also restricted her movements. Once he cornered her inside, there'd be nowhere else to run.

He pulled out the smoke grenade from his shield, aimed for the cavern, and threw. Julian grinned. He was already getting better at thinking things through.

The smoke grenade promptly bounced off the wall and smacked him in the face. Pale gas billowed through the air, completely obstructing his vision.

What the hell?

Had she done something to bounce it back?

Did Dynamic have a weapon like that?

No.

He'd screwed up and messed up the weight. The slit was painfully narrow, barely enough for a Mech to fit inside. Although the smoke grenade was small, the angle from where he'd thrown it was extremely unforgiving.

There was a resonant bang, and then the match ended. Emma had finished him off as he blundered through the smoke.

She laughed and laughed as they returned to the lobby.

"What the heck? What were you trying to do there?"

He groaned.

"Just not familiar with the smoke grenade yet."

"Yeah, I can tell."

"Want to go again?"

"Yeah, but first, tell me how you knew where I was."

"Oh."

He explained to her how he'd scouted out the map and various launch points.

"Since I was on the eastern side, I knew that you couldn't be there. So it was one of the other three, right? But since there's no good spot on one of the spawn points, I figured there was about a two-in-three chance you'd move to that niche in the wall."

"Huh. That's really smart. Yeah, I ended up spawning to the south. That's really good. I need to keep that in mind too. I thought it was the perfect spot, but now you mention it, an opponent definitely could have read me."

"Yeah, unfortunately, I ended up embarrassing myself pretty badly. Can't believe I messed that up."

She held up a finger.

"Not just that. It's alright to make a mistake and mess up the grenade. Maybe you'll choke in your match. But blundering around was an even bigger error. It guaranteed that I would get you. Next time, just calmly withdraw."

"Right."

He had improved his thinking, but he'd immediately panicked once things stopped going his way.

She sent him another invite, and he accepted it.

"Alright, let's hope I don't embarrass myself again."

The next stage was Beach, a unique land-and-sea field that presented exciting challenges for both snipers and their targets. The beachhead was almost devoid of cover—there was nothing but a few loose rock formations and a couple of palm trees.

In general, snipers would try and hide beneath the sea. The

coral reefs and shipwrecks meant that units could disappear nearly indefinitely. However, the same extensive cover also significantly restricted their sniping angles. The bullets tore through reefs and wrecks on their way to the target. If the sniper missed, they'd completely give away their position. Unlike other stages, like Canyon, Caverns, or Cityscape, there was no way to hide your shooting angle.

The combination of hiding places and complete lack of subtlety tested pilots who preferred assassination-based strategies. In general, Beach was a prized stage for teams that used a resupply strategy. In this clever gambit, one of the four Mechs took a completely dedicated support role, transferring their energy and ammunition to the other three players. In Beach, it was almost impossible to find a resupply point.

The specific stage was Beach 2, but unlike other places like Caverns or Colony, which had recognizable landmarks, the variant of Beach didn't make a big difference.

Julian launched onto the beachhead and carefully watched for a splash. But of course, Emma was too good for a beginner's mistake like that. She'd angled her launching cannon so that she'd directly appear underwater.

Fortunately for Julian, he'd see her if she ever tried to leave the ocean, and with his drones, he could safely find her position. Drones were one of the most potent weapons on Beach because there was no way to destroy them without giving away your location.

Julian set the three drones on their path and then waited.

It took only five seconds to realize his mistake, but by then, there was nothing he could do.

The drones splashed into the water and promptly slammed into the underground terrain. On such a complicated stage, he couldn't just set them on their path. He had to micromanage them. With no other means of getting vision, he was just a sitting duck on the island. After a while, Emma surfaced and gunned him down from behind.

"Dang it!"

They played over a dozen other matches, but Julian continued making stupid mistakes. Once, he exposed himself while focusing too much on managing the drone. He smacked himself with his own grenade two more times.

When he finally managed to get the drop on Emma, he choked and missed a spell cast, overshooting his stun and instantly giving away his position. He got more and more frustrated as the night went on. When he accidentally drove a drone straight into a wall, she stopped him.

"You're not improving, and you're just getting frustrated. I can tell you have a good idea with some of these approaches, but you just suck at using the new equipment. It'll be a lot more productive for you to just use it on your own first."

He sighed.

"Yeah. You're right. I'm just making way too many basic mistakes right now."

"Hey, it's not all bad! You scouted me out a couple of times. I think once you get the grenade throws down, you'll be fine. And yeah practice driving the drones and paying attention to several at once. And get used to casting spells. You know, stuff like that. You are getting better at thinking, though. Like you worked on it and got better, you know? It'll be the same here. Just practice the equipment and get better. Don't get easily discouraged."

She was right. Their practice wasn't helping him as much as it could.

Julian blinked.

"You know, it's a lot like what Tyler said. He said he didn't want to do March of Grunts with us because he had to get it right in a controlled environment. Like hitting stationary targets and then people not shooting back."

"Oh yeah, that sounds smart!"

He took a deep breath and tried to calm down. He still felt pretty embarrassed about his horrific performance.

"Don't worry. Take a break and log off. You'll feel better. I'll be free whenever."

She was right about that too.

Julian felt pretty burned out. His mind was totally fried. He flashed back to his last mistake, when he'd crashed a drone straight into the wall and had it explode in his face.

There was no chance the drone could have fit into that impossibly tiny gap. He hadn't known what he was thinking. He'd just thrown his hands up and hoped for the best, even though it was nonsensical.

It was only after he unplugged that Julian realized how hungry he was. He took another look at the time and then frowned. He'd played for over five hours without even realizing it. It was 11:30, and he still hadn't eaten dinner. Fortunately, the pizza place around the corner stayed open until three.

It was hard to tell if that place was him and Tyler's favorite because they made good pizza—which they objectively did—or because it was cheap, right by their house, and almost always open, which meant they got it whenever they were starving.

He knocked on Tyler's door and heard a familiar beep. The virtual reality headset of Overdrive responded to certain stimuli, such as knocks or doorbells. It also detected emergencies like nearby fires. The beep instantly alerted Tyler that someone was looking for him.

Moments later, Tyler emerged at the door. His friend gaped when Julian showed him the time. It was displayed on the Overdrive UI, but it was hard to pay attention to it when you played.

Julian was just about to ask Tyler if he was hungry when his friend's stomach grumbled.

"Pizza?"

"Yeah."

The friends ordered two pepperoni pizzas. As always, the food arrived quickly. The parlor was so popular that they pre-made pies in anticipation of upcoming orders. As the two best friends treated themselves to a very late dinner, Julian asked Tyler about doing drills.

"Yeah, I think that sounds smart. You should definitely do drills first before practicing with Emma again."

His friend could tell that Julian was embarrassed about his horrid performance.

"Don't worry about playing badly. You've never used smokes or drones before, and I think you mentioned you don't use Spell Titans too often either, right?"

"Yeah."

Tyler grinned and took another huge bite of pizza.

"See? It's just like how I couldn't shoot free throws when I first started playing. Of course, you can't use smoke grenades—you've spent the last seven years never touching one!"

Tyler told that story a lot. He was really proud of his free throw rates. His last year in college, he'd hit over 90%. According to him, he'd been at the low 30s when he first started in elementary school. Tyler was just a decent player overall, but at the end of the game, their school always gave him the ball when the other team was trying to intentionally foul. It was a very unusual honor for a center.

The two of them started designing various drills. The most important thing was for Julian to discover the eccentricities of every map. He needed to know the angle to through smokes and the best paths to send drones on. If there were paths where they could move in a straight line while staying behind cover, he wouldn't need to micromanage all of them at once.

Julian loaded photos of every map and variation onto his phone to study them even outside of the server.

The key to hitting smoke grenades was getting comfortable with the weight. Tyler suggested creating a set routine every time he used a smoke to ensure a consistent mindset.

"You need to make sure it leaves your hand the same way every time. It sounds like there's usually no need to rush. If he's in a cave, then he's going to be camped there, right?"

Tyler reminded Julian of his free throw routine.

"I fake a shot first, then do two dribbles. It could be the same thing here, you know?"

Julian remembered Tyler's fake free throw toss from when he went to games. He'd always found it funny, but his friend told him he'd learned it from various NBA pros.

It turned out there was even a research paper about it. NBA players shot about five percentage points better on their second free throw than their first. Steve Nash, a star point guard, managed to shoot ninety percent overall partially because of his special routine. Like Tyler, he would take a practice free throw without the ball before shooting.

Julian decided to do the same thing to improve his grenade toss. It was more important to be accurate than to be fast against a sniper.

They continued working through the night, designing different practice regimens for drones like piloting through narrow corridors or quickly identify safe spots where he could shift his focus. After all, it was hard to focus on four cameras all at once. Despite the alert system, it was still possible to miss critical cues like terrain damage.

Julian found some videos online that provided further guidance.

"And don't forget about the break period! You need to avoid burnout."

"Yeah."

He'd performed worse and worse as his matches with Emma

had gone on. It was important to spend time away from Overdrive.

"Maybe we can hit the gym tomorrow? Play some pick-up and lift."

"Yeah, that sounds good. Just text me when you go."

The invite from Dynamic would last for two weeks, and Julian could schedule for another week out, meaning he had three weeks to practice. He'd prefer to accept the challenge faster, but the most important thing was getting it done right. If he won, Julian would be in pole position to qualify for the Selection.

The next few days passed like a blur. Julian spent a lot of his class time learning about the maps. It made him feel guilty. He liked school and wanted to pay attention, but making the Selection was worth it. Besides, his inability to get a job wasn't because he didn't pay attention in class. It was because he had a threadbare resume and a painful lack of experience. If he made the Selection, he'd at least have a story that game companies would listen to.

But even more than that, Julian had come to realize that he had the chance to be legitimately good. He had the chance to be more than just some top five hundred player.

Julian thought about some of the startling moments during his close-range duels with Brandon. He'd gotten baited into making a mistake, but that wouldn't always be the case. If his game knowledge was better or if his skills were more diverse, Julian thought he could have won.

At the very least, Julian thought he could be a professional level melee support—a much better version of Alt3ration. He'd pretty much spent his time training for it by using an inefficient Ace-level Mech.

But he could be more than that too. Now that he'd learned so much more about Overdrive strategy and crafting, he and the Starlight R had much further to go.

[25]

Julian stared through the smoke. He concentrated more than he ever had before, furiously searching for any shift that would betray Emma's move to a new position. If she didn't run, he had her.

If she did run...

There!

The system for casting Spell Titan abilities was unlike that of any other machine. The look and feel of the special menu were more like a traditional RPG than piloting a giant robot. When he'd used it for the first time, it'd completely thrown him off.

But now, after two weeks of drills, it was just like any other action.

He selected Static Freeze and then aimed.

A surge of sparks streaked from his fingertips.

Thunk!

Emma's Mech crashed hard onto the ground. Julian swiftly moved toward the noise, moving from street to street with sure-footed steps. After his diligent weeks of study, he now knew the location of every building on Cityscape 3.

Emma had flown out from behind the massive office building. She'd fallen straight down afterward.

Left.

Right.

And then left again before they were on the same street.

He drew his cleaver, keeping his other hand free to cast spells.

If he successfully stunned his opponent, the shorter blade was the preferable option. Due to its force concentrating abilities, the cleaver could slice open the enemy cockpit in a single strike.

After the first week, Julian and Emma created a simple heuristic for which blade to use. If Julian landed a good hit with Static Freeze, he'd finish the fight at once with the shorter knife. If he missed, he'd use the longer broadsword to maximize his chance of landing a crippling blow.

He charged forward. The Spell Titan's lanky limbs kicked hard off the ground. Emma slowly turned towards him, but there was nothing she could do. The Static Freeze still restrained most of her movements. He plunged the blade in and out.

VICTORY!

He leaned back in his pilot's chair and grinned.

There was a bright flash, and then they returned to the main lobby.

"Nice!"

She pulled out her notepad.

"That's twelve of the last fifteen—and you've gotten five in a row. You're really getting the hang of this!"

She laughed.

"Man. It's hard to believe you were bonking yourself in the head with smokes just two and a half weeks ago."

Julian laughed with her.

One of the things that made Emma such an amazing teacher

was her genuine enjoyment at her improvement. She didn't view her losses as her defeats. She thought that meant she was training him well.

Julian had learned a lot during his self-created training camp.

Many players disdained the Support role. They thought it was much harder to fight on the frontlines and lead the team in kills. Plenty of pilots claimed that if they switched over to Support play, they'd be ranked far higher on the competitive ladder. Julian had once thought that way himself. After all, he had better control skills than Felix, yet his childhood friend was about two hundred ranks ahead of him.

Now he'd realized what a fool he'd been.

Even learning the fundamentals like throwing a smoke grenade or piloting a drone had taken him about fifteen or twenty hours of play each, and he was still far from an expert. The best Supports could hit nearly impossible angles with grenades by calculating how their tosses would bounce off of walls. Fortunately, Julian didn't need to be that good to beat Dynamic.

Once he'd figured out how to control the counter items, the matchup had become shockingly easy. Emma was an even more skilled sniper than Dynamic, but once Julian identified her position and made his approach, there was little she could do.

"You want to go one more?"

Julian shook his head.

"Nah, it's getting late. I want to sleep, so I'll be ready tomorrow."

He was beginning to feel the fatigue and burnout. There was no need to overwork himself to the point where he couldn't think anymore. He needed to stay sharp.

There was a bit of an awkward pause as they kind of mulled around. Then Emma gathered herself up.

"Well then. Good luck tomorrow. Get the win. I'll be watching!"

She logged off. Julian waited a moment, the tension tight in his stomach. If he won tomorrow's match, he'd put himself in the driver's seat for the Selection.

Then he reminded himself that it was a long path, even beyond this Selection. He just had to focus on getting better. Even if he lost, he knew how to improve. He was on the right track now.

Julian took a deep breath, and the tension slowly dissipated. Then he logged off too.

[26]

The next day, Julian logged onto Overdrive an hour ahead of time.

The first thing he did was check his messages—he had a few notes of encouragement from his friends, including Felix and Emma. Tyler had already wished him well earlier in the day at lunch. To Julian's surprise, Brandon had sent a note too.

Tyler must have told his old friend that Julian had a big match today.

The long line of encouraging notes helped alleviate his nerves, but only a tiny bit. He only had one message not related to his upcoming game. Emma was complaining in the Forever Fortress group chat about her failure to recruit beginners. Emma thought the Fortress's universal CALL GRUNTS feature and widely varied terrain made for the perfect training ground. Unfortunately, few new players took her up on her offer.

It was just due to a lack of trust.

The Forever Fortress featured player vs. player battles. Julian knew the Forever Brothers and their chosen guests would never bully new players, but not everybody realized that. Nobody wanted to get picked on when they were just getting started. It was why almost all the beginner guide missions were purely PVE.

Julian smiled wryly as he remembered Tyler's first mission. If Liefield had managed to keep the Challenge System, the cowardly pilot definitely would have spent his time picking on beginners. Julian had actually searched Liefield in the database out of curiosity, figuring that if Liefield managed to keep the Heaven's Boxer, he'd be able to climb the ranks quickly enough to get a rating. His old enemy still didn't have a profile. Perhaps the Mech really had been deleted.

Maybe that was why TiggerLuvr888 hadn't messaged him back yet.

Julian shook his head.

He had no time to dream about the Heaven's Boxer right now. If he won today's match, he'd qualify for the Selection.

He entered the Forever Fortress and quickly reviewed his Grenade and Drone maneuvers to guarantee that he wouldn't flub them during the battle. An hour was a reasonable amount of time to warm-up.

He'd thought about entering earlier. It wasn't like he had anything better to do. But he was wary of burnout, and he knew that there wasn't anything practice the day of the match could do for him. If anything, he was more likely to make a mistake and put himself on tilt.

His stomach had been tight all day, and Julian couldn't tell if it was lucky or unfortunate that he didn't have class today.

He'd spent most of his time pacing back and forth in his room, too nervous to do anything other than think about his upcoming battle. He'd felt the same way before last Selection. This wouldn't be his only chance to qualify, but things would be far easier if he won.

Perhaps this was how Tyler felt before basketball tournaments.

Julian entered the Forever Fortress, and then launched out to the planet. Although the ruined castle wasn't an official stage, the angles were quite comparable to those on Caverns or Cityscape. He figured those would be the two hardest maps. Although Cityscape didn't have the same cover as Caverns, Dynamic was known for playing exceptionally well on stages featuring urban combat.

He pulled out a smoke grenade and threw it, aiming to clear the very top of the castle wall. He tried to imagine Dynamic's Self-Supporting Sniper sitting at the very edge.

It promptly bounced back at him, filling up his screen with light gray gas.

Julian cursed and reminded himself of the warm-up routine.

Even though this wasn't a real match, he'd been so nervous that he'd forgotten all about it. Tyler did the same thing before every free throw—a deep breath, a fake shot, two dribbles, and another deep breath.

Julian's ritual didn't involve a dribble, but he did take a deep breath and a practice throw. The good thing about tossing an Overdrive grenade was that he could feign the toss with the smoke in his hand. When Tyler faked his basketball free throw, he wasn't allowed to hold the ball.

"Doing it right is better than doing it quickly."

Julian murmured his friend's mantra under his breath and drew his second smoke. Once he threw the smoke and started moving towards Dynamic's position, the battle would turn on a dime. But before then, he had all the time in the world. The most important thing was to throw the grenade correctly.

The second time, he nailed it.

Julian spent the next hour practicing his smoke grenade and drone usage, playing out various scenes from Cityscape, Caverns, and Colony. He figured those would be the most troubling maps.

When he finished, he pulled out the list of maps again and quickly reviewed them. Knowing where to move while staying behind cover was the key to winning this matchup. He was still unsteady when it came to thinking on his feet. The best way to make up for that was to plan things out beforehand.

Ten minutes before their match, the Dynamic's invite popped up again, asking Julian if he'd like to go to the lobby ahead of time. Julian entered the shop instead and refreshed his drones and grenades.

Then he quickly reviewed his status screen, making sure that he had everything he needed. Although it was a glass cannon, his new Mech had significantly more offensive strength than the Starlight R. Julian couldn't wait to see how powerful his Ace unit would get once he started crafting with it.

- General Data -
Pilot: Julian
Machine: SPG-1 Caster—Julian Custom
Class: Spell Titan
Sub-class: Attacker
Designation: Grunt Unit

- Statistics -
Melee: S-tier
Shooting: C-tier
Speed: B-tier
Maneuverability: B-tier
Defense: B-tier
Cohesion: A-tier

- Weapons -
Mana Gatherer Spike [x2]
Mana Dispersal Finger [x10]
Mana-Infused Beam Broadsword (Full Custom) [x1]
Mana-Infused Beam Cleaver (Full Custom) [x1]
Grenade-Carry Shield [x1]

Four Shot Revolver
Scouter Drones [x3]

- Abilities -
Thunderbolt
Static Freeze
Storm Surge

For one crazy moment, Julian briefly considered removing one of his swords, lowering his Credits total so he could buy a speed increasing item. After all, B-tier in Speed and Maneuverability would put him behind Dynamic.

Then he shook his head.

There was no need to second-guess himself. This was what he'd practiced with. He'd won his last five games against Emma using this strategy.

Julian entered the lobby and locked in his Mech.

Dynamic still hadn't arrived in the lobby, but a sudden bevy of notifications told Julian that he had fans.

He felt a sudden surge of nervousness. The list was much longer than he imagined. Guest 192 must have been Emma, and Tyler was there too, but he hadn't realized that Captain Maxwell and the rest of the Forever Brothers were also planning on watching.

Over thirty people were spectating!

What if he smoked himself again?

Emma sent him a message.

"Remember—just like in practice. I'll be mad if you lose. Means you think this guy's better than me."

That brought a smile to his face.

Tyler sent him a message too.

"'Just remember the routine. Everything's going to be alright. And don't forget the goal is long-term improvement."

That was right. It was just like in practice. And even if he lost —even if he didn't get selected this round—he was still improving incredibly quickly. He'd gotten so much better at thinking on his feet, and he was diversifying his game every day.

His time would come.

Moments later, Dynamic loaded in.

"Hey! Julian! Thanks for agreeing to fight. Sorry for the brief delay!"

Dynamic was a short man with blonde hair and a keen and intelligent face. His in-game outfit was a dress shirt and tie rather than a conventional pilot suit.

Julian smiled.

"Of course. Let's do this!"

As Julian had expected, Dynamic was using the Self-Supporting Sniper. The Mech's details were the same as what Julian had read on the Database. All Dynamic could see was Julian's frame. A shroud of darkness covered the SPG Caster's parts and weaponry.

Julian took a deep breath and reminded himself to stay patient. His lessons from his match with Tigger, his practice with Emma, and the drills he'd created to Tyler all came down to this.

If he played this right, Dynamic would have no idea what hit him.

$$[\ 27 \ ]$$

The stage was Canyon 2.

Julian couldn't tell if he should be relieved or disappointed.

Canyon was better than Caverns or Dynamic's signature Cityscape, but it was still one of the better maps for snipers. Julian immediately began calculating how likely a better stage would have been. Void only had a 5% selection rate, but when including more open fields like Beach, Sea, Skies, and Wasteland, Julian should have had about a 60% overall chance of getting a favorable stage.

He shook his head.

He was being stupid. The stage was the stage. Lamenting his bad luck wouldn't do anything at this point, and besides, the map was one of the ones he knew best.

Julian instinctively aimed his launch for the tall pillar on the far corner, which loomed in front of the long wall bordering the stage's side.

Julian caught himself. Instead of rushing his launch, he steadied his hand and carefully calibrated the launch cannon, ensuring that not a single inch of his Mech would be exposed.

Once he was certain of the firing angle, he locked the position in place.

During his previous match against Dynamic, he'd been so excited about a favorable spawn point that he'd set his launch too hastily.

The gangly Spell Titan was a perfect fit for that narrow alcove. The Mech's thin frame guaranteed that Dynamic wouldn't see him behind the wall, especially if Julian kept his hands steady. Even if he were spotted, the corner of the map gave him three clear paths to flee. There were straight paths to his left and right. He could also scurry around the pillar and streak for the hedge a couple of feet ahead of him.

But even though Julian got his perfect launch point, he had no idea where Dynamic was. Unlike Caverns or Cityscape, there was no one amazing sniping point.

Instead, Canyon was filled with imperfect positions. There were spots with excellent cover but mediocre angles and vice-versa. Instead of trying to guess where Dynamic had launched, Julian's best bet was to immediately send out his drones. Sniping on Canyon required constant movement from angle to angle.

The map was completely silent.

As soon as Julian set the drones to the ground, he lifted his hands off the controls. His Mech stood completely still. Julian took a deep and calming breath. To his relief, his palms weren't sweating yet.

Then he put his hands back in place and ordered the first drone to deploy.

The spherical mobile camera slid across the wall to his left. There were few obstacles, and the wall's looming shadow provided adequate cover. With a few additional keystrokes, Julian deployed the second drone to the opposite end of the corridor. Julian focused about eighty percent of his attention on the second scout. Its path was much trickier. Not only were there several loose rock formations, but the sun shone brightly along its route.

Until Dynamic spotted the SPG Caster, he wouldn't have any information about Julian's weapons. Julian hadn't fought in a competitive ranked match for over a month. All the reports claimed that Julian was the same one-dimensional swordsman he'd always been. Julian didn't want to expose his improved gameplay too early.

Every so often, Julian checked his primary eye cameras, which he'd trained at the pillar's very edge. It was the furthest he could peek without exposing his position.

The twin scouts reached the very edge of their cover. Any further movement would require them to bolt into the open space at the center of the stage.

But there was no hint of his opponent.

Julian bit his lip. Between the two of them, the scouts had covered eighty-five percent of the map. Should he push them further? If he forced the drones to keep moving, he might get better visuals. But more likely than not, he'd expose his equipment without getting much in return.

He shook his head and pulled up Dynamic's status sheet again.

Because Dynamic was using an Ace unit, Julian had the full scouting report. He carefully read through his opponent's design, double-checking for an unexpected change. The enemy unit had looked the same as always during the pre-match period. It was the same camouflage colored unit with a massive helmet covered with sensors and an enormous drone at the back. But perhaps Julian had missed something important.

His drones had covered almost the entire map. Had Dynamic splurged on a cloaking device?

He read through the list. The parts were the same as before.

Besides, Julian was being ridiculous. There was no way the Self-Supporting Sniper could have equipped a cloaking system.

Good shrouding—the sort that let you moved while staying cloaked—was incredibly expensive. It cost 80,000 Credits, enough to push the limit even for Ace units. It wouldn't be possible for Dynamic to keep his powerful gear while using a cloaking device.

There had to be some other explanation.

Julian sent his drones back the way they'd gone before. If his drones spotted Dynamic moving, they'd beep loudly, but for indicators like footsteps or scorch marks, Julian was on his own.

But there was no hint at all of the massive Mech. There were no footsteps on the ground or trails of smoke in the air.

Julian frowned.

Panic rose in his chest, but then he swallowed it.

There was no need for him to worry.

More likely than not, Dynamic had simply hidden in a spot outside Julian's visual range. If not for that, he might be inside some nook or cranny that Julian didn't know about. Julian had explored Canyon pretty carefully, but he only had two weeks of knowledge. A great sniper like Dynamic probably had been studying the maps for years.

Julian sent the drones back out again. This time, he propelled the third drone directly after the first, moving them both along the less crowded path to his left. Despite his worries, he kept the drone movement slow and steady. A sudden shift might betray their presence. As Tyler said, it was more important to do it right than to do it quickly.

Julian took a deep breath and then pre-planned his escape. He needed to move slightly out of cover to increase his view of the map. If Dynamic spotted him, Julian would drop a smoke grenade and then flee to the right. Once he got behind the large stack of rocks on the southern side of the map, he'd be safe again.

Julian knew the cover on Canyon 2 like the back of his hand. Confident in his escape plan, Julian subtly shifted his Mech past the pillar. He carefully scooched his hand forward on the trigger, maximizing his angle while still keeping the majority of his Mech hidden. The edge of his eye camera was pressed tightly against the rocky pillar. Even if Dynamic spotted him, Julian had enough time to raise his shield.

Dynamic didn't spot him.

The map remained completely silent.

Where was his opponent?

When his drones reached the edge of their cover, Julian anchored them to their positions, directing their cameras to get a clear view of the sky and high hills.

He switched to full control of the third drone and mused carefully.

If he smashed it into a wall, he might grab Dynamic's attention. If his opponent fired, Julian had a good chance of discerning the sniper's position. Between the improved viewpoint of his main camera and the two drones, he now had just over ninety-two percent of the map covered.

Julian shook his head again. The tension rapidly mounted in his throat and shoulders. He took a deep breath.

There was no need to rush. Faking his presence with a drone was an intriguing idea, but it was best to save that for later.

More likely than not, Dynamic was getting tense too.

Although things seemed frightening, the truth was that neither side had an advantage. The first one to do something rash would fall behind.

Julian stayed still and watched his drones.

He ignored the itch to send his drones past cover. Right now, Dynamic had no idea what was happening. If the skilled sniper spotted a drone, he'd realize what Julian was planning.

There was no need to take unnecessary risks.

Julian waited even longer.

When the match dragged past the thirty-minute mark, Dynamic grew tired of waiting.

Julian let out a long sigh of relief. He'd won the battle to avoid freaking out. It was no small thing to outlast a top 300 sniper.

The Self-Supporting Sniper started spraying missiles across the battlefield. Dynamic didn't know where Julian was, he just trying to flush him out. Julian grinned. Despite the veteran sniper's patience, Julian had gotten the best of him. Julian withdrew his eye cameras completely behind cover, relying entirely on his drones for information.

Stone shattered and exploded. Julian stared at the three streams of footage, furiously trying to discern the projectiles' source, but he still couldn't figure out where Dynamic was shooting from.

Whatever hidden nook his opponent was using, it was a good one.

He pulled up his mental map of Canyon 2. It was obvious that Dynamic was hiding somewhere near the edge of the map on the northeastern corridor. It was the only place Julian's drones hadn't explored yet. The overall direction of Dynamic's missiles confirmed Julian's suspicions, but it still wasn't good enough.

Julian stayed behind the pillar. He didn't make a single move.

It'd be worse than useless if Julian got spooked and charged only for Dynamic to get the drop on him and shoot him in the back of the head. Dynamic was just shooting randomly. There was an infinitesimal chance he'd hit Julian. Dynamic was just guessing randomly. The missile fire was currently directed towards the southwestern side. More likely than not, Julian's rival would run out of ammunition before finding the hidden SPG Caster.

Julian took another deep breath.

It cleared his mind and kept him calm. In the middle of some of these fights, he sometimes just forgot to breathe.

He reminded himself that he was in the driver's seat here. His opponent was panicking. Dynamic knew that Julian loved melee machines. He probably thought that it was Julian who found some secret way to sneak across the map.

There was no need to rush. Julian had a favorable matchup, and his modified Grunt helped him even more. The map was huge, and Julian was safe behind the pillar. Even if Dynamic lucked out and found his spot, Julian could drop a smoke and run.

He continued carefully observing the trails, but the guided missiles made it nearly impossible to determine precisely where the shots were coming from.

A few times, Julian thought he saw a shift in the wall, but he still didn't move. He only watched that spot more carefully.

He needed to be certain.

And then, there it was.

It was easy to hide where guided missiles came from. But after Dynamic ran out of them, bright red beams lanced across the skies, devastating the rocky walls. It took three shots of the beam cannons before Julian finally saw it. It was a strange cave with a shifting wall, almost like a pet door.

The Self-Supporting Sniper briefly crawled forward to shoot then immediately returned behind cover. It was a stupid map eccentricity, but now that Julian knew it existed, there wasn't much Dynamic could do against a proper approach.

Julian pulled out a smoke and took a deep breath. He feigned the toss, imagining the grenade entering the mouth of the cave right before the strange rocky flap closed again. He repeated the fake toss, making sure the calibration was perfect.

This was going to be tricky. Because Julian hadn't known about the secret door, he'd never done this toss in practice before.

But by now, he was intimately familiar with the grenade's weight, and the toss was similar enough to others he'd done in his drills.

Once he was fully prepared, Julian took control of the third drone. It was finally time to sacrifice it. He slammed it into a rock. Dynamic whirled at the echoing noise and drew his rifle. The shot was near-instantaneous.

The drone exploded, but before Dynamic could return beneath the flap, Julian threw the grenade and then charged forward, pushing his hands hard against the thrusters. The smoke shifted as Dynamic blundered uncomfortably inside the cavern. His opponent had no idea whether he should leave cover or charge.

Despite his excitement, Julian made sure to stay careful. He approached on a jagged path, guaranteeing that he always stayed behind some sort of cover. If Dynamic started firing, Julian didn't want to die to a random bullet. Emma had beaten him twice using that same strategy. She'd simply guessed the most likely path of his approach and sprayed. Julian knew that Dynamic was seasoned enough to make the same judgments. He carefully monitored the sky for any hint of the independent drone, but it was nowhere to be found.

Dynamic didn't fire, nor did he leave the cave.

By now, Julian was close enough to hear the footsteps coming through the strange fake wall. Julian raised his Mech's hand and prepared himself to cast Static Freeze, but no enemy emerged.

Instead, the footsteps went deeper and deeper. Rather than fleeing, Dynamic had pressed himself tight against the wall. It was a smart move. Julian wouldn't survive a straight charge into a heavy artillery unit embedded inside a cave.

Julian had thought that Dynamic might try and send out the drone as a distraction. Instead, he'd doubled down on his current position.

Julian stopped his charge before he reached the fake wall.

He probably could have sliced the cover apart with his blades, but that would guarantee his defeat. Dynamic would shoot Julian as soon as he showed.

The battle had changed, and Julian needed to think on his feet. The smoke cleared, but the door remained perfectly still. Dynamic clearly had no interest in leaving.

Julian took a quick inventory of his machine's abilities. He still had two drones and three more smoke grenades, but the supportive items weren't too helpful now that he'd found his opponent. He still had access to two spell charges and both his swords, but the firepower wasn't particularly useful because of Dynamic's cover. He also had the revolver, but it was only a backup weapon.

What could he do?

The door remained still. There were no more footsteps. Dynamic was deep in the cave now and perfectly entrenched. More likely than not, the barrel was trained right at the door for any sign of movement.

Oh.

Julian blinked as he realized what he needed to do.

He called both the drones back to him and soared high above the entrance, giving it a very wide berth in case Dynamic started firing.

Julian angled a smoke and dropped it right in front of the flap. Then he landed both drones at the mouth of the cave. The two plinks sounded almost like footsteps.

Julian drew his revolver and pumped all four shots into the wall, crumpling it to pieces. Dynamic's guns roared.

Julian drew both his swords and held them high above his head. He cast Thunderbolt on both of them. Emma's sword grew to enormous length and his own burned with raw concentrated power.

Then he slammed them onto the roof.

The entire cave collapsed on him, crushing his opponent to smithereens.

VICTORY!

Julian let out a long and relieved sigh.

Then he grinned as the congratulations messages immediately flooded his screen.

Dynamic smiled politely as the two returned to the lobby. The shorter man eagerly shook Julian's hand and vowed revenge before logging off. Moments later, Julian received a pair of new notifications.

The first indicated his changed ranking. As Brandon had predicted, beating Dynamic had moved Julian past the Selection cut-off. He was now ranked 492nd.

Julian took a deep breath and mimed a throw, smiling to himself.

This win felt better than all the others.

He thought about all his training with Emma and all his grinding with Tyler.

He thought about forging the two swords. He thought about all the drills and practice battles.

Even though he'd lost the Heaven's Boxer, he'd gained something much more valuable from playing with Tigger and his kids. He'd learned how to really play Overdrive.

This win felt earned.

And he knew that there'd be more coming.

Then Julian read the second notification on his screen.

TylerFord21: Hey, log off when you can. I just got some pretty exciting news.

Julian's warning sensor pinged as Tyler knocked on his door. He could vaguely hear his friend murmuring, but the immersive virtual reality world of Overdrive kept him from hearing the words until he logged off.

Julian exited the stage and then set aside his headset before opening the door.

"What's up?"

"I got a message from Tigger. Funny thing is, he didn't send it to me on the Overdrive server. He actually hit me up on LinkedIn. During your match, he shot me a message in-game telling me to look at my new job opportunity. I thought it was weird until I saw this."

Tyler handed the screen over.

Tigger's LinkedIn page was very poorly maintained. It still claimed he was a senior programmer at a data science company. After striking it rich off of Overdrive, Tigger didn't need to worry about stuff like his resume anymore.

Julian stared at the message.

Ray Chung: Hey Tyler. Hope you find this message. Please

show it to Julian. I'm sorry for staying silent for so long. If either of you qualifies for the Selection, please let me know. I will update you in person. I know how we can get the machine back.

Excitement and confusion battled furiously in Julian's chest. He loved the thought of reclaiming the Boxer, but he didn't know why Tigger was acting so evasive. Why couldn't he just type it out? Why had he sent it on LinkedIn instead of the Overdrive server?

Tyler had the same thoughts.

"Why do you think he sent it on LinkedIn?"

"I'm not sure."

Perhaps Tigger had the same worries Felix did about The Mechanical King.

"Some of the pros think the game owner is watching them."

"Oh. Weird."

Tyler read the message again.

"You qualified after beating that Dynamic guy, right?"

"More or less. I'm in the top five hundred now, but there's still two weeks until the Selection. I'm barely past the cut-off point. Someone could still steal the spot from me."

"Will they?"

Julian thought for a moment. Considering what he'd learned, he didn't think so. Dynamic was a top 300 player. He was barely on the edge of opponents Julian usually queued up against. If he could beat Dynamic, he could beat the players around him.

"No."

Tyler pointed at the screen and grinned.

"Good. Now there's another reason to make sure of it."

Julian smiled back. It was all thanks to Tyler that he'd turned his Overdrive fortunes around.

"I won't. I'm going to make it."

"Yeah?"

Julian nodded firmly.

"Yeah. And not just top five hundred either. Top eight. It's not just about the Boxer anymore. I'm going to keep working until I become a Fortress Master."

Thank you for reading *The Heaven's Boxer*, book one in Overdrive.

We hope you enjoyed it as much as we enjoyed bringing it to you. We just wanted to take a moment to encourage you to review the book on Amazon and Goodreads. Every review helps further the author's reach and, ultimately, helps them continue writing fantastic books for us all to enjoy.

If you liked this book, check out the rest of our catalogue at www.aethonbooks.com. To sign up to receive a FREE collection from some of our best authors as well as updates regarding all new releases, visit www.aethonbooks.com/sign-up.

JOIN THE STREET TEAM! Get advanced copies of all our books, plus other free stuff and help us put out hit after hit.

SEARCH ON FACEBOOK:
AETHON STREET TEAM

THE HEAVEN'S BOXER

THE POWER OF NINE

THE FONT OF LIFE

Don't forget to join LitRPG Addicts and come hang out with me!

I'm also very active and thankful for LitRPG Books and GameLit Society

To learn more about LitRPG, talk to authors including me, and just have an awesome time, please join the LitRPG Group

If you enjoyed this book, please leave a review!

You can find me on Facebook.

If you have any feedback or would like to join my mailing list, please contact me on my email: ryantang203@gmail.com

If you want to find more great LitRPG Books, check out the Amazon storefront!

Also check out the LitRPG Books on Facebook!

The GameLit Society is another fantastic group for LitRPG and GameLit discussions!